WISH YOU WEREN'T HERE

WISH YOU WEREN'T HERE

A Novel

CHRISTY SCHILLIG

alcove
press

This is a work of fiction. All of the names, characters, organizations, places, and events portrayed in this novel are either products of the author's imagination or are used fictitiously. Any resemblance to real or actual events, locales, or persons, living or dead, is entirely coincidental.

Published in the United States by Alcove Press, an imprint of The Quick Brown Fox & Company LLC.

Alcove Press and its logo are trademarks of The Quick Brown Fox & Company LLC.

Library of Congress Catalog-in-Publication data available upon request.

ISBN (hardcover): 978-1-63910-707-0
ISBN (ebook): 978-1-63910-708-7

Cover design by Heather VenHuizen

Printed in the United States.

www.alcovepress.com

Alcove Press
34 West 27th St., 10th Floor
New York, NY 10001

First Edition: May 2024

10 9 8 7 6 5 4 3 2 1

For Roarke and Hadley. You held my dream as if it were your own, and I can't wait to do the same with yours.

UNO

Ava

Ethan's long fingers cup my sweaty palm as he tugs me like a toddler toward the security check. He's nervous—maybe excited—I can tell by his pace. Anything beyond a strolling swagger is outside of Ethan Bennington's wheelhouse, so this breakneck sprint we are clocking has my heart rattling and my upper lip sweating. It's happening. I can feel it in my freshly painted but already chipped toes.

I would have chosen something a bit more romantic than the Philadelphia International Airport, with the smell of Cheez Whiz and the sound of unintelligible boarding calls, but I'll take it. Maybe he has signs hidden somewhere. Or an organized flash mob! I glance around at the people I'm passing, knowing that any Tom, Dick, or Sally could break out into dance at any moment. My slick grip slips a bit in his hand and I return my attention to the back of Ethan's beautiful head, focusing on the birthmark visible beneath his blonde hairline.

His free hand slides into his freshly ironed pocket for a second, and then reappears, tensing into a fist, finally stretching back out beside his lean, well-earned thigh muscle. I take a deep breath, looking for the outline of the midnight blue velvet box his mother had shown me last month while Ethan's twin sister, Tammy, and I sat on the couch in her closet, surrounded by racks of impeccably tailored Armani suits and Carolina Herrera gowns. It was humbling enough that every garment around me cost more than half a year's rent at my apartment. Then she'd opened the box in her hand.

The two-carat emerald cut diamond that lounged at the center like a lazy feline twinkled in time with the chandelier's crystals above us. And just before that familiar in-over-my-head feeling crept up into my chest as I stared at the glacier-sized ring, Ethan's mom spoke.

"*Been in our family for five generations,*" she'd explained in her imperious but soft voice, her crystal blue eyes that she'd genetically gifted to her twins misted just the right amount as she looked at me over the open ring box. "*Tammy and I couldn't think of anyone else we'd want to wear it.*"

I couldn't help preening a bit at the praise. Senator Olivia Bennington does not partake in unstaged Kodak moments often. My future mother-in-law is tough—Navy SEAL tough—but I can keep up. A stamp of approval from Olivia comes with more esteem than my impending summa cum whatever law degree from Villanova. And thus, job offers at the top firms in Philly are lighting up my inbox like a California wildfire on an August night.

All I have to do is get through this final coursework at the European Law Seminar in Urbino and fulfill my promise to Mom and then I can start my real life—the life I've been planning and working toward for the last five years. My checklist is rounding out nicely. Father-approved job? Check. Mother-requested experience abroad? Golden check. Everyone-approved fiancé? Rapidly approaching platinum check.

I step on the heel of Ethan's loafer, but he barely hears my apology as we swerve through a large group of what appear to be college students. A couple of the girls we pass do a double take as Ethan politely says "Excuse me," perhaps recognizing him from the recent cover of *Philadelphia* magazine standing behind his mother, one hand on her shoulder and the other locked with Tammy's as his chiseled chin juts out like a granite cliff. Three golden heads emblazoned against the dark background of the glossy cover. *The Bennington agenda: the power family takes on the lack of diversity curriculum in Philadelphia schools.* Power family. About to add one more to the mix.

Ethan squeezes my hand.

I'm gonna be the best fourth wheel this city has ever seen. Though, at the moment, anyone watching me brush the beads of sweat from my unimpressive cleavage while rolling my oversized suitcase behind me would think I was the Bennington's help. I can feel Tammy's phantom pinch on my arm, the one she always gives me when self-deprecation teeters at the edge of shame. Tammy is the best fringe benny any relationship could have. She brought back the laughter in my life right when I needed it most. And though it was tough at first maneuvering their sometimes creepy twin-synchrony, the awkwardness and walking on eggshells has been worth it. Now I'd walk across hot coals for her.

The sound of TSA barking orders about shoe removal signals that we are nearing security, and Ethan finally slows down and checks over his shoulder as if he's verifying that I'm still there.

"You didn't lose me," I tell him just loud enough for him to hear as he pulls me to the side of the corridor beside an expanse of glass that looks out over the planes tucked snugly up to their gates. *I'd follow you through worse, Ethan Bennington.*

He smiles down at me; a bright-neat line of orthodontia hypnotizes me for a moment until I remember what's about to happen. Seeing Ethan down on one knee might topple me like a Jenga tower. I release the handle of my suitcase and rest my free hand against the warm glass window, hoping it's thick enough to keep me from careening outward onto the tarmac.

"Ava," he begins. I want to shut my eyes at the sound of my name on his lips, savor the sensation of his breathy voice, but I don't want to miss a single detail of this. I want this moment engraved on my frontal lobe forever.

". . . when I met you four years ago, I knew—I knew that you'd always be there for me. And that devotion, that loyalty . . ."

We'd been randomly partnered at his Fraternity Olympics, and had hit it off hard and fast when it became clear no one could beat us at anything. His focus. My determination. Undefeatable.

". . . with Mom's reelection campaign starting and you being in Italy, I think this is the perfect time to take that step . . ."

I register for a moment that I'm still staring up at him. Perhaps Benningtons do not kneel?

The queen doesn't curtsy.

". . . to really see who we are. Push our own limits. Figure out exactly what we need . . ."

He reaches into his pocket. I try to exhale the fluttering in my stomach, the way my nerves are suddenly blurring my vision. I swallow the emotion, shape it into my will. No ugly tears when the photos start. Tammy had perfectly applied my liner just before she pushed me out of the limo. I must stay in control.

". . . so I want you to take this to Urbino with you."

His hand slides out and I blink hard at what he's offering me. This is not a midnight blue velvet box. This is a—what the hell is this? A piece of plastic? His words are starting to skip around my brain—bouncing frantically like children on a blacktop at recess. Push our own limits? Figure out what we need? I know what I need. And a plastic card is not it. But it somehow finds its way into my clammy palm anyway.

"What's this?" My voice seems to be coming from far away. I look around and notice there are a few people clustered to my left at a not-so-polite distance.

"It's a calling card." He gives me a patronizing smile. "I know it is old-fashioned, but I wanted you and me to have this time. We deserve this time, Ava. We've been so good to one another. So focused on each other. The card has five minutes on it. Enough for one call. That way we really have to stay true to the plan."

The plan? What plan? Certainly not my plan. Had I missed the changes while we'd eaten my farewell brunch with his mother this morning? I couldn't have. I avoided Tammy's thrice-proffered mimosas so I could stay hydrated for the flight. And when Olivia spoke, I listened. I'm tempted to pull up the picture of my "focus list" on my phone to show him that "relationship hiatus" is not one of the bullet points. What the actual f—

"One call. No texts. No emails. And whatever happens while you are over there, Ava, that's entirely up to you. I want you to experience everything Italy has to offer." Ethan's forehead dips toward me and his brows lift suggestively.

Experience everything.

There's the sound effect of a picture being taken from an iPhone camera and the noise makes everything click at once.

"Ethan, are you breaking up with me?" I ask with what I intended to be a light laugh. But the desperation in the sound makes me cringe.

"It's a break. Not a break-up. We just need some time to be—independent. To get the lay of the land—"

"The lay of what? You want to spend these four weeks getting laid?" My calm has slipped. I need to lower my voice. Breathe. The last thing I want is some random footage of me losing my mind as Ethan Bennington basically hands me a going-away box of condoms.

He takes my elbow and pulls me closer so I can smell the orange juice and mint on his breath.

"Of course not, Ava. I'm not looking for that—but if you have oats to sow—I want them sown before we"—he gestures between us—"move forward. I want us both to be sure. And this seems like the perfect time to do that."

He's barely even breathing hard as he rips my heart out of my chest.

I have no oats. I hate oats.

"I am sure," I whisper.

He tilts his forehead against mine.

"Then these four weeks will just make that certainty even deeper."

"So you're testing me?"

He shakes his head as he straightens.

"We. We are taking this time to remind ourselves of what we want," he says with such solid assuredness that I almost find myself nodding. That's his superpower. Conviction.

"Alright, Ethan. I hate this—"

"So do I," he interrupts.

"But I'll go along with it. For you."

"For us," he corrects.

I almost roll my eyes and say *whatever*. But this is Ethan, not my dad. He's my partner. My equal.

"One call," he reminds me, closing my fingers around the stupid card in my hand. The plastic feels heavier than the diamond I thought I'd be carrying across the Atlantic—the diamond that was meant to be a symbol of our future. Wrong symbol, universe. I was manifesting the shiny rock, not an obsolete piece of PVC. If I put a little pressure on it, maybe it'll turn into a diam—

Ethan reaches out and stops me just before I snap the card like a toddler.

"Right," I say, straightening myself and staring up at him. So much for the exorbitant daily fee I'm paying for international cell service. I'll have to use it all on phone calls to Tammy. He presses his lips together and suppresses a smile when he meets my narrowed gaze—sees the tight set of my molars at the corner of my jaw. He calls it my ball-kicking look.

"I'll miss that look," he chuckles, but doesn't cover his crotch like he normally does. I let out a measured breath, then lift onto my toes and kiss him. I put everything I have into the kiss.

It's a reminder.

A promise.

A fuck you.

And when he pulls away and sucks in a breath, his blue eyes three shades darker than they were before my lips hit his, I nod once and turn my back on him—equal parts punishment and assurance that he doesn't see my careful composure slipping like a scoop of ice cream from a melting cone. I turn and walk away, shoulders back and chin as high as it can reach without pinching a nerve.

A break? A four-week, oat-sowing, transatlantic break. This is Ross and Rachel on steroids.

I reach into my purse and find the tiny pill bottle Tammy gave me "just for emergencies." I believe the calling card/hall pass cutting into my palm constitutes an emergency. I'm tempted to call Tammy and check—no, to call Olivia and ask for her help—but I remind myself she's not my mother. She's his. The realization sends a pang of sharp, cutting grief beneath my sternum and I toss back the pill, dry-swallowing even though my throat has already closed up with the oncoming tears.

Four short weeks.

Twenty-eight Italian sunsets.

Less than half a summer.

The blink of an eye.

Why the hell is it taking so long for this pill to kick in?

DUE

James

When I pull to the curb at Bologna International, there's a clock hanging just over the arrivals entry above the oversized automatic glass doors. The neon red digits are flashing, berating me with the time. It might as well just spell out "you're an asshole" in all caps. I shift into park and leave the Fiat idling with the AC blasting so as not to make this girl's trip any more hellish than it already must be—thanks to me.

An hour late. Traffic around the coast had been unrelenting, even though I'd left before dawn. Not that I had a choice, with Zia Nina nearly dumping espresso down my throat as she shoved me out the door. Somehow, this girl was important to my aunt and uncle—a friend of a friend or something—which translated to me nodding immediately at their request and a three-hour drive through two regions of eastern Italy. Not that one can complain about driving through Emilia-Romagna. Unless one is a moron.

I grab the sign Zia made from the passenger seat, mouthing the name written in my Zia's loose cursive—Signorina Ava Graham. Decidedly American. Not that James was much better. But the moment I step around the back of the car, I can see the sign was an unnecessary touch.

"You are over an hour late."

It takes my eyes a moment to connect to my brain as I relate the unforgiving voice with the soft curves of this—woman. This is not a girl. Not some eighteen-year-old college freshman studying abroad for the first time. Hadn't Zia said she was in college? I trail my eyes down her bare legs to where one sandaled foot is tapping hard against the concrete then back up to where her arms are crossed tightly beneath her chest.

"Mi dispiace," I manage to choke out, wondering why my tongue chose Italian when the woman before me is so unabashedly American—phone in hand, taking a picture of my license plate like she's a detective at Interpol.

She checks the screen, nods once to herself, then slides the phone back into her pocket and turns on me, eyes narrowed so I can barely make out the color. Flecks of bronze in patina green. It reminds me of the fountain outside Palazzo Ducale in the late afternoon when the light catches the oxidized metal . . .

"Do you speak any English?" she asks slowly, her irritation with me growing by the moment.

I open my mouth to tell her of course, but I hesitate when she lifts a brow and tilts her head, loosening a bead of sweat that trails its way down her clavicle and under the dip in her neckline. Her buttons are askew and I start to point it out, but she shakes her head and makes a frustrated grunt, then yanks her bag off the curb with a thump as she bends to find the open button on the Fiat's trunk.

What the fuck, James? It's been a while since I've had to move on American time, but cultural pacing is not the issue here.

This—she—is not what I expected. Yes, she's a woman. A beautiful one at that—which she clearly knows by the way she holds herself and the look of genuine disdain she's giving me over her shoulder as she waits for the trunk to open fully. Yes, it's been a solid dry spell since Aleanna last spring. But there's something else about this woman. Something making my fingers itch for my camera.

I smile as I imagine her response to me requesting to photograph her right now. Have I ever been slapped by a woman besides Zia Nina?

I reach for her luggage to help, though honestly I don't know if this load will fit in the Fiat, but she beats me to it, shoving the thing in and making her way around the side as she murmurs to herself that "It's for the best we can't communicate because then you won't understand me when I call you an incompetent asshole for making me wait for over an hour after an eight-hour flight from hell."

I have to bite down hard on my lower lip not to laugh when she throws me a saccharine smile over the roof of the car, then slips out of sight into the passenger seat. I scratch at the stubble on the side of my cheek—no time to shave with Nina shoving at my back—and wait for a car to speed by before opening my door and sliding inside. I should tell her that I can understand her—apologize for my lateness in a language she can speak. Perhaps explain that I am not her hired help, but an actual, living, breathing human being. But something about the way she turns all the air-conditioning vents toward herself and widens her eyes at me as if to say *fuck off* makes me stop.

Instead, I buckle up and ask her profile, "Pronto?"

She pulls her nose up a little and then turns her body toward the window, shutting her eyes—the universal signal for shut up and let me nap.

And I can't help but smile as I shift into gear.

TRE

Ava

Whatever Tammy gave me is making my tongue stick to the roof of my mouth. I know hangovers worsen with age, but at the cusp of twenty-eight, I was hoping for a few more years before a little excess made me feel like roadkill post-vultures. Perhaps the champagne chasers pushed me over the edge. But really, who knew it could take so long for a pill to kick in?

My driver swerves around a mint-green Vespa as he takes another curve, and I'm definitely going to give this guy zero stars on whatever driving website he crawled out of. He's doing wonders for my headache—has even tossed me into the glass a few times with nothing but a muttered "me dis-pee-achay" to make up for the offense. The nap I needed is just one window concussion out of reach. An hour late and aggravated driving assault. My fingers itch to text Ethan again. But since he left my "I landed safely" text unread, another attempt would just leave me in the pitiful zone. Well, even further in the pitiful zone.

The truth is, this little "test" is so Ethan. He has this way of rationalizing the stupidest of ideas. When we planned our first hiking trip, he decided to have us dropped on a trail that was marked extreme by all the experienced hikers. One guy had written on the app, "Good luck not dying." And Ethan had said, "This way we will know if we are meant to be hikers." Like avoiding death should be the test for all skills in life. I'd twisted my ankle on a root mound about ten minutes up the mountain and he'd had to carry me back to the trailhead Troop Beverly Hills style. Needless to say, that was our last hike.

Why the hell did I go along with that stupid idea?

Because you always go along with Ethan's ideas.

I bet Ethan will want to have triplets. "Blah blah blah . . . Multiples will show us that we are really ready to be parents . . ."

"Che cosa?"

I turn. The driver's dark brows are pulled upward beneath his wavy hair, as he glances at me expectantly. Where does one get brows like that? Is there microblading in Italy?

Shit. I've been talking out loud.

"Oh, nothing, I'm just bitching about my boyfriend . . ."

The driver presses his full lips together. His nose is slightly crooked, "character crooked" as my mother used to call it. She'd make up an absurd story to explain.

Perhaps he'd busted it in a fight defending an old man from a purse snatcher.

Why was a man carrying a purse, mom?

Don't be small minded, Ava. Gender bias is so 1980.

What about a poorly timed head-ball in overtime of the World Cup?

She'd want to know which country he'd played for. Italy, obviously. Bronzed skin, thick lashes, dark eyes, lean build—Italian men are nice to look at, and this one is no exception. Terrible driver, but a fine specimen. Maybe I'll take a selfie with him to make Ethan suffer.

His mouth quirks up on the side and then he meets my gaze for a moment. We might not speak the same language but it's obvious he just caught me admiring the goods.

"It really is a shame you don't speak English because then you might be able to tell me what to do about my moronic man. You seem worldly. Like you've been with a few—"

His eyes are narrowed on the windshield. Am I really calling hot driver a manslut? This is Ethan's fault. And Tammy's for giving me drugs. My thumbs peck away at my phone, my eyes focused on her response to my "landed text," writing and rewriting the same question over and over. *Did you know?* She couldn't have. Oh God, what if she knew? I'm not sure what hurts more—that thought or the break itself. I quickly delete the words on the screen and recommence my babblethon.

"Well, you know what I mean. Italians are well-reputed lovers. So I'm sure you'd find my general tendency toward monogamy tedious and American. Apparently my boyfriend feels the same way. 'Experience the world,' he says. 'Oats to be sown,' he says." I let out a ladylike snort and look his way. "Got oats? Maybe, I should make a T-shirt."

I pull my attention away from his crooked grin and its culminating dimple to the hillside we are currently climbing, preparing myself for the switchbacks that are churning the champagne in my stomach. I go to grip the center console, but my hand lands on his hand on the gear instead as he shifts down. I pull away quickly and he chuckles.

"I know. Prude, puritan Americans. You have very nice hands, though. Very big. Are you driving me to Greece?"

We've been driving for well over two hours. Not that I can complain about the scenery. Just endless layers of green sloping up, up, and away into blue skies. I can see why this place produces artists like bunny rabbits.

Here and there the hills act like a pedestal for whatever architectural dream sits atop the bluff. The town we pass now appears to be a breath away from toppling over into the pasture below, soft earth-colored bricks defying gravity—an illustration from a Dr. Seuss book. The sun behind us lights the clinging village with an orange glow, and a shadow city spills across the valley behind the hill. It's all a bit like a fantasy novel—a land beyond Middle Earth. I can almost understand why my mother made me promise to travel here when my study abroad program became—impossible.

I swallow hard and reach for my purse and dip my hand into the front pocket, fingering the soft, worn edge of Mom's postcard, then turn my attention back toward hot driver. His obliviousness is a welcome distraction. The whole one-sided convo thing is kind of freeing. Talking to a man who can't understand a lick of what you're saying. If I wanted to sow those aforementioned oats, perhaps a language barrier would help. Something about the physicality of that would be extremely liberating. No words. Just bodies.

I'm feeling flushed and this car is absurdly small, so I pull one of his vents back toward me. He doesn't slap my hand away—just looks—amused?

"Ethan wants me to get it all out of my system—like there's a stockpile of sexuality somewhere inside of me that I can just sprinkle like seeds all over Urbino. Like I'm an Amazon warehouse just awaiting the right delivery men," I snort. "Such a man. No thought of the things that matter in bed. Like connection and respect and trust. Not that I'm complaining about Ethan in bed, though it would be nice if he was a little more vocal. And a little more adventurous. But no one is perfect—"

Hot Driver's jawline tightens as he takes a curve a little too quickly and I'm thrown close enough to smell his deodorant. Slightly spicy with a hint of something soft.

"You smell good. Really good."

Ugh, am I still drunk? He keeps on driving, his lips pressed tightly together as if he's focusing hard on the road. With all that focus, you'd think he could drive a bit better. I sigh. Back to my rant.

"The saddest part of it all is that I thought he was going to propose. So stupid, right? Pathetic."

There's a sudden heaviness on my shoulders, like gravity has doubled inside the car. There's nothing but the soft whir of the air spilling from the vents and I shut my eyes. Mom would know what to say. She'd wrap her arms around me. Let me feel sad, then say something brilliant and inspiring—or hilarious. There was always so much laughter.

A warm touch lands on my thigh and I open my eyes to see an impressive, bronzed hand lingering above my knee. I dimly register the fact that the car comes to a stop as I count the calluses against my skin. I pull my gaze upward away from the goose bumps forming on my thigh to find that we are parked halfway up a steep hill—the road we've been navigating has turned into nothing but dirt and stone that slips out of sight amid a cluster of bushy cypress trees.

Before I can ask where the hell we are, he whispers, "Siamo qui."

I nod, even though he makes no sense to me, and study the stubble that runs along his jawline. His eyes are looking right into me. *Siamo qui.* My lips try out the syllables.

He pulls his hand away slowly from my thigh, nodding, eyes on my mouth.

Then his door is open beside him. The interior is suddenly flooded with sound. A woman's voice. A dog bark-howling. Footsteps on gravel. The bleating of—goats?

I panic for a moment, suddenly sure my father's fears have actually come true. I'm the victim of some farming sex-trafficking scheme, but then I remember I confirmed the license plate with the one my advisor had sent me. And unless my abductor is a brilliant hacker, I am not being sex trafficked to a lonely goat farmer.

I look out the front windshield and take in the middle-aged woman in a long earth-colored dress who is clearly scolding Hot Driver. A dog—no no—the Beast from *The Sandlot* is circling him, his tale whacking against Hot Driver's thighs as he smiles down at it and scratches its dangling jowls. My head could fit in those jowls. The woman's gesticulating hands draw my attention back to her—mesmerizing me. She's the conductor at the Philadelphia Orchestra, but Hot Driver just kneels in the dirt and continues raking the Beast with those impressive hands, ignoring the woman's symphony over his head.

I open my door slowly and get slammed with a wall of heat and the smell of fresh hay. I open my mouth to assure her she doesn't need to yell at the driver—that I've taken care of that, but before I can make a sound, the angry Italian woman folds Hot Driver into her arms and then pulls away, mussing his hair with a deep laugh.

"I was worried, nipote! You are two hours late. Didn't Massimo buy me this dumb thing for a reason?" She holds up an old phone and pretends to toss it over her shoulder, then kisses his cheeks before turning her attention to me at the same time the Beast does.

I'm repeating her words in my head, making sense of them like they were said in a foreign language. But they weren't. My mind is muddy. The heat. The driver. The driver. All adding layers of muck to the swamp, but I know she's speaking perfect English—heavily accented, yes—but perfect nonetheless. She smiles at me just as the dog rams its wet nose up the back of my shorts. I try to push him away, but he just keeps burrowing between my cheeks, sniffing and snuffling loudly enough for all to hear. He's a horse. I spin, palm over rear, opting for agility over strength.

The driver whistles and the Beast retreats, satisfied with its knowledge of my ass, tongue happily lolling out of its massive jaws. Then the woman approaches with a single brow raised, slow steady steps on the dusty gravel drive. Her palms are out as if to say *don't run*. I'm still covering my butt with one hand. Another goat bleats and I rub my temple with the free hand.

"You must be Ava. I am Nina," she says, her smile stretching wider. Her hands land on my shoulders and I can see she has the same Italian eyes as Hot Driver—dark and knowing—but hers have fine lines that deepen as she smiles.

"What did you do to her, nipote?" She narrows those eyes at me as she kisses each of my cheeks. "You look a little—what's the word, James? Che è la parola? Piqued, no?"

I swivel slowly toward Hot Driv—James? Weird Italian name. He shrugs, one side of his mouth twitching as he lifts his brows at me.

"There are quite a few words I could think of to describe her," he says with a lazy smile.

My blood rushes to my face as he takes his time looking me over before continuing in eloquent, unaccented English, "But piqued works well enough, Zia."

QUATTRO

James

The American might have a better command of profanity than Zia Nina. And that is quite the achievement.

"What kind of asshole—"

"Stronzo," Nina provides in Italian.

"Stronzo"—she accepts the provision—"let's a woman they just met go on and on about the humiliating details of her love life—"

I lose track of the rant when Ava goes to drop the F-bomb and stops herself. Nina is assuring her that her restraint is unnecessary—that the four-letter word is her favorite in the English language. But their voices fade away and I catch myself wondering what filters would capture the coloring on the American's cheeks in this light.

"Nipote, do you have anything to say to our guest?" Nina asks.

"Hmm?" I pull my attention away from full lips and red-streaked skin and focus on the poorly hidden amusement on my aunt's face. Her tongue is about to poke a hole through her cheek.

"La donna è un'ospite di tuo zio, Gigi," Nina says. She's glaring at me for Ava's sake, but I can already hear the throaty laugh that will fill the air when she tells my uncle this story.

"I apologize for your misunderstanding and I hope you'll enjoy your stay here—"

"I'm not staying here," the American says. Her glare is real, burning my forehead like the midafternoon sun.

I shrug and open my hand toward Zia, who is obviously in charge in her long linen dress and apron.

"No offense, ma'am. But there's been a mistake," Ava says, more softly this time as she addresses Nina while reaching into her oversized purse. What is with this woman's bags? They could fit Verga inside. Where is that dog anyway? I want to give him a treat for the enthusiastic greeting he gave our guest's ass.

She pulls out a planner as thick as the Bible, with about thirteen colored tabs poking out from the side like rainbow bike spokes, then slides a folded piece of paper from the pages. "This is the apartment I rented. On Via Ma-zzi-ni."

Her Italian is shit. Who comes to study here with no command of the local language? She shoves the paper toward me and rattles on, her tone tight and angry again since she's looking my way.

"Modern. In the city center. No goats."

I take the paper without looking and slip it into my pocket.

"Nothing in Urbino is modern, dolcezza. And those animals over there"—I gesture toward the fields that slide down the hill where the sheep are grazing happily—"those are sheep."

Nina purses her lips and wipes one hand over the other—the Italian gesture for "it's nothing."

Ava blinks twice.

"The apartment is—how should I say—in disrepair, no?" Nina asks, then looks to me like I have all the answers. I didn't even know who I was driving until this morning when Nina handed me the sign, so there's no surprise that Nina's rented out the apartment without my knowledge. My aunt shrugs her shoulders and I shake my head and focus on Angry Smurf who is back on her phone for the thousandth time since we met. I'd love to take it out of her hand and throw it over the hill.

"If we are talking about the studio on Via Mazzini, then yes. Air-conditioner is broken and there's a leak in the roof," I add, then turn to Zia and lift my chin. "Which I could have handled had someone told me the apartment was being rented this summer."

I was under the impression that I was living here to fix up the guest house and help with the farm during tourist season. But this wouldn't be the first time my impressions were mistaken with Zia Nina. She and my Zio are the conductors, and I'm lucky if they hand me sheet music.

Nina makes a dismissive sound and the American looks to the sky. I hear her whisper something that sounds like "Why, Mom?" then she settles her gaze back on me.

"Can't I just put a bucket under the drip or get a fan with some ice . . ."

All of the fight has leaked from her voice. Her bare shoulders drop an inch and her words trail off. I have the sudden urge to tip her chin up. Just like I had in the car when she overshared her secrets.

"Don't be silly, carina. My husband and I will host you until James can fix it up." Nina steps up and puts an arm around the girl. "It is nothing. Dottore Pastore is an old friend."

"You know my advisor?" Ava asks, leaning into my Aunt's touch. Nina has that effect on everyone. Born nurturer. Keeper of lost souls like mine.

"Certo. How do you think you ended up here? He studied with my husband, Leonardo. Leo is the dean of the university here, but this can all wait. You must be tired, carina." Nina makes a dismissive hand wave and points up the gravel path then turns to me. "Gi, show her to the guest house."

I open my mouth to object and Nina widens her eyes and tips up her chin at me. I close my mouth. Nina turns and leaves, murmuring something patently false about a pregnant sheep and kicking up a poof of dust in her wake.

"Right. To the guest house," I murmur, tugging the ridiculously large luggage to my side before I set off again for the house.

"Could you fix my apartment tonight?"

I laugh.

"Right on top of that, principessa."

She ignores the sarcasm and keeps at it, though. Persistent little thing.

"I feel like that's the least you could do after—"

"Driving six hours to escort you from the airport?" I can feel her right behind me, her breathing growing heavier as I pick up the pace.

"I was going to tip you on top of whatever you got paid for that, but with the delay and then the lies." She sighs. "I'll double whatever they are paying you to fix my apartment."

I stop short and she runs right into my back. The American thinks I'm some sort of hired help. A butler, maybe? Family chauffeur? How entitled is this woman? I think back to my exchange with Nina. She only used the word nipote when addressing me, and for all the Italian the American knows she could be translating that word as manservant.

Our collision makes me drop the handle of her overpacked suitcase, and it wobbles then falls to the gravel at her feet with a thump, sending dust and dirt onto her toes. She stares at her luggage, shuts her eyes, and takes in a deep breath that makes her chest rise so it's nearly touching mine.

"Listen, Signorina Graham," I start.

She clears her throat and I find her staring at my jaw. I start again. "I'm not sure who or what you think I am—"

I stop. Her eyes are darker than they were at the airport, more like the needles on the cypress trees that line the path up to my Zia's. Her brows pull together, forming two little indents above her nose. My fingers go to my chest where my camera usually hangs, but I find only fabric.

Ava must think I'm finished because she takes over. "I think you were my driver who was over an hour late. Who then lied about speaking English and sat soaking up all of my personal information like some sort of villainous sponge. And who finally just manhandled my belongings like a gorilla," she says, pointing to her fallen luggage.

Villainous sponge? I'm biting hard on my lip so I don't smile and piss her off further, but come on. I know I should apologize. She's Zio's guest—and my uncle is the best man I know. But the clipped tone. The privilege that oozes out of her like the chocolate from the center of Zia's lava cakes.

"Fine. I'll fix the apartment tonight for five hundred euro," I tell her, surprising myself with the obvious lie. I lift my brows and hold out my palm. "Deal?"

She makes a sound somewhere between a growl and a sigh, puts her hand in mine without meeting my eyes, and then reaches down and lifts her handle.

"I'll show myself to my room," she says.

"You can pay me tomorrow," I tell her back as she takes off in the direction of the house murmuring the word stronzo over and over again. There's a wet mark on her ass from where Verga drooled all over her, and I know I'm smiling like a lunatic as I look after her. But that exchange was the most fun I've had since—

"What did you do to her, Gi?"

Zio Leo steps out from between the trees, a bouquet of sunflowers in one hand and pruning shears in the other. My favorite camera, a gift from Nonna, hangs around his neck. He's smiling so wide I can see the gold tooth in the back of his top row of teeth. His thick dark brows are lifted to that hairline that refuses to budge. Sneaky, handsome old bastard.

I shrug and he puts his hand on my shoulder.

"Women, no?" he offers, following my gaze to where Ava disappears around the final curve of the path, stumbling a little when Verga goes down into playful puppy pose like he's about to pounce.

"Did you take any pictures, Zio?" I ask, nodding toward his chest.

"Certo," he chuckles. "There was much to capture during the arrival of our guest."

My uncle presses the flowers against my chest. "Forse, these will help?" He reaches into his back pocket and pulls out an envelope. "Another note from London."

I take the sunflowers even though I know they won't help, and then shove the envelope in my back pocket to be filed away with the others.

"You know, Gi. You might consider what the man has to say. A sabbatical could be good for you."

He runs a hand through his thick gray hair then removes my camera strap from behind his neck and lifts it up and over mine, patting my sweaty chest once as I look him over. The man is always impeccably dressed, even at home on the farm, a mix of Professor Indiana Jones and Robert Langdon, but with an Armani twist. Always dressed the part. Three-piece suits are apparently the uniform of a dean of a five-hundred-year-old university.

"I always consider it," I lie. "But my family is here."

We start to walk, our strides matching despite the five inches I have on him. It's muscle memory—this pace we keep—ingrained in us from two decades of walking together side by side to and from the city proper and campus. When I was a boy, he never left me behind. And now I return the favor.

"And we will be here when you return. That is what family does," he says, putting a hand on my shoulder.

But we both know that the second part of that statement isn't always true. It's time to change the topic.

"How long is she here?" I ask, keeping my tone as even as I can while lifting the camera to cover my face as Zio studies me.

But Zio speaks seven languages fluently. He is a master of communication. Has degrees in words that I don't even know the meaning of. So whatever I'm trying to keep out of my voice, I have little chance of hiding.

He lets out a throaty chuckle and pats my back twice before letting out his signature sigh.

"Long enough, Gi. Long enough."

CINQUE

Ava

Not even half a day's travel freshly dumped and a lying asshole welcome committee could ruin the charm around me. The moment I round the curve, the Beast still tight to my side despite my shooing motion, I almost forget that the two men who stole my dignity even exist. As much as one can forget being humiliated twofold—but this. This place is a fairy tale.

Tan and gray stone stacked together in varying patterns, evergreen painted shutters hanging like ornaments, burnt sienna tiles sliding down the roof, and ivy—so much ivy, dripping from every window as if mother nature were standing inside the oversized openings pouring it out of a bucket.

I realize I've let my luggage fall much like the ape did moments ago, but I leave it as I follow the Beast's wagging tale toward the side of the villa. I run my finger against the stone and sniff the chalky residue left behind. Smells like ancient dust. Earth. And goat—excuse me, sheep. I tangle my hands in the ivy, let it twist between my fingers. Shit. I hope this isn't poison ivy.

There's a distant barking. I've lost sight of my canine guide. The tinkling murmur of water on water pulls me around the back of the villa, and I find myself two steps from toppling into the bluest pool I've ever seen. The water is cascading over the far edge of the Olympic-size rectangle, down to a place I cannot see, both because it disappears out of sight and because my eyes are fixated on the view beyond—golden hills roll down and over one another, flanked by dense woods. It's a sea of sun-kissed, grassy waves. Spotted here and there by green puffs of trees with fluffy white sheep resting in their shade.

I lift my phone to capture a picture and nearly drop it in the water when I hear, "Ciao, bella. Ti piacerebbe nuotare con me?"

I shield my eyes from the sun and turn to find a teenage boy lounging poolside in the tiniest Speedo to grace this planet.

"I'm sorry. No hablo Italian," I try, mentally kicking myself for not sticking to my Duolingo when the fact that I used Spanish registers in my addled brain. Between interviews and studying for finals and the MBE, something had to go.

I attempt to reach about half the wattage of the boy's smile to make up for my incompetence. His curly dark hair is overgrown and he runs both hands through it doing nothing to keep it in check. He stands and gestures to my body.

"Allora, did you bring a bathing suit?" the boy asks in perfect English.

Note to self: everyone is multilingual except you.

"Yes, I did, but—"

"Is it a bikini?"

His thick eyebrows lift over his perfectly rounded brown eyes. The picture of innocence.

"Massimo, entra in casa prima che ti colpisca con questo cucchiaio!" Nina's voice reaches us loud and clear from inside the house as the shutters fly open. She's waving a spoon, and a moment later the smell of garlic and olive oil smack me straight in the gut. I hear it growl in response. The Beast whines and tilts his head at me.

"Calmati, Mamma. Sto arrivando!" he shouts back, then turns his white teeth back toward me like a shark and sweetly says, "Va bene. Bikini later then, no?"

I don't even have a chance to answer the little creep before he's scampering through a huge set of wooden double doors that have been left ajar. The Beast chases after him, tail wagging like crazy.

Nina points at me with her spoon, then points to a tiny faded stone building at the far side of the pool. "There, Ava. That is the guest house. You've now met my son Massimo. Che fortunata!" She rolls her eyes heavenward and I laugh. Had to give it to the kid. Hitting on an older woman was creepy, but it meant he had some balls. They might not have descended yet, but—

"You seem to have lost James, no? The guest house is open." Nina says.

I turn my attention to the guest house and the way it dangles precariously over the edge of the hill, threatening to spill over like the pool water.

"Sì, I lost lo stronzo," I murmur. "Grazie, Nina," I say louder.

She gives me a knowing smile. "Dinner at eight, but I left you a tray of formaggi, prosciutto, e pane in il piccolo fridge," she says, and salutes me with the spoon, then disappears back inside the huge window frame.

I turn to my temporary home. It's small. Quaint. Also covered in ivy. A huge glass double door takes up most of its front. Not a great entryway to protect from peeping Massimos.

I carefully make my way around the water, though taking a plunge wouldn't be an entirely unwelcome break from this heat. This definitely isn't the modern apartment in the city center that Pastore helped me rent, but there are worse things than a little voyeurism and some olive oil–scented country air. I'll just have to adjust some of my itinerary with the distance from town. But surely sharing housing with the dean should give me some invaluable insight into the seminar.

I hear my mom laughing at this shitstorm of a day and for the thousandth time in twenty-four hours I can't help but wish she were here beside me, in this place she spoke of with awe, the place she made me swear to visit. She'd smile and pull me close and tell me again that "*Life doesn't care about our plans, love.*" Life certainly didn't care about hers. But that's just a reason to plan harder. Control what you can.

I take in a deep, humid breath and yank open the heavy glass door with a heave. I'm welcomed with a blast of frigid air. No problems with this air-conditioner obviously. The inside is surprisingly spacious. The clean white cathedral ceiling stretches high above my head, the joints and beams stained a soft grayish-brown. Or perhaps not stained at all. There are built-in bookshelves on both walls that flank me, books of every color stacked neatly together, interrupted only by a few windows and a litany of black-and-white photographs that are framed with the same barnwood that runs throughout the space. The natural light streams over the cloud-like comforter on the huge iron bed. There's a thin wooden door in the corner that must lead to the bathroom. But the true selling point of the space is the view. The far wall is a plane of spotless glass, a window overlooking the endless slopes and soft summits. I trace the rolling lines with my finger in the air and let out a sigh.

Perhaps I was a bit hasty with my negotiations with lo stronzo. I wonder if I'll see him working around the farm before he returns to sleep under whatever rock he came from. I picture him shearing the sheep—his huge bronzed hands moving back and forth over the wool. Though he definitely didn't smell like a shepherd. He smelled fresh—spicy clean. Ugh. I told him that. In English. A language he clearly understands.

I curse Tammy and her pills one last time and shake myself out of the cringe to close the door behind me, not wanting to lose any more cold air. Obviously, my intrusive farmhand thoughts mean I'm delusional from the hours upon hours of travel. Or maybe they are sent from deep within my subconscious as a revenge plot against the man across the pond.

I head straight for the mini fridge, plucking a piece of cheese off the tray Nina left on the top rack and nibbling at it as I kick off my shoes. It's sharp and flaky with a nutty aftertaste, and I want to gnaw on an entire wheel, but the bed is calling. I fall into the down pillows and let them fold around me. A night or two here might be a nice adventure—something to write home about on Mom's postcard that's burning a hole in my purse lining. Something to distract me from the lingering hurt and rage I feel toward Ethan right now. The sting of betrayal at the thought that Tammy might have known his intentions. The dread of telling my father about the job I accepted without consulting him. I consider using my five minutes just to call and curse Ethan out, but I'm too exhausted to even move, let alone creatively cuss. And my phone is in my purse at least three feet away.

My eyes feel so heavy. Jet lag and hangover are teaming up to swallow me. I can hear them high-five beneath the throbbing at my temple. And though the worst thing I can do is submit, there's not an ounce of fight left in me.

The air whirs softly from the sleek split AC unit above the bed. A little catnap and then—more food. Let's see what all this buzz surrounding authentic Italian cuisine is about. Just as I'm about to give in to the sleep, my eyes catch a pop of color above the desk. A bouquet of gorgeous sunflowers. My mom's favorite. I drift off with the image of the buttery petals on the inside of my lids.

SEI

James

We are well into our secondi piatti when the American graces us with her presence.

She's freshly showered, her skin still flushed from the heat of the high-pressure triple showerhead I installed in the guest house last year. I love that thing. I imagine our guest loving it as well and shift in my seat, trying to refocus on the plate in front of me but failing miserably.

Her hair is blown out around her shoulders, no more messy travel bun, and the navy dress she's sporting is tailored perfectly to every curve on her body like a second skin—so well fitted that I can perfectly make out the outline of her phone in her hip pocket. Could she not just leave that thing in the guest house? She's probably waiting for it to ring at any second with a groveling idiot on the other end begging her for forgiveness.

My uncle clears his throat and taps my arm, and I notice he and Massimo are standing to welcome her. I push up from my seat expecting to see her eyebrows lifted at me with haughty disdain, but she's not even looking my way. Her hand is outstretched to my uncle.

"Dean Russo," she says. "It's a pleasure to meet you. Thank you so much for hosting me."

Zio pulls her inward and plants a kiss on each of her cheeks.

"Any student of Pastore's is welcome here. Especially one with the acclamations that he has given you. It is our pleasure."

She turns to Nina with the same genuine smile—one that has yet to be sent my way—and says, "This all smells so delicious, Nina. My stomach woke me up and saved me from sleeping straight through the night."

"Sit here," Massimo tells her with a devilish smile, pulling out the seat beside him. Nina gives him the look and pulls out the seat next to me instead as she stands.

"Sit, carina. Mangia. I will get the melanzana," she says, putting her hand lightly on Ava's shoulder and then making her way into the kitchen to fetch more eggplant.

Everything about the woman taking the seat beside me screams impeccable manners. Where were those manners with me? Apparently, I was deemed unworthy.

"You are finding the guest house comfortable, no?" my uncle asks.

Ava nods and the flame from the lantern at the center of the table catches the gold in her hair as her head moves. There's a shadow dancing in the tiny indent below her clavicle. My fingers itch again. But my camera is in the kitchen.

"The guest house is beautiful. Obviously, you and Nina have impeccable taste," she says gesturing to the space around us. Everything in the dining room is handcrafted—some things, like the olive wood buffet and the bench surrounding the stone fireplace, were made by my uncle and me. Others come from my Zio's and Zia's travels through Italia.

My uncle presses his lips together and looks my way, lifting a brow, silently asking if he should redirect the American's compliment my way. I shake my head subtly. The woman doesn't need to know that I designed and built the guest house. We need to keep her arsenal limited or she'll be requesting updates and remodels when we move her along to the apartment.

She finally glances my way, following my uncle's gaze. Her eyes narrow, possibly wondering why the family butler is sitting at the right hand of the dean.

"I thought you'd be working tonight," she says softly enough for only me to hear.

I dip a piece of bread into the wild boar ragù left on my plate and take a bite, chewing slowly while she waits for me to answer. Being stuck at a table with me is nearly breaking the pleasant manners she's perfecting—seemingly for my aunt's and uncle's benefit only. I dab my mouth with my napkin and she lets out a sigh.

"I decided there are more important things than money," I say at full volume. "Like having dinner with my family."

I pat Zio Leo's arm and he rolls his eyes.

There's a fleeting moment where Ava's soft green pupils dilate and her lids lift as understanding hits her, but she grits her teeth into a smile and nods.

"That makes sense. It wasn't adding up why such a kind and generous family would keep someone like you around," she says, her voice low. She takes a sip of the red wine Massimo has filled to the brim, not spilling a drop and keeping her eyes on mine as she drinks. Impressive. "But now—knowing you are their blood—they have little choice in the matter."

My uncle makes a sound in his chest that I know is a suppressed chuckle, and Max kicks me beneath the table. I turn to meet my cousin's stare and he waggles his eyebrows at me. Twelve going on twenty, that one. I throw a piece of bread at him and he picks it off his lap and eats it with a grin.

"Well, it seems you and my nephew are acquainted, no?" Uncle Leo says, gesturing between Ava and me. He meets Nina's eyes over our heads as she enters from the kitchen.

"Certo. Very acquainted," Nina confirms. "That is why Ava needed to learn all of those Italian profanities today." She throws me a wink and slips back into her seat at the head of the table, motioning with her hand for Ava to take more.

"You will find, Ms. Graham, that James comes and goes as he pleases, but will never miss a meal," Zio Leo tells her. "Though in the summer he's a more constant fixture." That about sums it up. I nod once.

"How charming," Ava mumbles as she forks a huge piece of eggplant onto her already full plate. She's never going to eat all of that. The woman weighs less than my dog when she's soaking wet. "So he's like your own version of Uncle Eddie from *Christmas Vacation*."

I groan. Of course she'd pick my uncle's all-time favorite American movie. He has a thing for Chevy Chase and forces us to watch his movies at least once a month. He's nodding vigorously, smiling wider than I've seen in some time.

"Essatamente, Ms. Graham. Well said!"

"I think Nina might need help in the kitchen," I grumble, standing up to get the hell out of the line of fire, though I'm used to this gently barbed banter. Ball-busting is a tradition at this table, but I really just want an excuse to find my camera. The moonlight is doing incredible things with the shadows tonight.

"How can I need help nella cucina if I'm right here, James?" Nina asks, making a hmmm noise after.

"I'll do the dishes." I go to grab Max's plate across from me and he snarls. Zio smacks the back of his head and hands me his.

Like clockwork, Verga appears beside me, his tongue hanging out the side of his mouth, ready for its job.

"What kind of horse is that?" Ava asks, fork halfway to her mouth.

Nina chuckles.

"A Clydesdale," my uncle answers.

"Verga is a Neapolitan mastiff," I correct, patting his head with my free hand. He was a gift from my Zio and Zia.

"You named him Verga. How dark. Why's his face all messed up like that?" she asks, then shoves an impossibly large bite of pasta into her mouth. She chews slowly and her lids fall closed, the first bite of Nina's pasta temporarily flooding her senses. Her expression sends me spiraling back to my first bites here, Nina beside me in the kitchen directing me what to taste and how.

Ava lets out a soft sound and I have to look away, choosing Verga as the safest landing spot. Handsome, loyal boy.

I lift a brow at Ava.

"His face is perfect. Mastiffs have wrinkles. You know who Giovanni Verga is?"

She stops chewing and meets my eyes. Swallows hard. I follow the line of her neck back up to her mouth.

"You assume because I can't speak the language, I can't read the country's authors?" she asks.

I shake my head, but hold her stare and say, "Of course not. Only an ignorant ass makes assumptions about language abilities."

She narrows her eyes at me, clenches her jaw until a tiny divot appears at the corner. She looks like she wants to kick me in the balls. I hurry out of the dining space before she can get up to do so and nearly trip on Verga, who is waiting for me to put the plates down so he can lick them clean. Conversation continues at the table and I make sure to make a lot of noise so it doesn't seem like I'm eavesdropping.

"I'm so excited to meet the lawyers and professors I'll be working with," Ava says.

Brown-noser.

I imagine my Zio smiling kindly at her as I try to grab the licked plate off of the floor and Verga shifts his hind quarters to block me. At least he didn't snarl like Massimo.

"Actually, Ms. Graham," Zio begins, "we have some sad news about this year's seminar. It seems that most of the lawyers were at a conference in Nuremberg this past week and have fallen ill with some sort of contagion."

Everything is quiet for a moment. No forks on plates. No polite chatter or pass the pecorino. I realize I'm bent over, stopped in mid-motion, both hands on Verga's flank ready to push with my eyes so wide they might fall right out of my head.

Ava's voice finally breaks the silence, shaky and soft. "Surely the seminar is just postponed for a week?"

Silence.

"Right?" She's barely audible.

My Zio lets out a long sigh. "Sfortunamente, no. We just got notice that the seminar is canceled completely."

I flinch a little, waiting to hear the sound of Ava's head explode. She's had a day. Asshat boyfriend giving her a hall pass. Apartment rental a no go. Now her program of study canceled. Shit—and me. I played a part in her hellish day. I don't have a second to sit quietly in my guilt before Zio Leo's booming voice reaches me again.

"Not to worry, cara. Pastore has given me explicit instructions to take care of you, and I have worked out a course of action, which I'm sure he would approve of, but he is a bit off the grid at the moment. You will assist in un'altra classe and receive all the credits that were promised for matriculation. No problem at all. Any professor here would welcome a student like you."

I can feel Ava's reluctant relief through the stone wall and I find my own shoulders loosening with my uncle's words. This woman does not seem to flex and shift easily. I wonder how many pages of that absurd planner she'll need to rip out with these changes.

I wrestle the plates from Verga, who, in all honesty, has given up the fight, and stand to wash them. I turn the water on and refocus on the task at hand, washing hard like I can scrub away the nagging guilt for adding to this poor woman's shitty Italian welcome. Surely, Zio will take care of her at our university. There are many political science classes to choose from—Professore Giugno teaches one on Italian government. The American will be fine.

I turn off the water and leave the dishes to dry, turning to find my camera on the butcherblock counter. That camera was once the only thing on the planet that could make me miss dessert. I tell myself it still is. I have not been chased away by a sharp-tongued hellion.

I lift the strap over my head, roll the lens twice between my fingers, then turn it in my hand to look at the picture Zio took earlier on the display screen, for the thousandth time today. The picture of the scene in the driveway comes to life when I turn the dial.

Ava is partially concealed by my shoulders, her eyes tiny slits of fury, her skin flushed, her finger pointed at my chest. There's the hint of my dimple beneath the dark stubble on my cheek and part of the profile of my nose—the bump on the bridge from being kicked in the face during a calcio match—apparent from my Zio's angle. He captured the exact moment that she called me a gorilla. I chuckle at the image and bring the viewfinder to my left eye as I walk outside.

Time to scratch that itch.

SETTE

Ava

Someone has tipped over the fuck-with-Ava dominoes, and I'm wondering how many more are left to fall.

I lick the chocolate from my fork and try not to groan—especially with Massimo across the table waggling his bushy brows at me every ten minutes. Nina has given me three little lava cakes—count them, three. As if she knew that the only thing that could bring me back from the ledge was her little mounds of gooey heaven. Italy, thus far, has taken my well-crafted plan and used it as toilet paper. One wipe by Ethan. Two wipes for my apartment and my coursework. And three wipes by the absent asshole, James. The study portion of study abroad is making lazy circles in the flushed toilet, and that awful spin in my head that I haven't felt since after Mom is making it hard to breathe.

My mother's voice gently nudges me to *remember why I'm here.* As if I could forget.

Though in reality I only promised to travel here, not stay. So contractually, I could call it a day and head back. Clean up the mess with Ethan and work out a way to earn my final credits at home.

The second the thought lands I feel sick to my stomach like I did when I was little and tried to hide something from her. Nothing twists the soul like guilt.

Maybe regret. Regret hurts too. Lucky me. I've got both swirling together like a twist of soft-serve ice cream.

And then someone dipped that soft-serve in a hard chocolate shell of anger.

I want nothing more than to call my advisor and get some reassurance about these impromptu changes, but he's on an adventure expedition in the Galápagos. So I have to trust Leo and go with the terrifying flow. I'm more she-who-engineers-the-levees-to-control-the-flow. But I can adapt. I must.

I chew the last bite of cake slowly—consider lifting my plate for a lick, but when I look around to make sure no one is watching, I find Verga staring at me from beneath his skin flaps. He whines and I put the plate back on the table.

Nina and Leo have left me with their pervy tween son, and he's watching me eat like I'm a rare zoo animal at feeding time.

"Do they not have chocolate in America?" he asks. His teeth are so perfect.

"Do they have braces in Italy?" I ask.

"You like my smile, no?"

Oh shit. Do not encourage. Do not engage.

I put my plate on the floor for Verga and ignore the imp.

"Dogs cannot have chocolate," he tells me, wagging his finger twice at me. "Luckily there was none left on that plate after you made love to it."

I scrunch my nose as I push up from the table. Time to escape. Nina has put me under strict instructions to take a walk up the hill path after I finish my espresso, and I'm unsure if anyone in their right mind would defy Nina. Though she did tell Massimo to leave me alone and, alas, alone I am not. But he's obviously not in his right mind. My gaze settles on the bushy-headed boy as I round the table, being careful not to give Verga or him access to my ass.

"I don't think the normal rules apply for this dog. I'll see you around." I finger wave goodbye.

"Don't forget you promised me a swim," he calls after me.

I pick up my pace and elongate my stride as far as it can stretch in my favorite dress, heading straight for the path in the woods that I have yet to explore, hoping not to be followed by prepubescent hormones. I pull my phone from my pocket, check that the ringer is on for the one hundredth time today, and then slide it back in its place, feeling pathetic for thinking that maybe I missed his call. *Stay present*, my mom reminds me, and I let out a long breath and focus on the scene.

The gravel and dirt is lined with shepherd's hooks as it leads uphill through the trees, and hanging on each one is a tiny black lantern that casts a fan of soft light out toward my bare toes. The light is entirely unnecessary tonight with the full moon above, but the décor adds a sense of safety in the darkness.

The thought has barely grazed my brain when there's a rustling in the leaves beside me. My hand goes to my hip where my purse always hangs, chock full o' Mace and rape whistles that my dad thrusts upon me along with the crime rates in Philly every time we meet up for dinner. He can't seem to comprehend the idea that the Main Line doesn't really count as the city proper. The movement stops for a moment. Are there bears in Italy?

The leaves explode in the darkness and a huge wrinkly-faced mastiff bounds out of the brush toward me and leaps majestically through the air. I'm admiring said leap when two front paws connect with my chest, copping a generous feel, and I plop gracelessly on my ass. His tongue accosts me—gives me the kind of facial I'd pay hundreds for in Center City—while I try to karate chop him off of my chest. I'm a fly compared to him. I start to just play dead when the sound of a whistle fills my head and I think I'm imagining my rape whistle. But then the Beast is gone, up the hill and out of sight, leaving a trail of floating silvery dust in his wake.

A dark figure makes its way toward me down the hill, through the dust, and I'm reminded of that time when Harry catches Voldemort drinking unicorn blood. Except I'm the unicorn.

As Voldemort approaches, I notice he's holding a camera in front of his face, the click of his finger in rapid succession just audible over the chirping crickets.

"You alright?" he asks.

"Voldemort would have been better," I murmur, picking myself up off the path with as much dignity as one can muster after being mounted by a dog. I ignore the proffered hand and wipe off my dress.

"Verga has taken quite a liking to you," James points out, snapping away as I fix my hemline.

"So it would seem."

"Follow me," he says.

"To further humiliation?"

His hand closes around the skin above my elbow and I suck in a sharp breath. I mutter some lie about his hands being cold, but James doesn't let go, just lifts his mouth into a lopsided grin and then tugs me softly up the path.

"No more humiliation. I've decided to tolerate you," he tells me. I notice that the hand that isn't holding me still has the camera balanced firmly in its grip. His fingers are rolling along the dial on the lens, restless and eager.

"How magnanimous of you," I murmur. "You're a photographer then?"

He looks at me for a moment, shakes his head a little, then lets out a frustrated breath.

"You realize how American it is to make everyone fit inside a single box," he asks—no, tells me.

I consider shrugging off his hand, but it is sliding down toward my wrist and I'm not sure I have the will. But then I picture Ethan's long, elegant fingers and nonchalantly slide my wrist out of his calloused hand.

"You realize how condescending you are, right? Would you prefer art-eest?" I ask, making sure to top on some extra sarcasm.

"I'm a lot of things, Ava. Most people are. Get used to it," he says.

But I've stopped listening to him.

The earth has ended—dropped out from beneath us—and a fortress is rising from below us like it's an extension of the rocky hills it was built upon.

"Is that Atlantis?" I whisper.

James chuckles, a low, deep sound that shakes the air around me.

"Urbino," he says, his voice soft. Reverent.

And I can see why.

The walled city appears to be built of gold—thousands of lights illuminate the sawdust-colored stone that stretches in every direction, peaking here and there into bronzed turrets and duomos that seem to reach into the stars above. It's a castle—no, it's more. More welcoming. A palace? A kingdom? It's unlike anything I've ever seen.

"I've seen it on my postcard, but . . ."

My thought trails off as I trace the expanse of the walls with a finger in the air, dipping down and around the hillsides that surround it.

"The image rarely captures the reality," James says, and I sneak a glance at his profile.

He lifts the camera to his eye just as I notice the way his top lip rests just slightly over the bottom.

"Enjoying the view?" he asks, turning the camera on me.

"I've seen better."

He's snapping away and I roll my eyes and turn back toward Urbino and all of its splendor.

"It seems quiet down there," I say to myself.

"In the summer, yes. When the semester begins it gets a bit more boisterous," he explains.

"College town."

He nods. "Something like that."

This is the longest we've gone without insulting one another. I'm about to point that out when he speaks.

"You seem a little old to be a college student," he says.

There goes that. Patronizing shit.

"I'm twenty-eight. And I'm graduating from law school. Not college."

"Don't get huffy. It was just an observation." He turns toward me and lets the camera fall to his chest.

"Huffy? You mean like leaving a family dinner because you can't handle some light teasing?"

He smiles. Steps forward. And I realize I'm standing on my toes to try to match his height and I'm still falling short. Annoying. I left my heels on the porch.

"Yes, exactly like that." His voice lowers an octave. He steps forward again and the lens from his camera is an inch from my chin. I don't budge.

"Why Italy? Surely there were better law programs than Urbino's?" he asks.

And here it is. Once I pull the mom card, there's no putting it back in the deck. He's watching me like I might hold the answers to the universe. I open my mouth. Close it. Turn back toward the view and pull out my phone from where it's tucked in my dress pocket.

"I made a promise," I say, voice thick now, trying to pull up the camera on my homescreen to ignore his probing gaze.

He makes a low sound in his throat and I can smell him—it's lemon, that scent I couldn't put my finger on earlier. Mint and lemon.

"Interesting. Una promessa . . ."

His Italian is as smooth as Nina's lava cake. I glance back up to find his lens trained on me again. I lift a brow.

"You will be deleting the pictures of your dog taking advantage of me," I tell him.

He grins, his eyes so dark I cannot find where pupil becomes iris. I turn my focus back out to Urbino and hold up my phone to capture the memory, pressing wildly at the red button like it can protect me from his presence beside me.

He leans into the empty space beside my ear, his breath and the breeze mingling along my neck.

"Certo, dolcezza."

The roll of those Zs slides down my spine and my eyes fall shut. My mother told me the language was intoxicating, and she didn't lie. I can feel every sound slipping along my skin—teasing and caressing. I take a small step forward to escape the sensation easing down my back, and James's hand shoots out to grab me. The shock of his touch sends my phone up and out of my fingers.

My eyes pop open and I look down just in time to see the glimmer of my rose gold case bounce over the edge of the cliff and plunge into the darkness below.

I stare after it for some time trying to make sense of what's happened. Someone has placed a hex on me. I'm cursed. I pissed off a deity. I turn toward James, and his eyes are round, his lip pulled between his teeth as he watches me like I might explode into a thousand angry pieces.

I let out a breath that might have been in my lungs for an hour and look up to the sky.

"Ava, I'm—"

"You knocked my phone over the cliff," I cut him off.

"That's not exactly what—"

"Why did you do that?"

"You were going to fa—"

I put up my hand for him to shut up.

I want to take all of the bubbling anger in my chest out on him, and if he says one wrong word, I'm scared of what I might do. Maybe send him tumbling over that cliff after my phone.

"At least now you won't be tortured by having to check to see—"

The sound that comes out of me is a mix of Xena Warrior Princess and the sound a motor makes when you run out of gasoline. He takes a step back and holds up his hands. I turn my back on him and head back down the path, walking as quickly as my bare feet allow, ignoring the happy prancing mastiff that's at my side. I need to crawl into bed and wake up on the other side of this god-awful shitstorm of a day. I need to recover, recoup, and replan.

I need to stay the hell away from James.

OTTO

Ava

My wits have fully recovered (almost) and I'm ready to face day two.

I will no longer let the chaos of this place control me, nor will I let Ethan's shortsightedness ruin my plans for our future together. I'll give myself one more day to cool down, then I'll use that five-minute calling card and someone else's phone to do what I do best—convince and persuade. As for Italy—I'm gonna beat her crazy ass into submission. Gonna make this country my bitch. I'm determined to give my mom the authentic study abroad experience that I promised—but my way. Controlled. On my terms.

So I've put the bullshit that was yesterday behind me with a solemn promise to stay wine-free and pill-free for the near future, and got a fullish night's rest (not including some pesky graphic dreaming and a few sheep sound wake-ups), and I've showered (albeit a far colder shower than the first), and dressed in my most professional pencil skirt and blouse and twisted my hair into a no-nonsense updo. This is my take-me-seriously-or-else outfit. My don't-fuck-with-me outfit. My—

"Ms. Graham." There is a gentle knock on the guest house glass and I turn away from my reflection in the mirror to find Dean Russo outside with a tray in one hand. My room-service-from-a-dean outfit.

I push the door open with a smile.

"Buongiorno, Dean Russo," I say.

Yep. I practiced my Italian from the phrase book my mother gave me years ago. Well into the night, because I broke the jet lag rule by taking a nap—and it took hours to settle the anger from he-who-shall-not-be-named. I refuse to be the only monolingual human in every room here.

"Buongiorno, Signorina Graham," he says, matching my smile and handing off the tray with an unnamed pastry and a steaming cup of cappuccino.

I take the tray, inhale, and nearly faint. "Oh my goodness. This smells amazing." I turn and place the tray on the small table by the door. "Grazie."

"I was hoping you could take it to go, veramente. I'd like for us to walk to campus together," Leo says.

Walk? This is *not* my walking-for-miles-in-the-sweaty-countryside outfit. I glance down at the ridiculously overpriced pumps Tammy forced me to borrow and see their future demise. I can still hear her clucking at me and shoving them into my perfectly organized suitcase. "*There is nothing the Italians respect more than fine footwear.*"

"I'd love that," I say. "Let me just change my shoes."

I kick them off, slip into some flats, and grab my purse and the goodies from the tray, double-fisting like a pro.

"Pronto?"

"Sì," I nod, trying not to slosh any cappuccino on me as I kick the door shut behind me.

It takes us a bit to find our rhythm as we make our way around the pool and onto the gravel road that James drove in on. My purse has to be shifted several times, and my stride is limited in the tight skirt, but eventually we fall into an easy pace that lets me enjoy the warm, foamy beverage without the threat of outfit ruination. We wind along the hill in companionable silence, nothing but the sound of my ladylike chewing and slurping to interrupt the peace around us. I go to wipe foam off my lip and I realize it's sweat. It is too early in the morning for it to be this hot.

"Fa caldo, no?" Leo asks, reading my mind or my lip sweat. "This heat wave has made everyone restless. Even the sheep cannot sleep."

"I hadn't noticed," I lie. I'd had to put ear plugs in to drown out the bleating.

"Fortunamente, the amphitheaters are air-conditioned. You'll find most of the students arrive at class early and stay late because their dormitories are not."

I smile. "Perhaps they are just eager to learn."

"Ah, yes. That must be it." He winks my way and I marvel at the fact that I can't find a single bead of sweat on his tanned face. He's dressed to the nines. Gray linen suit pants without a single wrinkle, a matching vest, the jacket slung over his shoulder. He reminds me of the guy from the Dos Equis commercials. The Most Interesting Man in the World. We come to a fork in the road and he nods to a little stone wall in front of us.

"Leave your mug there," he instructs. "We will grab it on our way home."

I do as I'm told.

"Is that the way into Urbino?" I ask pointing to the road not taken.

He nods. "Sì. Forse, James can show you the city today."

I count to three before I answer. I don't want to reject the idea over-eagerly, and be she-who-doth-protest-too-much.

"I always like to get to know a city on my own—form an independent opinion," I explain.

He lifts his dark brows at me. His eyes are a dazzling shade of blue, lighter than the pool water at the villa. Finally, he pulls his lips downward and makes a sound like "vabbè," lifting his shoulders to his ears, palms out and forward.

It's the Italian gesture for *whatever.* And I like it.

"Vabbè," I repeat, mimicking his movement.

He chuckles.

"Not bad," he says.

Campus comes into view as we round the final curve, and I'm surprised by the modernity of it all. Walls of glass and brick topped with cement make a dozen little boxes set into the hills that rise above us. They seem to be squatting all around a gray paved courtyard where the massive central building sits.

"Benvenut'alla nostra università," Leo says, gesturing to all of it with his hands.

The contrast of the architecture from what I witnessed the night before has me reeling a bit as I follow him across the expansive cement space toward the double metal doors leading into a huge circular building.

"You will be assisting our summer course with the highest enrollment," Leo tells me over his shoulder. "Pastore will approve this, naturally, when he returns—he told me you were up for any challenge."

I nod, wishing that I could hear this approval firsthand, but asking Leo for further information seems like an insult after all that he's done for me. The sun catches the white in his hair and blinds me as he pulls open both doors to the main building. A rush of cold air smacks me and I hurry inside onto the tile floor, looking around at the high glass curves of the wall that stretches along my left side.

"This center circle houses the lecture halls," Leo says, his shiny leather shoes making a satisfying click on the tile that echoes off the ceiling three stories above my head. I wish I'd worn my heels so I could make that sound. That sound is power.

He leads me to the right.

"Eccola," he says, opening his palm toward another double door. "This is it."

I take a deep breath and nod. This is what I'm good at—what I love—structure and school and impressing the hell out of people. Taking initiative and accomplishing more than asked. Plans and checklists and syllabi. Time to do my thing.

He opens the door for me and I step inside a huge semicircular amphitheater that stretches down and around to a center pedestal. I look over my shoulders to find that there are two balconies behind me on either side—like an opera house. Almost every seat in the space is full, and when the heavy metal door shuts behind Dean Leo and me, close to a hundred heads turn toward us.

"Salvete, studenti," Leo says in his booming voice.

There's a murmur of greeting and I lift my hand and give an all-encompassing wave. My hand freezes midair when my eyes land on the annoyingly handsome man standing at the pedestal at the bottom of the theater. In perfectly fitted gray pants and a crisp white button-down with a thin wine-colored tie, he no longer could be mistaken for the hired help. Behind him, a huge projector screen is alight with an image of Urbino at night. It is the exact angle of the city that this man showed me last night. It takes my mind a moment to understand why he of all people would be standing below at the epicenter of the lecture hall. His dark eyes widen and his lips part slightly as he takes me in, then he shakes his head once and narrows his eyes at the handsome older man standing beside me. And like that—snap—it all clicks into its dreadful, unwanted place.

On a breath, I hear myself whispering. "No. Nope. No. You've got to be kidding me. This is f—"

"I will leave you to it then, no?" Leo says loudly, drowning me out as he pats my back once.

I barely hear the sound of the metal door swinging open and closing behind me with a thud over the blood rushing up my carotid artery to my brain. The spin I felt last night at the table starts again.

"Welcome to art history," James says into the microphone. "I am Professore Massini—"

I back toward the doors hoping I can get a moment to collect myself outside, but James has other plans.

"—and this is my assistant for the four-week course, Ava Graham."

I wish his balls were within kicking distance.

NOVE

James

I don't knock before barging into Zio's office after class.

"You are completely out of line—"

He holds up one elegant finger and removes his reading glasses.

"Professor Massini, remember who we are here—in this place," he says softly, gesturing to the tome-lined walls and the expansive window that overlooks the dorm-spattered hills.

I take a breath and turn to shut the door behind me. He's right, of course. As always. It's entirely unprofessional of me to attack the dean of academics about his choices. I should wait, attack my uncle upon arriving home, instead. But there's no way in hell I can sit with this for another minute.

"She knows nothing about art," I say, sinking into the leather chair across from him.

He tilts his head, questioning.

"Who? A student? Surely that is why she is taking your course."

Mio Dio. Is this really how this is going to go?

"Signorina Graham. She's studying law," I explain for the benefit of the act my uncle is staging.

"I see." He steeples his fingers. "So she who studies law cannot also study art? That's very narrow-minded of you, Professore."

Zio has dabbled in so many fields of study that we have a filing cabinet filled with diplomas and certifications. I'm barking in the wrong forest and this suddenly feels a lot like my conversation with Ava last night about fitting people into boxes.

"She has no interest in art," I amend.

"Did you ask her that?" he muses.

I don't move.

He turns his lips down.

"Then don't be absurd, James. Everyone is interested in art." He smiles, and I'm suddenly twelve again, my feet dangling from this same chair as I watch my uncle work on his thousandth dissertation.

I let out a breath and try to find the right words to explain why I cannot have Ava Graham in my amphitheater all summer, glaring at me from behind the students' heads, distracting me from my lectures with—whatever the hell it is that makes me need to grab the camera. She's infuriating.

"She challenges you," my uncle says, leaning across the desk. "And it has been some time since I've seen that."

"Ha! I don't know if I'd use the word challenge, Zio," I say.

Vexes. Enrages. Maybe even confuses.

"It is done, Gi. There were no other courses on such short notice," he says, then pats the papers in front of him twice and then swirls his hand in the air. "Forse, she will help you 'mix it up' a bit."

What the hell does that mean?

"Mix it up?" I repeat, mimicking the twirling hand gesture.

"Sì. Your syllabus has gotten a bit—what's the right word?"

"Solid? Refined? Watertight?"

He pulls his lips to his nose and then puts a finger in the air.

"Stale."

I lean back in my chair, gripping the handles made of ornately carved mahogany. Stale. Like the leftover bread Nina leaves on the counter in a basket to make crostini. I watch my uncle for some sort of remorse, some acknowledgment of the insult, and he just lifts his hands and shrugs his shoulders.

"Yet another reason why you might consider accepting Signore Davenport's offer in London. Think of the lectures you could write while passing the time in the Victoria and Albert or Kensington Palace, all while pursuing what you love—"

I put up a hand to stop him before he gains momentum.

"I should really get to work on my stale lectures."

I stand.

"Thank you for this meeting, Dean Russo. As always, your feedback and expertise are invaluable to me," I say, glancing at him over my shoulder as I reach for the door.

"Certo, Professore. Any time."

Oh man, I cannot wait to tell Nina this. Maybe she'll make him sleep with the sheep.

"Gi," he says just as my hand lands on the handle.

I knew he'd break first. Apology time. I meet his steady gaze.

"Please send Signorina Graham in when she's ready."

He gives me one last shit-eating grin and I choose not to throw his stapler at him. The moment the door to his office is shut behind me, my eyes find her, ankles crossed demurely as she stares up at me.

She pushes up off the divan slowly, eyes on mine. "You know I can fulfill this role with my eyes closed?"

Part of me wants to open the door so Zio can witness this. Part of me knows it will only further confirm his decision.

"Great. You can start by heading into town and getting to know the subject matter since you'll be grading the seventy-four assignments they'll be bringing to class tomorrow," I tell her.

The students were released after introductions and syllabus questions to capture their favorite "artistic moment" in Urbino and write a thousand words explaining why it resonated.

"I think I can handle seventy-four thousand words. That's the length of the romcom I just finished on the plane," she says, looking bored.

I step toward her so that she has to tilt her chin up to meet my eyes and I see her chest still. But she doesn't step back.

"Do you know anything about Renaissance art?" I ask.

Her lips turn up in a tight smile. "I know that if they allow you to teach it here, it can't be too difficult to master."

I bite my lip. Nod. I notice her gaze dip down to my mouth. I remember the way her eyes closed as I leaned toward her last night before she nearly stepped off that cliff. I need to get away. Fast.

"The dean is waiting for you," I tell her, turning my body and gesturing toward the door.

She lifts a haughty brow and pushes past me.

"I'll see you at dinner. Unless, of course, you'll be hiding in the woods again behind your camera." She tosses the words over her shoulder without looking at me before she knocks lightly on the dean's door and lets herself in.

I breathe in deeply—try to clear my head, but the smell of the lavender shampoo I put in the guest house is lingering in my uncle's waiting room. I walk outside and lean against the brick wall. Take a deep, not-so-cleansing breath.

This woman is a menace.

There are lectures to be written, a new batch of art to be catalogued and inspected at the museum, and a thousand photographs to be sorted through. My career. My art. My family. Yet, somehow, she's made her way into all three and she's been here for a little over twenty-four hours.

I push off of the brick wall and hope to God that Nina will distract me from this spiral. And for the first time in years, I start the daily walk home without my uncle.

DIECI

Ava

The stone that holds up the massive archway that hovers above the cobblestone street leading up into Urbino's city center reflects a pinkish hue in the late afternoon sun. The walls, the turrets—every piece of the town seems to have shifted from the gold in my memory of last night to a soft blush. I want to bottle the color. Paint my nails with it so that every time I see my hands I remember what they've touched.

I pull my hand off the stone and rub my thumb to my fingertips, imprinting the sensation of something so old and so solid. There's no time to dawdle here. I must stay focused on the task at hand. There's five hundred years of Renaissance art history to catch up on in these walls. No way in hell am I going to let Professor Assholio catch me unprepared again.

After pleading my case to Dean Russo, it has become painfully clear that there's no escape from this assignment. If I want the international studies credits needed for matriculation, I've got to assist in a class that covers some aspect of a foreign culture. There was a moment in the conversation when I nearly pulled the mom card and explained that this class would bring up too much grief, but I bit my tongue and kept the panicky feeling in my chest locked down. It's not like I can avoid art forever. Especially while I'm in Italy. Besides, Leo assured me this was the only possibility.

So I've laid out my plan into three simple, foolproof phases:

> Phase 1: Get to know the city. The paper map in my left hand was procured after a few terrible attempts at Italian conversation at the visitor's booth a few hundred yards behind me, where they also sell bus tickets. I believe I have a one-way ticket to Pesaro now.
>
> Phase 2: Capture images. Leo has lent me a camera that looks like it belongs in a museum. Extra bonus is that it belongs to James and I have an inkling that he wouldn't like me using it. So I'm going to use the hell out of it. I will catalogue every piece of art known to Urbino. And basically dive head first into whatever said art might stir up inside me.
>
> Phase 3: Gather information. There's nothing James knows that Google doesn't. Please see the aforementioned paper map where I have circled an internet café for art research—and maybe some light Ethan stalking.

I bump into a woman as I stare at the map and she murmurs, "Americana," like it's a contagious disease. I dump the map into my purse.

Point taken.

I step beneath the archway, the momentary shade doing nothing to quell the swelter, and look up along Borgo Mercatale, the infamous entrance street of Urbino. As much as I love my pumps, this climb would cramp the finest of calves. And the uneven stones would eat my heels for breakfast. The road is narrow and I'm reminded why the Italians drive such tiny cars. The street is lined with four-story stucco buildings, each painted a varying, soothing, earthy shade with a pop of seashell pink sneaking in every now and again. There is no space between them, they are stacked together like the book spines on the shelves in my apartment, so tightly packed that the shift in color is the only sign that one has ended and another begun.

I begin the steep trek upward, noting the group of older gentlemen in hats smoking cigars outside of a tiny osteria. Kate Middleton would be proud of their male millinery. One looks my way and smiles—blows out two perfect rings—the scent of them reminding me of my father.

I wave the last puffs of smoke away and continue the climb. My quads are already burning. Oooooh. Wine in a window. I read the sign—or try to. Enoteca. This is not part of the plan, but there's no harm in picking up a bottle now for Nina since it says they'll close soon for dinner. And I'm sure there's art to be catalogued in here.

I dip my head and step under the low entrance, and I'm immediately greeted by the glorious combo of cool air and dim lighting. There are bottles everywhere—in the wall-to-wall shelving, on the floor at the base of the shelves, along the bar. The only break in bottles is a few framed black-and-white photos that remind me of the ones in my guest house. I start to lift the camera to snap pics of them. If wine could be a country, this would be its capital. My fingers are twisting the view into focus when an older gentleman appears on the stairs that lead down into the belly of the wine shop.

I'm staring at a round, smiling face with two tufts of white hair over each ear that transition into a beard that Gandalf would envy.

"Salve!" he says.

"Hi—ciao. Buongiorno," I stammer.

Three hellos for the price of one.

"Do you need help?" he asks, saving me—or himself—from botched Italian.

I look around, prepared to grab at random, and get back to the mission, but he is making a clucking noise at me and shaking his head as he approaches.

"Vieni. Devi gustare. You taste," he says, so close now that I can see the twinkle in his dark eyes and smell the slight odor of hard work and garlic, perhaps from his lunch. Somehow the scent works for him.

"I am Franco," he tells me. "You are?"

"Ava," I tell him, sidestepping to give him room and nearly knocking over a row of bottles like dominoes.

"Down you go, Ava," he tells me, and he slips around me to get behind. A warm hand finds the small of my back and he ushers me into the depths of wine heaven. Something tells me Franco would not accept a refusal, so I just pray that I'm not going to find plastic wrap all over the walls and floor as I descend. But instead I am surrounded by brick walls and wine barrels lit by a few Edison bulbs hanging from ropes.

He immediately goes to work setting up two small wine glasses on the small olive wood bar mounted against the bricks.

"Lambrusco," he tells me, as he fills each of our glasses. I'm transfixed by the color of it. And the tiny bubbles that bounce upward in lines.

He lifts his glass and his white brows, then inclines his head toward my glass. I lift it and mimic the way he swirls the pink elixir, ignoring the tiny amount I lose when it sloshes over the rim.

"Salud!" He taps his glass to mine and down it goes, sending a rush of effervescence up my sinuses as I wrinkle my nose. It's delicious, but sweet. Very unlike the dry reds Ethan and I are accustomed to.

"Non ti piace?" he asks and I'm trying to translate the words in my brain, but he doesn't give me time to process.

"Try this," he instructs. And there's a fresh glass in front of me, this time with something light gold. "Verddichio," he says as he hands it to me. I repeat the word, failing to roll the R, but nailing the short click of the hard C. He nods and turns his lips down. The Italian *not bad.*

We toast again and this time I slow down and enjoy the crisp taste of the liquid on the back of my tongue.

"Squisito, no?" he asks.

"Mmmhmm," I murmur around another mouthful.

"Prossimo, you will try my favorite. La Vernaccia," he says.

I finish off the glass and put both hands up.

"I won't be able to make it up those steps if you keep pouring," I laugh.

He is unfazed. His white hair ducks out of sight and there's the sound of rummaging in the cabinets. He pops back up and drops a basket filled with long, dry breadsticks on the counter. He beams at me.

"That will fix you," he says, wiping both hands together. "And I will make you espresso. Mangia."

I don't have time to argue before he's off fetching the espresso. This man is a mover and a shaker. He reminds me of the White Rabbit. Which makes me Alice—perhaps these wines will shrink me. Or gigantify. I giggle. Shit. Do not get buzzed, you lightweight!

I break open the wrapper and gnaw on the hard breadstick while I look around before Franco returns. This place is like the

Land of the Lotus-Eaters and I wonder if I'll make it back to—whatever it was I'm supposed to be doing. My crunching echoes off the low ceiling as I stop in front of one of the black-and-white photographs.

There's something mesmerizing about these pictures. The subject of this photo is a little girl. She's staring at the camera, her dark eyes so wide, I step back so I don't get sucked into them. At first you see innocence, but as you study her—the set of her jaw, the glimmer of liquid hovering just above her thick lower lashes—you can't help but wonder what she knows. What she's seen. A shudder runs through me and I turn to the next wall.

And then my heart stops beating. My half-eaten breadstick hangs from the corner of my mouth, then gives up its purchase and falls to my feet.

There's an acrylic painting of Urbino at sunset hanging before me. Just another landscape to most. Albeit an enchanting one. I run my hand along the wide brushstroke of coral that forms the walls of Urbino—mimicking the flick of the wrist I'd seen her make a thousand times—that stroke more familiar to me than my own reflection.

"Ava, cara. Are you alright?"

Franco has appeared beside me, arms laden with wine bottles that clink together like wind chimes as he balances the tiny mug of espresso in his hand. The scent of it grounds me a little.

I nod, my finger now tracing the signature at the bottom right-hand corner. I'd tried so hard when I was little to make my cursive look just like that, practicing over and over in those old composition books the teachers gave us.

"You know the artist?" Franco asks, his tone more somber.

I nod again and hear my voice from somewhere very far away. "She was my mother."

UNDICI

James

Dinner should have been a relaxing break with Ava markedly absent. Conversation about our first day of summer semester should have bounced freely across the table. And Nina should have been scolding Zio about his foolish placement of our guest as my TA.

But even Verga is anxious, pacing back and forth out on the front porch like a hungry lion.

Nina has her phone at the table. Of all the things she's whacked me for, this is the one that makes me rub my head now in memory. Massimo is watching his mother with wide eyes, shocked by her blatant negligence of her own rules as she taps away with her right thumb like she's stamping her fingerprint over and over. At this rate, she may have a text message composed within the month.

"Do you worry about me like this when I go into town?" I ask. Though I can't believe I'm admitting this, I only made it through the antipasti before the pit in my stomach could not be pawned off as hunger.

"Sì," my Zio says just as Nina says, "No."

Nina gives him the malocchio but continues stamping her phone screen while she explains, "Gi, you have been here far too long to make me fret like this. She is new. And she looks the way she does—"

"She does look the way she does," Massimo says with a wide smile. Head smack from his left. Zio's never sting like Nina's. They feel more like encouragement.

"I'm sure she's fine, Zia. Are you saying she's better looking than me?"

This time everyone says "Sì" at the same time.

"As if you haven't noticed," Max shoots.

"Vero, Gi. We have noticed you noticing," my uncle adds.

E tu, Zio? E tu?

I choose to focus on the bread I'm balling between my fingers and transplant myself back into this afternoon, when I was at ease driving through the country, stopping only to capture something when it demanded to be captured. Cool as a cucumber. Breeze in my hair. Snapping blissfully away.

"Ahhh. Bene. She's at Vincenzo's with Franco," Nina tells us, leaning back in her chair with a hand over her chest.

"Alas, the lost treasure has been found," I murmur, ignoring the flash flood of annoying relief in my own chest. "Can we have dessert now?"

Nina clucks.

"I need you to pick her up," she says, topping off her wine glass. She takes a long sip, and I notice my Zio doing the same out of the corner of my eye. She motions between them across the long table. "We've had a bit to drink. These curves can be dangerous—"

"The only danger is you two and your devious nonsense." I stand and toss my napkin at Massimo. It bounces off his forehead. "You wanna come?" Be my chaperone?

My Zia shakes her head. "No. No. Maso, you have things to do—"

"No I don't."

"And Vincenzo mentioned Ava might be a bit ubriaca, Gi. So be prepared." She finishes with a dismissive hand wave.

"She's drunk?" I ask, trying not to laugh.

Nina lifts her shoulders and opens her palms.

"I'll walk then," I say, whistling for Verga. "She'll need the fresh air."

Though it'll be a lot of fun to watch her normal swagger teeter out of control. No one at the table gives a shit about what I do now that Ava is accounted for. They are all digging into the dessert that I am missing for the drunk American. I get a nod and a wink from my uncle as I pass through the front door and tell Verga how much I appreciate him.

"Just me and you, buddy." I get beneath the wrinkles by his ears and he pushes his head against my thigh. "You wanna help me pick up the drunk American?"

And he's off. Kickin' up dirt like he's Seabiscuit racing for the Triple Crown as he disappears down the road and around the hill. And I'm alone again. What. The. Fuck.

Admittedly, there is something charming about the American—if she doesn't despise you, of course. Even the students were taken by her as she sat beside them and listened to their ideas for what they wanted to write about for the assignment we gave today. When she's not fixating on some contrived plan, she is a natural people pleaser. Until she looks my way.

I touch the worn leather strap around my neck, twist the dial of the camera to bring it to life, and center the giant illuminated keystone of Porta Valbona as soon as it comes into view. A few buses are left in the huge square outside the city's walls, dropping some of the college students off after their trip to the beach in Pesaro. The smell of suntan lotion and exhaust fumes hurries me along through Borgo Mercatale as the students chatter about which bar they'll meet at after showering. No matter that it is nine PM on a Monday night. To be young.

I ignore the young potential drunks and focus on finding the nearing-thirty-already-drunk that is unwittingly in my charge. It takes only moments to find her outside of the tiny osteria two buildings up Via Mazzini as I pass beneath the archway.

I stop. Lean into the shadow that runs beneath the stone, lift the viewfinder and let loose.

She's wearing a man's homburg hat—Franco's from the looks of it—her hair still twisted like earlier beneath the straw brim that turns up in the front. And she's smoking a cigar, one far too large for her tiny frame; she wets her full lips, takes a drag, bright eyes wide on Vincenzo across from her. Her brows lift as her mouth makes a tiny O and she tries to mimic the donut holes Vincenzo makes across the table. She's so focused on the task at hand, her body leaning over the iron table scattered with empty plates as she studies her mentor, that she doesn't even notice when I get close enough to capture the way her nostrils dilate as she exhales carefully. She succeeds in making a round puff, no O in the center, and her face lights up with excitement as Franco pats her shoulder in encouragement. I lower the camera when I see Verga lounging beneath her feet. She's kicked off her flats and is stroking her bare toes into his fur. I try to compose my face into something that masks the wonder. Who the hell is this? Surely not the uptight American who wrinkled her nose at me at the airport.

I pull out a chair at the table beside Vincenzo and he puts his arm around my shoulders onto the back of the iron seat. Franco tilts his head toward Ava and widens his eyes at me, lifting his gray brows up into a question. Verga doesn't bother to move.

"Where have you been hiding this charming little thing, Gi?" he asks, pointing his cigar at Ava. She pushes the tip of her index finger into her cheek and twists and tips her hat at me with her other hand.

"I take no responsibility for that." I nod toward her as she fills the wine glass in front of me from the bottle of Vernaccia. Franco's favorite wine.

"You didn't make it very far into the city," I tell her as she tops off the rest of the glasses.

"The wine in the window spoke to me. And then Franco got me drunk." Franco puts his hands up in surrender. "A wine store just inside the gate is entrapment, no?" She smiles at Franco and he nods his agreement.

"And you?" I poke Vincenzo's meaty flank. "How'd you get into the mix?"

He shrugs, his suspenders lifting and falling as he purses his lips beneath that impressive silver mustache. Vincenzo taught me to cook when I was sixteen. And Franco. Well, Franco taught me to drink when I was fourteen. Ava was in far better hands with them than with me.

"She must eat," he says, standing and collecting the plates.

Ava stands from her seat and nearly tips over on the cobblestones before Vincenzo steadies her.

"I can help," she protests, and Vincenzo's deep laugh drifts into the open sky.

"You can help tomorrow when I make you coniglio in porchetta," he promises.

Ava looks at me and grins. Then whispers, "That's bunny rarebit."

"Okay, Elmer Fudd, sit down before you end up with a concussion," I tell her, pointing to the chair and, surprisingly, she does as she's told, just as Franco excuses himself to check on the shop. I glance over my shoulder to find the shop window completely dark and decidedly safe.

"How much Renaissance art did you learn about today?" I ask her. The light from the single candle on the table keeps catching flecks of emerald in her eyes. If her at-ease smile hadn't already transfixed me, that color would have done the trick. I look away, reminding myself what lies beneath that beauty.

"So," Ava begins, her S only the tiniest bit softened by the wine. "Funny you should ask that. I learned a lot about the work of a local photographer. Talented man. Well-liked by the locals. I doubt he runs in your circle."

She flicks her wrist and waves off her sentence, trying hard not to laugh at her own sarcasm. She's seen some of my work.

"Anything they told you about me is a lie," I say, letting the crisp Vernaccia slide over the back of my tongue.

"Well, that must be true since it was all good."

How is she still this quick after this much wine? I count the empty bottles on the table as she leans back in her chair.

"Your photos," she starts, then looks away as she finishes more softly. "They are incredible."

I shake my head. "Alright. Something's not right. Let's get you home before you say something you'll regret."

"No, Dad. Please let me stay." She widens her eyes, puffs out her lower lip. Then takes another sip of wine and rolls her eyes. "Did Nina send you?"

"Yes. She was worried," I say.

She winces a little bit and then tilts her head. "Well, if someone hadn't tossed my phone over a cliff, I could have texted her."

"Maybe said phone would have remained safe if you'd left it in your pocket and weren't always checking it to see if what's-his-face called," I say, and her face falls like I've stuck a pin in her.

"What a dick," she whispers. At first, I think she's talking about me, but then she pulls her shoulders back and meets my gaze and I realize she meant him. I nod my agreement.

"Besides, I wasn't checking to see if he called," she lies. "I was setting up my Italian Tinder. Tinder-o."

I nearly spit out the sip of wine at the smile she gives me. This Ava is terrifying. I should get the hell out of here, but this conversation is the most fun I've had in a long time.

"Italians don't need Tinder," I tell her, pressing my lips together when she raises her brows.

"Is that so?" She runs her finger around the rim of her wine glass. "How do Italians find lovers if they aren't sending dick pics over an app?"

"Jesus, Ava," I whisper as a group of college kids hustle by. I narrow my eyes at her, watch the smile falter a little, the corner of her lips pulls down. The wine has given her the softest blush along her neck.

"What?" she says, touching her face. "Why are you looking at me like that?" She glances toward her reflection in the window of Vincenzo's osteria, wrinkles her nose at herself.

"I'm just thinking I like you better this way," I tell her when she turns to face me.

"You like me better drunk? That's a little pervy, Professore."

I chuckle. Shrug.

"Vabbè," she provides, and I nod.

"Is that how you met Edward?" I start softly, knowing I'm treading on dangerous terrain. "He doesn't sound like the type to send you—"

"Dick pics," she finishes. Making sure to harden the Cs at the end more than necessary.

I bite back my smile.

"It's Ethan. And you're right. Though I'm sure it has more to do with fear of ruining his mother's campaign if it were to surface." She's studying my face as she speaks. "His mom's a senator. Great lady."

"A senator's son? Sounds like a lot of pressure."

She presses her lips together. Sighs. Places her chin in her hands.

"Let's not do the boyfriend chat tonight, k? Let me forget for a bit."

I duck a little to meet her gaze that has drifted down below my neck.

"Are you asking me to help you forget him, dolcezza?" The words slide out of their own volition. I reach for her hat. Tip it back so her eyes are no longer in its shadow. They sparkle like the Vernaccia in her glass.

She stares at me a second, and I'd give anything to hear her thoughts. She glances down at my mouth and swallows. Her teeth slide along her bottom lip, then release, popping it back into place. I can't form a coherent thought.

She reaches for her wine glass and downs what's left and fixes her smile back in place.

"The wine will do the trick—for now," she adds with a wink. "Let's talk about you, no?" I lift my brows and she mistakes that for consent.

"You grew up here with your aunt and uncle?"

Ah shit. Here we go.

"I grew up in Brooklyn with my Nonna, but I moved here when I was ten—when she passed," I clarify, watching her face change from interested to saddened. She has zero emotional filter right now.

"I'm sorry," she whispers. And mio Dio does she look sorry. She looks like she's about to cry. I force myself to look up the cobblestone street.

"You came over here by yourself? At ten years old? That must have been terrifying."

I shrug. It was. But she doesn't need to know that.

"Nina and Leo were here. Believe me, I was never alone," I say.

She nods, understanding how impossible it is to be alone with two personalities so big.

"You must have been incredibly brave," she says to her wine.

"Bravery is making a choice despite your fear. I had no choice."

Her hand falls on top of mine and I study her expression as she registers that she's touching me. Her eyes widen, and she pulls her hand back so fast an empty wine glass clatters against the table.

She stands, too quickly, and through willpower alone, barely teeters. I imagine her stubborn ass could will herself sober if she chose. She's a tiny whirlwind right now and, despite myself, I can't help but enjoy the view. Verga immediately pops up by her side, looking up at her like she's the sun. Poor shmuck.

She strides away, lifting her purse over her shoulder as she passes and slipping her flats back on her toes, both arms out to balance as she pokes her head inside the restaurant and yells goodbye to Vincenzo. She makes her way down the hill and back through the archway. My traitorous dog doesn't follow at first, just looks at me, and I swear in that moment as he takes in the stupid grin on my face, I can hear him repeat my thought right back at me.

Poor shmuck.

DODICI

Ava

Groups of college students are passing us heading back into the city from the dormitories in the hills. I compliment them despite James's shushing as he tugs me in the direction of the villa with his hand covering his face.

"Ladies, looking good—damnnnnn, Gina. Wear that dress!"

"You're going to regret this tomorrow when one of them is in our class," he tells me over his shoulder. I make a face at the back of his head when he turns. I don't get drunk like this often—must uphold Bennington standards in public. But being over four thousand miles from home feels like an invisibility cloak on top of the glorious wine haze. Everything feels warm and soft. Fuzzy at the edges. And I'm not wasting it.

"They don't recognize me. I'm incognito," I say, tipping Franco's hat down over my eyes, then immediately tripping over Verga because I can't see.

"You're literally wearing the exact outfit you wore to class today," he says, finally releasing his death grip on my wrist.

"Wanna switch clothes?" I pretend to lift my shirt up and he yanks my arm harder. "Calm your hormones, Jamesy. A little girl-on-girl positivity is allowed and encouraged."

He lets out a dramatic breath and I give him a saccharine smile.

"You're dangerous when you drink," he says to himself, putting distance between us so that he's on one side of the curving road and I'm on the other.

"Fun dangerous? Or like liability dangerous? Oooooh, my mug!"

I reach for the white ceramic mug I left on the wall that morning and hold it up to him. He lifts his brows, one side of his mouth slightly higher.

"I'm very thirsty," I tell him. I drop the dry mug in my purse. "Do you have any water?"

"Your brain reminds me of *If You Give a Mouse a Cookie* right now," he murmurs. "I'll get you a whole pitcher when we get back if you're good." He gestures with his hands for me to pick up the pace or do a somersault. Definitely one of those.

I do neither. I make a smooching sound and Verga comes to my side of the road.

He laughs. "What the hell did you do to my dog?"

I stop yanking at Verga's wrinkles and look across the street.

"I think your dog has more to answer for than I do! He violated my ass and then mounted me in a shrouded wood."

James chuckles and whistles the Beast back over. Are we reenacting the Jack Nicholson–Greg Kinnear scene from *As Good as It Gets* when the dog has to choose?

"I carry bacon in my pocket," I lie, heading back up the road.

"Are you quoting Jack Nicholson?"

I ignore him, pretending to be unimpressed by his movie trivia.

"Can I ask you something?" I muse. I hear the snap snap snap of his camera and I look over to find it aimed at me. Again.

"No."

I push on unfazed. "You really should get permission to do that." I point at the lens. "And how old are you? Thirty? Thirty-three?"

"Can I have permission to photograph you? And thirty-four—"

"Yes, but nothing kinky." He chuckles. "Ooof. You're getting up in years. So I happened upon something in Franco's wine dungeon and I'm wondering—" I pause and look up to my left—and bam—there he is in all his rugged Italian glory. I've veered to his side of the road. "Oh, hey there."

He shakes his head, a few long dark waves fall to his forehead, but I can see he's gnawing on his cheek. I'm amusing him. Amuse-bouche.

"So anyway, I was wondering about a painting down there in the sex dungeon, and you being the art boss, I thought you might know something about the artist who—"

"Annette Barrett's painting?" he asks.

I trip on air. Hearing him say my mother's name makes my mind spin. Or the ninth glass of Vernaccia is making my mind spin. I nod, unable to make words. Then look away as he searches my face.

"She's a bit of a local legend. An artist who studied here for a year and discovered her muse in these walls. Maybe even fell in love, according to the rumor mill—" He pauses and puts a hand on my arm. "Are you alright?"

I must have frozen. The lanterns that line the villa's drive light half his face as he looks down at me. There's a *Phantom of the Opera* thing going on with the shadow. And I'm Team Phantom all the way. I refrain from humming "Music of the Night" and watch two tiny lines appear above the bump on the bridge of his nose. His concern shakes me. I push onto my toes and run my finger over the bump, noticing his pupils widen at my touch. His eyes are so dark and unanswerable, like the girl's were in that photograph. His photograph.

"How did this happen?" I ask, my voice like sandpaper. I need that pitcher of water.

His other hand circles my wrist as I pull my hand away from his face.

"Calcio—soccer." He swallows, and I watch his Adam's apple dip down and up, the muscles around it clenching with the effort. But still he stares down at me.

I knew it. A soccer break. I smile and tip closer to him, so close that I could brush my lips to his if a strong wind chose to blow. Or a strong dog chose to walk by.

He breathes my name and the heat from the night air creeps under my blouse, down over my navel, pooling deep in my belly. I want to hear it again, but he uses my wrist to keep me still as he steps back.

"You've been drinking," he says.

"I've been drinking," I confirm.

"You need sleep."

"I need sleep." I sound like I'm being Dracula-ed. Am I being Dracula-ed?

His thumb circles the soft skin on my wrist and the pooling warmth down below becomes a painful pressure. What the fuck am I doing? I pull my hand away, but I can still feel his touch.

"I'll see you in the morning," he whispers, his eyes never leaving mine.

Brain. Words. Tongue. Go! "Sure thing, boss."

He gives Verga a look and purses his lips to whistle, but then thinks better of it and turns to disappear onto the porch and through the front door of the villa.

"Shizzzz," I say, sounding more like a released balloon than a grown-ass woman.

Verga nudges my hand and brings me back to reality. I lift one foot to make sure I haven't grown roots into this spot. Then the other.

It isn't until I've plopped on top of my comforter fully clothed with a hundred pounds of soft wrinkles beside me and the room spinning like the Gravitron that I realize I never got that pitcher of water I'd been promised.

TREDICI

James

The students look like they're crawling out of the grave. All but the select few locals who are used to the Italian social clock are wearing their tourist hangovers like neon flashing lights, slumped in their chairs with their pitiful bloodshot eyes unfocused and the noxious fug of alcohol wafting from them in gusts. They aren't going to make it. And there's no way in hell I'm wasting one of my favorite lectures on a bunch of hungover zombies.

I click off the projector and the picture of my hero, Federico da Montefeltro, dissipates to blackness on the screen behind me.

"Alright, people. Listen up. I get it. Second night abroad—you want to party like the locals. Start your night at midnight. Dance into the morning in fabulous footwear. But this"—I gesture with an open hand to all of them—"this is not what a local looks like. Luca, do you mind standing up?"

"Certo, Professore."

Luca stands easily and faces the crowd. His facial hair is freshly groomed. His gray pants are perfectly tapered. Shoes quite probably shined this morning. A few girls and guys lean in to whisper something to a neighbor. Luca doesn't even bat a lash. Kid looks like a million bucks. An Italian Ryan Gosling. He smiles. Points to a few people in the seats a few rows above him. And sits back down.

"Thank you, Luca. That is what a local looks like."

At least they are smiling now. Still hungover. But smiling.

"Here's the deal. You have one hour to go get espresso, eat something greasy, take a shower, whatever you need to do to not look and smell like"—I pull up my nose and open both hands toward them—"this. Meet on the West Hill at exactly nine AM."

There's a communal sigh of relief that still reeks of vodka and about fifty thank yous thrown down at me from above. I wave them away and gather up the stack of assignments they've left behind. Typically, we do the architecture lesson on the third day, but it's too beautiful outside today (and the smell inside is making me nauseous) to be stuck in this amphitheater. And now if someone vomits, we won't need to clean it up.

Ava shows up when the room is cleared out.

She pushes through the doors calmly, as if she took a huge settling breath before doing so, and looks around, then stares straight at me. Her hair is wet, twisted up into a bun on top of her head, and she's wearing a long cotton dress. She makes her way down the steps with her eyes on me, chin up. The armor's back in place and she looks just like the spoiled, expectant American I picked up at the curb. The urge to poke at that armor is impossible to resist. Especially now that I've caught a glimpse of what's underneath.

"You missed the entire class," I tell her.

"I'm never late. Honestly, I haven't been late since—"

"You're late now."

"I really don't want to apologize to you—"

"Then don't."

"But obviously it is completely unacceptable for me to be late on my second day."

She looks like she's in pain. And it's not the hangover. I'm enjoying this way more than I should.

"It won't happen again. I don't usually drink like that. And without my phone"—she glares at me and I shake my head—"I had to use an alarm clock from Nina that was set to the twenty-four-hour European time. It just won't happen again," she assures me and I know I shouldn't be smiling because she's genuinely apologetic and obviously embarrassed, but I can't stop thinking about how this is a completely different person standing in front of me than the one I escorted home last night.

"Ava, as much as I enjoy seeing you grovel—"

"I'm not groveling."

"You need to lighten up a bit. This is an art history class, not a prison. And you are in Italy, not boot camp."

She narrows her eyes at me, but nothing about her stance relaxes.

"Where did you send the students?" she asks, taking a few steps closer to me.

"To sober up. We are having class on the West Hill at nine." And there's the smell of the lavender shampoo. I can smell it from ten feet away. She's stopped on the final step, either to keep her distance after last night or to even out our heights.

"Listen," she starts. "About last night—"

Here we go. This should be good.

"Which part? The part where you tried to kiss me or the part where you stole my dog?" I take a step around the podium and weigh the thick stack of essays in my hand. Feels like a shit-ton.

Her nostrils flare like they did in the picture I took of her exhaling that cigar. But she doesn't bite.

"I have a boyfriend. A serious one." She pauses and waits for me to interrupt. I don't. "And we are going to get engaged when this little"—her hand twirls in the air like she's swirling cotton candy onto a stick—"this little hiatus is over."

"Right. An oat-sowing hiatus from your quiet as a mouse in the bedroom future fiancé," I clarify. It's a bit below the belt, using the things she told me in the car against her. But she's pissing me off with this Little Miss Perfect act. In fact, the only time she's not pissing me off is when she's drunk.

Our gazes meet, hers narrowed and closed. Angry even? She's unbelievable. I feel like she's hit me with her car, backed over me, and is revving her engine for the third pass, all while hanging out the window demanding that I apologize for being in the middle of the road.

"To recap," I begin. "I have now escorted you home twice with no thank you. One time in which you insulted me repeatedly and the other in which you threw yourself at me and now you want to set the record straight for me?"

She scoffs. "Threw myself at you? Don't be ridiculous. I can barely tolerate you. I just booped your nose. Boop."

She reaches out with her finger to demonstrate, and I swat it away.

"Thank you for walking me home, James," she says in a monotone, robot voice that indicates just how little gratitude she feels toward me.

"You're welcome," I say, reaching out and touching her nose with my fingertip. She tries to hit my hand but misses and nearly drops the papers.

"I suggest you drink that coffee and eat that croissant Nina sent for you. It's on the desk down there." I make my way up the steps, careful not to brush past her as I go. She wants to avoid me, and the feeling is fucking mutual. I have zero room in my life for a spoiled American, no matter how fun she is when tipsy and how photogenic she might be. "And, Ava."

When I turn she's already got the croissant in her mouth, half of it ripped off like it was fought over by two ravenous dogs.

"Hmmm?" she asks, pausing her chewing.

"Maybe you should use that calling card and clarify all those little details you just told me with Senator Edward. Seems like he's the man with the plan."

She flips up her middle finger and takes a sip of the coffee, smiling around the rim of the mug.

"Oh, and also, Ava. I'm not interested," I say, taking my time with the last three words. "See you at nine, dolcezza. Try not to be late."

I push through the door and head straight for my office, where my camera sits beside an empty cup of coffee. Somehow having the last word after that conversation didn't bring me as much relief as it normally does with her. There's a painful niggle deep in my gut, like the time four-year-old Massimo karate-kicked me in the nuts after watching a Ralph Macchio marathon. Except this time it's not Maso's foot doing the damage. I just need to get behind the lens, then I can shake her off.

I lift the camera and let the light and shadows chase away the anger at having my summer hijacked by the stuck-up American.

QUATTORDICI

Ava

Sun plus hangover equals sweat-covered throbbing temples. Multiply the sum by James's amused sidelong glances and seventy-four papers awaiting my attention. Calculator error.

What a mess. Even my foolproof steps didn't work yesterday. I catalogued all of six pieces of art. And one was my mother's.

Life's messy, baby girl. Look for the beauty in the mess.

I look up at the brightest blue sky I've ever sat beneath. Did you sit here, Mom? Paint on this hill? Life's only messy when I step away from myself. When I veer off the path and invite in the chaos. When I drink too much and let people in too deep and lose focus.

You mean when you actually live?

"Enough!"

I stand from the blanket James brought me and about a hundred eyes turn my way. Talking out loud to my dead mother is not a good way to get back on track.

"Something to add, Signorina Graham?" James asks with a crooked smile.

"No, sorry to interrupt."

He nods at me, eyes narrowed, and I turn my attention back into the town.

The view from the West Hill is magical—surreal even—transporting you straight back to the centuries where these walls had a higher purpose than admiration by the onlooker. We are perched just above the west wall, giving us a peek right into the streets that are filled with year-round residents. I feel like a soldier looking down from her post.

I know all the intimate details about someone named Marizio and his lover from Pescara, after this juicy gossip was yelled by a woman dangling out of her third-story window, stringing her wet laundry on a line while talking to a man below walking his dog down the street. I also witnessed a cat fight. Not like the demeaning kind men imagine women having. I mean an actual tornado of feline screeches behind the little pizzeria I'm going to visit ASAP based on the smells reaching me from their open windows and doors. I get why the cat was territorial about that piece of real estate.

James's voice pulls me back to the hill as he points to the twin turrets of the palazzo. He's got these kids hanging on his every word, brains open and ready for the next knowledge bomb to drip out. His passion for this subject—and this city—are as palpable as the scent of that pizza that's making my stomach twist and grumble. The way his hands move as he gestures to whatever landmark he's describing and the way his long gait stretches as he circulates around the blankets where the students sit cross-legged, staring up at him like sunflowers turned toward the sun. It's all very annoying.

"Do you have anything to add, Signorina Graham?"

Ugh. He keeps doing this. Why in the world would I have anything to add? Well, if I'd stuck to the plan and learned the city yesterday instead of learning to blow smoke circles while pretending to be Puff the Magic Dragon . . .

I could point out the pizza place to them. Surely they'd appreciate that. But then there might be a line.

"Nope. I think you covered it all. Does anyone have any questions?" Smooth, Ava. Deflect to the students.

I shield my eyes and look for a raised hand, hoping that they recognize the pleading look in my eyes telling them it's lunchtime. Please give me the freedom to roll down this hill into the hot mozzarella awaiting me below. But they don't need the reminder. They are just as hungover as I am.

"Alright, then," I clap once. "Lunchtime! Hydrate, everyone. And four fewer alcoholic beverages tonight."

James watches me dismiss his class, his eyebrows pulled together and up over that damn bump on his nose. It was a boop? What the hell is wrong with me? It's him really. He's scrambling my brain like the chef at an omelet station. Though having my veins filled with white wine didn't help the situation. I feel dizzy at the thought.

"See you all in the morning. Luca, keep them in line tonight," James tells them as they attempt to stand from their positions on the hill. Luca smiles down at us and pops up from his blanket. Kid looks like a dark-haired Ryan Reynolds. The rest of them look geriatric as they groan and head off toward the cafeteria.

James doesn't bother to say goodbye before following the zombie horde back toward campus. I zero in on his back.

"James, can I get in this way?"

He pauses almost like he's considering not turning around. Interesting. Seems like I've twisted up his panties with this morning's conversation. Or am I completely overinflating my effect? Maybe he's just tired of me taking up all of his free time.

"Are you heading back to Franco's?" he asks; his eyes are trained somewhere over my shoulder.

"Eventually. I need to apologize for drinking all his wine and return his hat. But first. Pizza," I say, pointing to the little shop that is now bustling with patrons. Shit. They're gonna eat it all.

"Head to the right and stay along the wall. There's a sally port about a hundred feet up. If you hit the bastion, you've gone too far," he says, turning back toward campus.

I don't have a second to ask what weird language he's speaking because he's disappeared over the crest of the hill.

"Have a good day," I yell after him. Definitely twisted panties. And can I really blame him?

I scoop up my bag and shove the towel in it so it covers the stack of essays in the manila envelope I stole from James's classroom. Last thing I need is pizza grease dripping on the papers to add to this man's impression of me. Everything I value has gone out the window since I stepped foot in Italy. Professionalism. Punctuality. Dependability.

I'm going to redeem myself—grade the heck out of these papers. After food.

I repeat his directions in my muddled brain, whispering to myself as I go.

"Sally port. Sally port. What the fuck's a sally port? Aha!"

I make my way through the opening and lift my nose in the air, picking up the scent of tomato sauce and garlic immediately. The streets at this end of the city are even narrower.

Dozens of cars are parked perpendicular to the wall behind me. A vintage clothing store across the street with its door open has Tom Petty's voice crooning "Free Falling" from inside. Beside the shop, the soft blue shutters of the neighboring business surround a window that claims to house an internet café. I make a mental note of the street name, Via Porticale, and head straight for the pizza shop in view up the alley.

There are emails to be sent. Dreaded emails. One to a best friend who I miss dearly despite the fact that she could be complicit in my current state of heartbreak. One to a father who wants to know every update about my career path. And maybe one pathetic check-in with Ethan?

The thought of waiting for a reply from him makes my skin crawl.

I refocus on the research that needs to be done on one Annette Barrett. Seems she chose not to share all of her study abroad details with her beloved only daughter. Nothing more depressing than having to google your own mother—besides the previously mentioned pathetic check-in email. But again, first, pizza.

I attempt my shitty Italian with the poor woman behind the counter and am rewarded with a wrinkled nose and upturned hands. Right. Just point. She nods at that and scoops the beautiful slices up with her wooden peel and pops them into the hole in the bricks that are erupting with flames. I was speaking fluent Italian last night with Franco and Vincenzo. How does one lose fluency so fast? Does sobriety block access to language processing?

Before I have time to puzzle out the neuroscience, euros are being removed from my palm and the most gorgeous sight known to man is being pushed across the counter at me. I pocket the change that I don't bother checking and grab the pizza, hovering over it like there might be a seagull waiting to accost me from above. Google time.

By the time I swing open the glass door to the café, half of my pizza has disappeared and I'm resigned to the fact that I'll need to head back up the alley to get like nine more slices. I stop at the counter where a young man with blue hair is studying the screen of his Mac Air like I don't exist and ask for a half hour of internet. He gives me a card, points to an empty computer that looks like it's from my dad's college years, and takes my money—all without looking up. Impressive.

I slide into the swivel chair and down another slice before wiping my hands and getting to work.

The second I'm logged into my Google account, I'm bombarded with unread emails. Most are trash, sales at stores that conned me into giving my email address, a few event notices from Villanova, several emails from Tammy, one from my advisor's secretary reminding me he's away, and a few capitalized subject lines from my father.

"Shit," I whisper.

I purposely avoid my father's emails, swallowing the guilt right down with the cheese, and open the one from my advisor first, which is just a generic I'll be out of the office email. I hover over the one from Tammy—subject line F*** HIM. Promising title.

Aves,

I swear I had no idea. I'm embarrassed to share DNA with him. I love you. Please call me.

Always,
T

The relief at her ignorance settles into the empty spaces in my chest. The betrayal from Ethan was bad enough. But if she'd known, that might have ripped out a piece of my soul.

I click on a more recent one from her.

Ava,

You need to call me. We need to talk about the gala . . .

Love,
T

Why would she want to talk to me about her mother's charity gala? Maybe she met someone. A little rush of excitement pushes through me and I hammer out a reply.

T,

It'll all be fine. Ethan and I will work it out when I get home. Phone has gone over a cliff, but I can't wait to hear about the gala. Pizza here is orgasmic.

Wish you were here,
Aves

It *will* all be fine. I just need to give Ethan that space to remember what we are. I hit send and let my cursor hover over my father's emails. I take another bite of pizza for strength and then click at random on one from this morning titled JOB OFFERS.

Ava,

I know you don't have much longer to decide, but I think we should discuss the options again. The moment you get this, you need to call me at my office. 989-634-5242

Be safe,
Dad

My stomach flips at the idea of having to explain to him that I accepted a job offer without running it by him first. He'll be hurt, no doubt, but I'm a grown-ass woman and I needed to handle it on my own. Coupled with this trip that he never supported, there's no way in hell I'm making that phone call any time soon.

I decide to ignore the four other emails from Dad and head to Instagram for some light Bennington stalking instead. I log in and click on Tammy's gorgeous face at the top so that her story fills the monitor. A small pang hits me beneath the ribs when I see her at her mother's charity gala on the steps of the Franklin Institute. I haven't missed a gala since we met. But it seems Bennington life goes on without me. Tammy's wearing the gold dress with the ribbed bodice that she bought at D&G on our girls' trip to NYC last month, and damn do I mean she's *wearing* it. Her hair glimmers over her shoulder almost the exact shade of her dress, and she's so distracting I barely even register Ethan beside her. But then I do, and I can't unregister him. He's wearing his tuxedo with the onyx silk lining, the one I helped him pick out at Saks before his graduation ball. He looks as dazzling as ever. Golden hair not a centimeter too long and parted perfectly, blue eyes directly on the photographer, stature of a god.

The next photo takes over the screen, and I see Tammy sitting at one of the tables set up in the Benjamin Franklin room at the Franklin Institute. She's giving the camera a wink with a glass of champagne pressed to her lips, and just before the photo disappears I see Ethan's golden head in the background. I quickly click Tammy's icon again and reload the story, holding the cursor down to pause it when the photo reappears.

I narrow my eyes and lean into the screen as if I'm looking at a Magic Eye until my hungover brain can make out exactly what I'm seeing on the dance floor. I put my thumb and pointer finger to the screen and open them, trying to enlarge the picture until I realize I'm not on an iPhone and I've just smeared grease all over the monitor. I can't tear my gaze away from the gorgeous redhead in the emerald green dress with her hands linked behind Ethan's neck. It's just a dance. Surely Ethan danced with dozens of women at the gala. Even when he and I attended together I'd had to lend him out like a library book. But something in my pizza-filled stomach twists. I've met this woman before—Eleanor or Eliza—something old school like that. She's a resident at Jefferson—her father is the chief of something—very important. Very influential. Very worthy.

I start clicking like a woman possessed, trying to find more photos, and sure enough there she is again in the background of a photo of Tammy and Olivia. She's laughing at something Ethan has said, her fingers wrapped around his bicep. The bicep my hand belongs around. And another one of Tammy at the table; Ethan isn't looking at the camera, he's twisted in his chair. His full attention on Eli-whatever's face like she's giving him the secrets on how to rule the world. I hit the plus button in the corner, zooming in until the image is so pixelated the blurring hurts my eyes. There—I touch the screen again—right beneath the white tablecloth, this woman's bare knee is pressed right up against his.

What the actual fuck, Ethan? Is this what Tammy wanted to talk about? *If you have oats to sow* . . . His voice floods my head. Was this all part of his plan? Oh God. Was he seeing her—before? My heart drops into my pelvic floor, and the last bite of pizza slides from my plate. And when I see the delicious cheese hit the floor, that's when I get really pissed.

QUINDICI

James

It's one of those beautiful crisp nights that fools your body into getting excited for fall too early—makes you crave open fires and warm sweaters in the middle of August. I spent the earlier part of my afternoon at the museum, looking over the newest acquisitions that Silvia, the curator at the Galleria, managed to obtain from Firenze on lease. She's masterful. And now we have four portraits by our own Raffaello di Sanzio to display for the fall, with two more on the way. There's something so fulfilling about art finding its way back to Urbino—the city that shaped and nurtured the work's creator.

The later part of my afternoon was almost as satisfying, playing Massimo one-on-one at soccer while Nina refereed from where she milked the sheep. I've been schooling the kid since he was in diapers, same mop of black curly hair and huge white chicklet smile. Though I hate to admit it, it might not be long until the tables are turned. Maso's getting stronger—the ball tighter to his foot every time we play. I've got a year—maybe two—to keep him in his place. And then we are all in trouble.

"Gi, could you let Ava know we are leaving?" Nina yells out the window.

I stop rocking in my favorite chair on the porch and watch my peaceful afternoon drift into the past. There's no point in saying no to Nina. And besides, the more I contest their obvious meddling, the more she and Leo see reason to meddle.

I take my time around the side of the house, replaying our conversation from this morning. "*I have a boyfriend. A serious one.*" Right. No wiggle room there. No blurred lines. Just a big red stop sign and a shitload of attitude. Why didn't I tell her I'm not interested? Or that her presence is nothing but a splinter just beneath the skin?

The low-hanging sun reflects off of the glass of the guest house doors and I knock twice, even though I can tell she's not inside. A small, silly pang of worry strikes me as I remember her brow knitted together in confusion this afternoon when I saw her last. What if she got lost searching for a sally port?

More likely, she's out cataloguing artwork or creating some sort of checklist for her time here, her ridiculous planner tucked under her arm. Or maybe she's working on the details of her absurd relationship arrangement with the jackass. Either way, her whereabouts do not—should not—concern me, so I step to the side of the guest house and take my time with my camera and the view, letting the pressure beneath my finger give way to the satisfying click of a moment captured. Sunsets like this make me crave watercolors, but I know my brush could never re-create that shade of orange, the way it burns the underbelly of the soft pink clouds above it. Only the camera can get that right.

Massimo destroys my moment of peace by yelling at me from where he is walking out of view along the driveway behind the cypress trees. At least his voice cracks a little, so I can smile as I sigh. I lower the camera and focus on the screen, clicking through my recent images while I try to close the distance between me and my family as they make their way toward the city walls for dinner.

There's no doubt that the best pictures on the reel are those I've taken of Ava, and it's not just my knack for portraiture. As a subject, her range makes the series of photographs fascinating. There is constant transformation—the Ava that she wants the world to see, and the Ava that is hidden underneath. The dichotomy makes the work impossible to ignore. And she's stunning—lit from within.

Which just makes her all the more infuriating.

"Oh, Gi. That's gorgeous. She will want that," Nina says, leaning in to see the picture I'm studying of Ava looking down into Urbino's streets from the hill beyond the wall. Her eyes are wide, the green popping with the grass on the hillside, and her lips are slightly parted in awe.

"A Mortal's Glimpse of Olympus," Zio Leo says. He has a habit of naming all of my work. And doing it well. Which makes him insufferable. "You should send that to Signore Davenport."

"Zio, per favore," I plead.

Since he "accidentally" opened an email from Greer Davenport, the owner of *The Post*, who wants me to sign with his magazine, Leo has been unrelenting. The arrangement requires me to live locally in London, and I'm not interested in leaving Urbino—leaving my family and my career.

"There is an entire world out there, Gi—"

I put up my hand. "I've seen enough."

"You can never see enough," he counters.

"Leo," Nina warns.

Time to change the subject to the only thing they like talking about more than meddling in my professional life.

"The American must have left without us," I tell them, ignoring their shared glance.

"No," Massimo says. "She never came home. I kept an eye out."

"You kept an eye out while I was embarrassing you at calcio? Maybe you should get a job, Maso. So you have less time to—you know—stalk guests?" I punch him in the arm and he points at my camera.

"I'm the stalker?"

Little shit.

I lift the camera. "This is art. Not creepy puberty hormones."

Massimo kicks some gravel at my heels. "I'm sure that is what all of the great serial killers think."

Nina chuckles and I throw her a glare that she just lifts her brows at and waves away. My paltry effort hardly registered with the Queen of Glares.

"I hope you are not giving her too much work, Gi," Leo chimes in. "We want her to really take in what Urbino has to offer."

I grunt and choose not to acknowledge the fact that I've given her 74,000 words to look over in her first week here. She basically begged me for them.

"She took in most of the wine Urbino has to offer last night with Franco," I tell him. "Perhaps you should have put her in a class with lower enrollment if you thought she couldn't handle the work."

He purses his lips. "I believe that woman can handle anything you send her way, Gi." I hold his gaze for as long as I can, then look back toward the view as he continues. "And good for her. She should imbibe as much as she wants. So long as she has saved us some for dinner tonight. Vincenzo said he procured some of the most exquisite white truffles he's seen this season." Zio closes his eyes, touches his fingers to his lips. Truffles and Petrarca are the two things that cause my uncle to speak in reverent tones. Which in turn causes my aunt to roll her eyes deeply into her skull.

"It is not as busy tonight," Nina comments as we pass through the entrance onto Via Mazzini.

"My students are nursing hangovers," I explain.

Both Nina and Leo nod their understanding. In the fall, when the university reaches full capacity, the city buzzes with an energy that could sweep you away faster than a rip tide after a hurricane. But in summer, that energy ebbs and flows at half its power, depending on the moods and whims of the student body on campus.

Our usual table outside of Vincenzo's osteria is set for us with a small placard that says RESERVED, four candles lit beside bottles of white wine sitting in cylinders of ice. Six places are set, Franco occupying one of them in the hat that Ava wore the night before. I look around for Ava as Franco stands, removing the hat, and Vincenzo appears from within to welcome us.

Vincenzo kisses and embraces us with the same warmth I remember from boyhood, the kindness exuding from his every pore toward me even as a strange American child fresh off the boat. But then his wife was alive to double that warmth and welcome.

"Gi, you look lost, no?" he says in his booming voice. The other patrons don't look up, a sure sign that they are locals who are used to the deep resonance of Vincenzo's volume. "Ahhh," his finger goes up and he gives me a nod. "She has gone to make a phone call."

I don't even bother asking who he's speaking about because five knowing pairs of eyes are on me. Massimo's eyes are accompanied by a wolfish grin. I look to the sky for help.

"I'll let her know we are here," I say, dropping my gaze to the haphazard stones at my feet as I begin to climb the hill toward the pay phones in the piazza.

I'm glad she's phoning home. It means she took my advice—decided to call home and figure out what the hell her douche of a boyfriend expected from her. I try not to feel too satisfied at the fact that my words reached her this morning. It's not like it changes anything. She's still an entitled brat and I'm still not stupid enough to get wrapped up in her emotional wreckage.

I nod and wave hello as I pass students and locals alike, but my mind keeps pulling toward her—to what she said—how he responded. Did she take hold of the situation? I can't imagine this woman as a back-up singer at someone else's concert. She's got a zero-shit-taken policy that's as visible as a traffic light. At least for me.

The tinkling of the small fountain at the center of La Piazza della Repubblica reaches me before it comes into view over the stone crest of Via Mazzini. The iron tables set up on the near side of the square are filled with students and tourists clustered beneath the white umbrellas, partaking in a very late apertivo or a very early nightcap. The portico of white archways outside of the Collegio Raffaello glow with bright lights beneath, happy chatter drifting outward from the open doorways where students sip espresso and plan their evenings. I look to my right and find the familiar sight of the eight pillars that seem to hide the space behind them where something as mundane and modern (comparatively) as pay phones dwell. I step into the shadows, the tinkling of water and conversation fading away behind me the moment my eyes settle on her golden head.

She's sitting on the smooth tiles that run the length of the portico, her back up against the brick façade where the pay phones are mounted every four feet, her knees hugged against her chest. She looks up when I'm standing over her, and the look in her eyes curls my fingers into a tight fist. I'm torn between two equally insane instincts—wrapping my arms around her and finding Edward and beating the ever-loving shit out of him.

I should walk away, run back down the hill, but I crouch so I'm nearly at her level and hold her gaze in the shadow.

"Do you want to talk about it?"

She shakes her head twice and hands me the piece of plastic that the shithead sent her across the Atlantic with, and I try to imagine what sort of man could pull a stunt like this—what kind of man this woman would allow to make her feel this way. It takes everything in me not to crack the card in two. But I slip it in my pocket and keep studying the way the unshed tears in her eyes make them swim—the green is the exact shade of the Tyrrhenian Sea off the coast of Sardinia. Her face here in the shadows looks like a black-and-white film star's. This photo, if I were shite enough to take it, would be the best of my life so far. Possibly the best of my future life.

As if she can read my mind, her eyes lower to my camera dangling against my chest.

"Do you want to eat and drink wine?" I try, then hold out my hand to help her up.

A smile slowly tugs at the corners of her mouth, but falls again as if the effort is too great.

"The answer to that is always yes," she whispers, her voice thick as she settles her fingers into my palm. I yank her up and she bounces off of me gracelessly. Her uncomfortable chuckle unclenches my fist, and I put my hand out for her to lead the way back down the hill.

"I didn't call him," she says as she passes me, glancing up to study my expression, searching for—approval?

"And it wasn't because I couldn't figure out the stupid pay phones," she adds.

I keep my lips pressed together until she looks away, then I breathe. Breathe out her scent. Breathe out the gut punch that took me off guard after seeing her pain. Breathe her out. Out and away.

She didn't call him. Is that supposed to be a victory? Some sort of restraint or feat of strength? Some sort of signal to me? I might be fluent in Italian and English, but this—Ava-ese—is way beyond my reach. She's a breadbasket with cake inside it. Or a cake filled with vegetables. Either way you never know what you'll get when you reach inside. And apparently I'm a moron, because I keep reaching inside despite my better judgment.

I watch her step out of the shadows, past the white umbrella–covered tables, back into the lights streaming from the shops and windows lining Via Mazzini, smiling at the bottega owners who stand in their door greeting their customers. And just like that, she's lifted her infuriating shield, stepped back into her armor, and is marching away while I'm left wondering why the hell my insides are still twisted from seeing her hurt, when the only thing I should be feeling is inconvenienced that I'm dealing with the baggage that I just promised myself I'd avoid.

SEDICI

Ava

There is a lull in the conversation as Vincenzo and his apprentice, Raffi, set down the final plate on our table before wishing us an emphatic "Buon appetito" and hurrying back to work. To this point, I've done a damn good job of not thinking of Ethan with the redhead. I deserve an award for not simmering. Accolades. Someone should compliment me.

"You look very lovely tonight, Ava," Massimo says.

Damn it. Not him. Someone else should compliment me. Someone who wasn't born decades post-Bieber.

I shove a bite of heaven into my mouth and nod my thanks to the teeny-bopper warily, reminding myself not to look directly into his eyes. James punches his cousin on the arm and I send him a glare. I don't need another rescue. He's already got home court advantage and a fifty point lead after seeing me in the fetal position with zero dignity left intact. I don't do outward displays of emotion. The only way I keep my feelings is bottled, but somehow the man I can't escape got to see that bottle crack and leave a messy Ava-shaped puddle beneath the pay phone. Honestly, at this point there's no way to remedy the impression I've made on this man. So I'll focus on the food.

I'm eating rabbit. No. I'm eating pork stuffed with rabbit. I spin the fork in front of my eyes, marveling at the combination that has just sent dopamine rushing to my brain like a jackpot. It's the Italian turducken. But oh so much more.

"Ava," Franco begins, pointing his fork at Leo beside him, who is chewing so slowly that I wonder if his tooth has fallen out and he's trying to find it. "Did you tell Leo that your mother is Annette Barrett?"

Leo freezes. His eyes open and he swallows the bite he'd been so carefully enjoying.

"No," he says, his voice dipping on the O. "That cannot be."

He narrows his eyes at me and I look to Franco, who is nodding and smiling at him. Leo is lifting his cute little reading glasses onto his nose. Studying me like I'm an ancient illuminated manuscript. He sighs. "Mamma mia, certo. I did not see it. But there"—he points with two fingers—"gli occhi—sono essati."

I'm looking between Franco and Leo with a cheek full of rabbit-stuffed pork. They are rambling in Italian so quickly I can't even pick up the spaces between the words and sentences. I look to James for help. And immediately see that he will be none.

He's gazing at me with a sort of intense awe that I'd love to take credit for.

"Your mother?" he whispers.

I nod, remembering I never really clarified why the hell I was asking about her last night. He's obviously having an art nerd moment. Poor guy.

Leo laughs and pulls his attention away from his friend and back to me. His hands are a whirlwind of movement. They are giving me vertigo.

"How appropriate, then, that you should be placed in this program, where your mother studied all those years ago," he says, nodding. "It is fate, no?" His eyes are twinkling so brightly that I can't help but think of that star that Jiminy Cricket has to make a wish on. Or is it Pinocchio? "Tell me, cara. How is she? I can only hope she visits us while you are here!"

I swallow the lump of pig-rabbit and stare at him. Words, of any language, are eluding me. They always do when it comes to my mom.

"She's," I try. When was the last time I had to say these words? "She's—um—no longer with us," I finish, looking down at the most delicious thing I'll never eat. My appetite has flown the coop. Or my appetite has flown to a neighboring coop, because the wine is suddenly looking pretty appealing despite my low thrumming headache.

"Ahh, Ava. I am so sorry, cara. So very sorry," Leo tells me. Nina is rubbing my back in a way that makes me want to curl up in her lap and sleep for days, and Franco is topping off my wine glass.

"It's okay," I lie. "Please, just eat before your food gets cold."

I want to ask a thousand questions. About my mom. About her art. About it all. But, watching the light in Leo's eyes fade into dullness after informing him of her loss, stopped me in my tracks—reminded me of how Dad's heart had plunged into deep freeze with the same news. Yet to be thawed despite my attempts to be a human blowtorch.

I'll ask my questions later. When I'm not still spiraling from the pictures of Ethan and Red. When James isn't gawking at me like I'm the descendant of Van Gogh. Now is not the time to go traipsing through my mom's Walter Mitty shit.

Leo meets Nina's eyes beside me and nods once before returning to his plate with less enthusiasm than before. I want him to enjoy his magic truffle thingies. That was the plan.

But there I go. Ruining a perfectly amazing dinner with my inability to handle my shit. According to my ex-grief counselor, I'd never be able to handle my shit unless I let myself grieve. Whatever that means. When she—after she passed, it had been so much easier to jump back into school. Create the plan. Check those boxes. Dive right into the life that I could save and somewhat control—my own.

And I'm here, aren't I? Fulfilling that promise I made to her. That has to count for something. Some sort of grief step on the list. Maybe even two.

I look up to find James is still staring at me with that same awe. No sadness or pity there—thank goodness. Just some sort of misplaced wonder.

I take a long sip of wine and glare at him over the rim of my glass.

"Do you draw or paint?" he asks softly, studying my hand around the stem of the wine glass as if he might find the answer to his question on my fingers.

I place the glass back on the table and slip my fingers back into my lap beneath the napkin, then shake my head.

"Neither," I tell him, crossing my arms over my chest. He tilts his head. Narrows his eyes as if I might be hiding something.

I could add presently. I don't draw or paint, presently. Or even since. I could clarify with since. But that just opens up this li'l moment for further conversation, and we are already well beyond our daily limit of pleasant words betwixt us.

Nina leans in from beside me and whispers, "You seem exhausted, cara. If you'd like to head out early, I can make your apologies to Vincenzo and bring you home the tiramisu."

Mio Dio. Tiramisu. The Italian word for mouthgasm.

Sit across from James's questioning and intense gaze for the rest of the evening and avoid awkward conversation about my mother, or have Nina-room-service deliver billowy clouds of mascarpone being drowned in fresh, hot espresso after I take a triple-headed shower to wash off Ethan's potential betrayal?

Though the idea of being left alone to my thoughts is almost as terrifying as the way James is looking at me.

I lower my eyes to my lap, and Nina sees right into my exhausted, battered brain.

"Ava, I think you need to go rest," she says loud enough for all to hear.

Not a single person argues with Nina. In fact, they all say their goodbyes as warmly and casually as possible, and get right back to their food.

My apologies and gratitude are waved away, and I'm almost to the archway when I hear Nina's decisive tone pipe up again.

"James, you will walk her, no?"

Oh, Nina. You sneaky, sneaky woman.

"And miss dessert again? I don't think—"

I keep moving, pick up the pace, too emotionally exhausted to witness the standoff behind me between James and his aunt, but I can't help regretting my decision to not look back when I hear the distinct and gratifying sound of someone being smacked in the back of his hollow head.

Naturally, that joyful noise is followed by unwanted but familiar footsteps.

DICIASSETTE

James

We are one hundred meters from the guest house when Ava finally breaks the silence between us.

"Can you stop looking at me like I just told you I'm the queen of Genovia?"

"I didn't realize I was looking at you at all," I lie. She has this trail of freckles along her chin that reminds me of Orion's Belt. "And what the hell is Genovia?"

Ava murmurs something about me being culturally illiterate and focuses her attention back on the road. I study her profile.

Annette Barrett's painting *Urbino Under Storm* was my first memory of art—of beauty, really. It hung in Nonna's small kitchen in Brooklyn—watched us eat dinner together every night beside the empty place setting my grandma left out just in case, ever-hopeful that my mother would join us. That painting with the ghostly white pallor of the palazzo against the deeply bruised sky that I'd catch Nonna gazing at while she stirred the marinara—that staple of my childhood. That had been Ava's mother's work? Until I was eight, I had believed that Urbino was surrounded by walls of snowy ice because of that painting. And, of course, my Nonna did nothing to dispel my beliefs. She'd encouraged them.

To this day I smell her marinara when snow falls in Urbino.

"Really, James?"

My viewfinder goes black and I realize she's put her hand in front of the lens. I hadn't even realized I'd been taking pictures.

"I'm sorry," I mutter, but she's already stormed off. "Ava—"

"What?"

She's got her shoulders pulled up to her ears, her chest pressed outward, her elbows akimbo. All puffed up like a house finch taking on a hawk.

"I'm sorry about your mom," I tell her, taking a step into the shadow of the cypress trees. Ava seems to command light and darkness according to her mood.

"It was a long time ago. I'm fine, really," she says looking upward. I keep my hands in my pockets to resist the pull of my camera. I know that time doesn't heal a wound like that. The loss of your mother is something you feel over and over again, like a circle of Dante's Inferno.

"And I'm sorry about whatever happened today with Edward."

She looks straight at me. Narrows her eyes as if she's assessing my sincerity. I imagine her pulling a cord that opens a trapdoor beneath me as she yells *liar* down into the hole.

"Are you sorry—about Ethan?"

She steps forward, her tone suddenly curious. The way she says his name is like she's cursing. Her body language shifts—her puffed-up anger relaxes into something warmer—more languid. I should step away, but the way she moves—tilts her head to the side, teeth tugging at her bottom lip—has me frozen where I stand. My gaze slides to her mouth, then down her chin, past the constellation of freckles and along her neck. My fists clench and unclench at my side as I imagine how soft she'd feel. The chorus of "O Fortuna" breaks through the sudden thickness around us, and she jumps back as I pull my phone from my pocket, still watching her.

I tear my gaze away from her and look at my screen. It's Tommaso, the owner of Il Pinguino, a college bar in the center of town. I run my hand along my jaw, trying to find a positive explanation for this call. An explanation that doesn't end in a headache for me.

There is none.

I accept the call, tapping the speaker button.

"Pronto," I say.

The noise from the bar seeps into the quiet of the night like we've opened a bag of pissed-off hornets. The bass is bumping and the sound of laughter and yelling makes Ava put her fingers to her temples. I feel her pain.

"Gi, ho bisogno di te," Tommaso yells over the din. "Gli Americani . . ."

His voice gets swallowed by shouting.

"Va bene. Sto arrivando," I say, already making my way back toward town.

Ava's footsteps crunch behind me. I turn and look down at her.

"Go to bed," I say. "You don't need to deal with this."

She lifts a brow. "Yeah, I do. I'm your assistant. I'm literally supposed to assist you."

"In the classroom, Ava. We aren't Batman and Robin," I say.

She lets out a laugh, and it's ridiculous how much the sound pleases me. I walk away faster, but she just hurries after me.

"I think I'd rather be Catwoman—the Anne Hathaway one."

"I don't have time for this. What if it's a fight? I don't want you to get hurt," I say.

She waves me off like I'm an overprotective dad. Or a horsefly.

"I do kickboxing and tai—"

"Ava!"

I stop and she steps forward and clenches her jaw, her eyes wide and chin up, as she pokes a finger into my sternum harder than necessary.

"I'm coming, James. You think I can't handle a little Italian scuffle. I'm from Philly for fuck's sake." Her eyes drop to where her finger is pressed against me and she lets out a long breath, then adds quietly, "Besides, I need a distraction."

She shakes her head like she's physically trying to remove something from inside and then looks back up at me. I let out a long measured breath and turn back toward town, calling over my shoulder, "Fine. Let's go, Robin."

I don't bother to look back and watch her eyes crinkle in the corners when she giggles behind me. And when she starts singing the *Batman* theme song, I just keep my focus forward—away from her—where it needs to be.

DICIOTTO

Ava

The moment we step through the port-of-sally-whatever, I can hear the low bellowing bass. I can feel it shaking the inside of my head and vibrating over my skin. James leads us up a shadowy alley with strong Jack the Ripper vibes that would normally terrify me, but with his broad shoulders blocking my view and his quick steps forcing me to hustle, I don't have time to even look around and acknowledge the haunting surroundings.

"When we get there, I want you to let me handle it," he says.

"Mmmhmm," I say to his back.

"I'm serious, Ava."

"You're always serious, James."

His fists clench at his sides, but he doesn't turn around.

My brain starts to rattle and I know we are close. The opening chords of "Juicy" hit my ear, and the music feels a little less invasive at this distance and a little more inviting. The bar is entirely made of the old stone that comprises most of the town, but instead of one single entrance, there are three huge semicircular drop-down garage doors. James squats and lifts one high enough for me to duck under, and the moment I do it's like I've stepped into an underground club.

The garage door drops behind me and I barely hear it over Biggie's chorus. The inside of the bar is broken into two rooms—the bar room where a dozen red leather booths line the back wall, and what appears to be the dance room where a small platform peeks out above the cluster of gyrating students with their drinks held aloft like torches. Torches that are spilling all over their heads and clothes, but they don't seem to mind.

I see a handsome older gentleman climb over the bar and push his way through the crowd. He looks stressed. Or distressed. Both, really.

"Gi!" he yells.

James puts his hand on the small of my back and guides me toward him.

"Gli Americani," the man gestures to the bar. "They will not get out from behind the bar."

I lift onto my toes and take in the four girls who are mixing drinks while they dance and shake. They are all in our class. And they are working that bar like they've been trained at Coyote Ugly. I try not to smile when the one named Jennifer sprays a guy reaching for her friend Sam's ass across the bar. Looks like they've got shit under control.

Tommaso gestures toward the other room, where everyone is singing the lyrics as they sway. My rib cage suddenly feels too tight as I watch their happy faces laughing without a care in the world. This would have been me at twenty-one if I hadn't canceled my study abroad summer. The thought sends an unfamiliar yearning through me, and I force my gaze away to focus on Tommaso.

"And they have taken over la musica," he yells, his bushy eyebrows disappearing into his thick hair.

I squint and find a student named Jessica on the platform with a pair of headphones on, dancing above the singing crowd. There's a dark-haired, olive-skinned man behind her that might be the only one in the bar who isn't dancing—including me. James's hand stills me by the shoulder and I look up at him, pressing my lips together so hard they might bruise.

"Alright, Tommaso," James yells. "We will handle them."

I widen my eyes at James. Is there really something to handle here? A couple of girls helping out behind the bar and another who appears to be working the crowd with her music doesn't seem like a problem for the dynamic duo. I start to move my hips again and James shakes his head and lowers his mouth near my ear and says, "You deal with the music. I'll handle the bar."

"If I'm not back in ten, save yourself," I say, trying my hardest to be serious. James ignores me and heads for the bar, leaving me to shimmy my way through the drunk crowd. I stay along the wall, trying not to draw any attention to myself, and I'm doing a damn good job when chaos breaks out at the bar.

"Shot! Shot! Shot!"

Everyone is pounding on the bar top and I make out James shaking his head while Samantha pours a shot in front of him. I can tell he's working hard not to smile; his dimple does the pop-and-hide thing as he leans in and says something to the students behind the bar. They all nod in unison and James lifts the shot and throws it back. The cheers are deafening.

My partner has gone rogue, it seems, but then the four girls make their way out from behind the bar and James turns in my direction, scanning the dance floor for me. I slide and sway to the platform so he doesn't catch me watching him with this stupid smile on my face. When I'm close enough, I tap Jessica's foot until she looks down and sees me. Her face breaks out into a huge smile and she pulls me up as she grabs the microphone and emcees over the music.

"Special guest everyone! Miss G is out tonight!"

Everyone's hands go up in the air and I shake my head, trying not to laugh. They are chanting my name like I might do a solo performance of "Lose Yourself" on the platform. I feel like I'm about to deflate a bouncehouse with twenty toddlers in it.

"Jessica!" I yell, but there's no way in hell she can hear me with the headphones she's stolen from this poor schmuck behind her. He makes a hand signal toward her that can only mean *what the actual fuck*.

I tap the side of my head and signal for her to take them off. She leans in.

"You have to give this man his job back," I tell her in her ear.

She pulls back and looks at my face, shaking her head with a horrified look. Then she leans back in and says, "Miss Graham, I can't. It's bad. He only has like five songs and they are from the nineties."

I swallow my laugh and try not to be offended at her calling out my birth decade, then lean in to tell her the song she's playing is from the dreaded nineties, but I can tell it's a lost cause. My eyes find James sitting at the bar, his arms folded across his chest, one brow lifted as he watches me as if he knows exactly what I'm about to do. I hear Jessica repeating the word *please* over and over beside me, and I mouth the words to James over the sea of heads. "Abort mission."

He shakes his head and lifts his camera, aiming it at me. I shrug and smile, then lean into Jessica and tell her, "If Tommaso signals you, cut the music and help him. Deal?"

She nods and I wink at her. She holds up her hands in victory. Everyone cheers, and the song blends into Lizzo as I make my way down the platform steps and back toward the bar, where James is grinding his teeth so hard that I see the muscle along his jaw twitch with the effort.

"Am I kicked out of the Justice League?" I yell at him.

He gestures toward Tommaso like he defers the decision to him, but the man is so swamped with orders he can barely look up. James leans over the bar and says something to him, and Tommaso gives me a thumbs up and waves us away.

"You ready?" he yells. "Or do you want to do some more dancing?"

God help me, I do want to do some more dancing. That craving for freedom hits me again square in the center of my chest, but I can't submit. I'm in charge of these younguns and there's no faster way to blur the line of authority than the running man.

"Will Tommaso be okay?" I ask, changing the subject.

"I think he was better off with the guest bartenders," James yells over his shoulder, pulling me toward the garage doors.

"Shouldn't we offer to help?"

James lifts up the door as I scoot under.

"We just did," he says as he straightens. "Well, I did."

I roll my eyes.

"Jessica said he had five songs on loop from the—gasp—nineties!" I put one hand on my heart and one on my head like I might swoon.

He lets out a low chuckle and I straighten.

"Did you just laugh?" I ask, looking around to see if it could have come from anywhere else.

He sighs, then turns and heads back down the haunted alley without answering me.

"Back to the Batcave," I tell his back. "Very unorthodox for a vigilante to take a shot before completing a mission."

"The shot was part of the mission," he grumbles. "I think it's quiet time now, don't you?" James asks, snapping a photo of the shadows spilling across the stones at his feet.

"Sure thing, boss." I zip my lips and then study him as he retreats into his photography. I watch him drop to one knee and aim his camera up at the walls of Urbino, the moon hanging low just above their reach. I watch him point his lens out over the hill-sides, his bottom lip pulled between his teeth as his finger presses down over and over again. He doesn't make a sound.

It's clear in the way he moves, the way his body relaxes with each shot, that this is what he loves. That photography to him is what painting was to my mother.

The silence lasts until we get to the first cypress tree that lines the driveway to the villa, and then, emboldened by the shadows, I ask, "Why haven't you made photography into a career?"

He doesn't answer, and I look up at him to find a sliver of moonlight cutting across his cheekbone as he stares out over the fields toward the distance.

I narrow my eyes at him and push. "It's clear that you love it. And you are extremely tal—"

"Could we not do this?"

His eyes flash to mine and I can see I've struck a chord. Naturally, I want to strike it again. Several times.

"Ahh. I see," I say. "You get to know all of my secrets, see me at my lowest, but I'm not good enough to hear yours?"

He stops at the side of the house and turns to me, eyes narrowed.

"You don't see. There's nothing to see," he says. "Telling some-one your life story because you believe a driver can't be bilingual doesn't make you not good enough. It just makes you—"

I put up my hand. "Don't you dare. You don't get to just hurl insults and deflect every time I ask a serious question that you're too scared to answer."

He steps forward, and I have to tilt my head back in order to keep eye contact, but there's no way I'm looking away first.

"A serious question?" His voice is low, just loud enough to reach me above the cicadas. "What is it that you love, Ava? Law? Is that what sets you on fire? Or did you choose that career for some other reason? Maybe the same things you saw in Edward? Money? Prestige? Veneers?"

I open my mouth to speak and shut it again. His brows lift in a knowing smirk that I want to smack right off of his face. But before I even have a chance to defend myself, he mutters something in Italian and turns his back to me.

"It's rude to talk about someone in a language they don't understand," I call after him, wincing. I sound pathetic—like a petulant teen.

"Then learn Italian, dolcezza," he says just before stepping through the front door and closing it behind him.

"Good night to you, too. Stronzo!"

But he doesn't hear me. The porch light turns off and I'm left with a burning anger in my gut and nowhere to release it as I make my way to the guest house through the dark. Somehow this anger still feels better than the rest of today's emotions. So when I plop into bed, my eyes on the single square of light coming from the second-story window of the villa, I turn the heat up under that anger and let it simmer.

DICIANOVE

Ava

Everyone is being too kind. I suspect it has to do with the Mom conversation at dinner the other night. Or maybe I've grown unaccustomed to random acts of nurturing.

Nina keeps sneaking extra baked goods and fresh fruit into my purse.

Leo has interrupted class twice in the last two days to steal me away, once for a tour of campus that was long overdue, and once to show me a photograph he found of my mother and her art history professor sitting at a picnic table with a bottle of wine between them. The man looked vaguely familiar to me, but Leo assured me he was no longer residing in Urbino.

Even Massimo has been on his best behavior, barely leering when five of his tweeny buds came over for some pool soccer yesterday afternoon. He even swatted one of them when the little bro said something under his breath in Italian as I walked by. I will definitely bring head swatting back to America. Best souvenir ever.

And then there's James, who is pointedly ignoring me in all ways possible. If I catch him watching me in class, his eyes are narrowed and he looks like he wants to throw the projector remote at me. If I could flip him off in a professional manner, I would. But I refuse to add to his arsenal.

He's also been absent from family dinners. Nina hides it well, but I know she's pissed about it. Apparently, James never misses dinners, and I can't help but wonder if he's working hard on the apartment so he can get me the hell out of his family life. All of this in mind, you can imagine my surprise when his MacBook Air appeared on my desk with a note saying: *Until you get a new phone.* But maybe Leo forced him to play nice. Or maybe James was kicked in the head by a sheep and forgot he despises me.

I turn my focus from the paper I'm supposed to be grading and run my fingers over the keyboard of his Mac, pulling up the email Tammy wrote to me yesterday to reread it for the thousandth time.

Aves-

I'm not speaking to him. He swears up and down that he's not seeing her and I wish I could tell you I believe him, but I feel like I don't even know him right now.

It's time for you to stop thinking about him and focus on you. Go. Get. Yours. If you haven't already . . .

Lost without you,
T

She knows full well I'm not getting mine. I scroll down to my reply email—a screenshot of flights from Philly to Bologna in the hope that one will somehow fit into Tammy's crazy schedule. Between photo shoots and galas for Olivia and her volunteering at the children's literacy camp, it's a miracle she even has time to email me.

A huge glob of drool lands on the essay to the left of the keyboard. After checking my own lip, I look up to find Verga reading over my shoulder. I've been grading these godforsaken papers for eight hours, lying on the floor on my stomach picking at the bread and cheese I brought home from town. I've gone through two of my favorite ballpoint pens. Still I have at least thirty left to go.

I remind myself that this is nothing compared to the endless hours I'll put in at Grant and Stanley when I start there in September. Of course, I'll be getting paid for that. Handsomely. I'll have told my dad by then and he will accept the fact that I'm not working at his firm. And I'm sure Ethan will have worked whatever this is out of his system by the time I get home, and life will be moving onward according to the original plan. I just have to get through these next few weeks without losing any more of the little dignity I have left.

I picture James's narrowed eyes as he asked me what I loved—as he accused me of caring only about veneers. It's not a crime to be ambitious. And wanting finer things doesn't make me greedy. Why am I thinking about this again?

I roll onto my back and look up at my canine companion.

"Could you tell your dogdad that he's a pompous prick, Beasty?"

Verga tilts his head, then lies down on the stack of papers.

"Maybe you could bite him!"

I scratch his ears the way he likes and he immediately lolls backward to give me access to his belly. Verga has slept with me every night this week. I'm thinking of booking him a flight back to Philly with me. In a seat. As my comfort animal.

"Bite who?"

James is watching me from the porch like I've conjured him. He steps inside, and I almost pull out the vampire rules and tell him he can't since he's uninvited, but it's too late. Ugh. This is why you don't leave doors open. But the weather has been too gorgeous to shut out. Maybe I should make a pros and cons list. Crisp air vs. threat of James.

"Am I ever going to get my dog back?" he asks.

"Verga prefers to avoid possessive pronouns. 'My' is objectifying to him," I say, using my nails along the dog's barrel-sized rib cage.

"Well, since I used to clean up puppy Verga's shit in the house so Nina didn't make him sleep in the barn with the sheep, he's going to have to deal with some objectification," James says.

He's standing over me. I know because his shadow from my desk lamp is stretching all the way across the hardwood floor and then disappearing into the glass that spans the back wall. I don't look up.

"Are you done ignoring me now?" I ask, pretending to read.

"No. This is work related." His foot nudges Verga off of the stack of papers. "How many do you have left?" he asks.

"Not many. A few. Thirtyish," I murmur, pulling Verga back over the stack by his legs.

"Christ, Ava. Are you rewriting them? You've been holed up in here for two nights—"

"Missed me?" I finally smile up at him and immediately regret it. He's freshly showered and shaved. His shirt sticks to his pecs in a way that's bordering on sinful, and I imagine touching his jaw. It probably feels like velvet or—

"Just give me the rest," he says, bending over to grab them.

I smack his hand, probably harder than necessary, and Verga stands up too fast, alarmed by the sound, knocking his hindquarters right into my face. Now I'm as acquainted with the dog's ass as he is with mine.

"I'm almost done with them, you bossy stronzo," I say, scurrying onto my knees and pulling the papers back.

James watches me with a crooked grin that I want to knock straight with my fist.

I place the papers behind me and rush to stand the moment I recognize I'm on my knees in front of him, turning my face so he can't see the flush that image has caused.

"I don't need your help," I say, brushing the dog hair off my bare legs.

"I didn't say you needed it. I just don't want to get smacked for keeping you from all that Italy has to offer," he says, pointing to the view. I don't need to follow his finger. I've memorized the way the sky turns from orange to pink to purple at this time of day, the way the hills beneath it slide into darkness with the change like they're slipping beneath a favorite blanket.

"I think I've seen enough of what Italy has to offer," I murmur, turning back toward my desk that suddenly needs to be tidied up.

James scoffs.

"You've barely made it past the piazza. You're at the tip of the iceberg," he says.

"Well, when the tip is enough to toss your life into a blender, why would you go looking for the rest?" I am trying to find something to look at because he's boring a hole in the side of my face. I pick up my mother's postcard and tuck it into the cover of the Calvino novel I'm reading so that he doesn't see it. A week in Italy and not a word written. *Fill it when the words find you.*

Words aren't finding me, Mom. But a bunch of bad shit found me. One of the bad shits is staring at me right now, making my skin feel too tight.

James takes a step closer in my periphery and I squeeze as close to my desk as I can. The guest house is suddenly far too small. It needs another point of egress. Or one less wall.

"Italy didn't toss your life into a blender. You can't blame a country for things going wrong in your life."

I can smell his goddamned soap. I might as well be in the shower with him. Wrong turn, brain. Reverse. Reverse! The edge of my desk is leaving an indent in the front of my hip bone. I sidestep—smooth as a pothole—toward the built-in shelves.

"Here we go. Are you going to call me ignorant again? Or wait—how 'bout fake? Which insult would you like to launch, James?"

He lifts his brows and pretends to mull it over. I roll my eyes.

"Nothing has gone according to plan. You threw my phone off a cliff. My law seminar died of *E. coli*. And my rental in town center is probably floating away toward the Adriatic Sea by now since you seem to be in no rush to save it," I say, trying to keep my voice steady while I restack books that were perfectly stacked. But I can see his reflection in the glass that covers one of his photos hanging on the wall.

He shakes his head, sending a dark, wet curl onto his forehead. "I'm not going to dignify any of those accusations with a response. But questa è la vita, dolcezza. Life has its own plan for you—"

He sounds like my mother. *Life does not care about your plan.*

"—And don't worry about the apartment. Besides, if we are pointing fingers, let's not forget about the man who started this spiral—"

"Can we not do this again?" I ask, turning, my eyes finally settling on his. And now they're stuck there. Damn it.

He nods and lets out a breath. I breathe right back at him.

"I actually didn't come in here to fight, dolcezza. I really just came in here to help grade," he admits, stepping away.

My muscles relax—a snake finally uncoiling after a threat. I watch him run his hand along my perfectly tucked sheets and my abdomen tightens. The sight of his fingers on the thin white cotton. Threat! Threat! What is wrong with my libido tonight?

"With what happened the other night—" He lifts his brows and looks me over. "Just let me grade with you. I swear we don't have to talk. You'd be saving me from the wrath of Zia. If she finds you in here grading when they get back from date night—" He gives a fake shudder, lifting the stack of papers off the ground and splitting them into two piles.

I look down at the two stacks, each pile still too thick for my liking, then back up at his lifted brow. I don't want to accept his help. It feels like admitting defeat, and I should send him back into hiding.

But instead I let out a long breath that almost blows the top paper from the pile on the right. I take the smaller stack and try not to smile when he laughs at my choice, then I sit at my desk with my back to him and attempt to settle in. But the truth is, there is no settling when James is around. My body does the opposite of settle. It perks up, wiry and alert and on edge. Even in class, I've been hyperaware of every move he makes. Every passionate explanation of Urbino's art. Every angry look he sends my way. It's maddening. And I need it to go away.

I pretend to focus on this student's experience at the botanical gardens. But focus is a pipe dream. The scratch and scrape of his pen on paper. The pensive sounds he makes from the back of his throat. The swoosh of every page turned makes me more aware that he's here, sharing this tiny space with me, tasting the same air as I am, smelling the same scent of lavender from the open curtain of my glorious shower.

I force myself to reread the paragraph about the composition of the three-tiered landscape. But the words just flit and float over where they need to reach. Because my entire body is humming, like a swarm of monarchs flapping their wings all at once, trying to keep warm.

Maybe I'm just lonely. That's all this is. Or maybe I do have oats. Obviously, the man is attractive. I'm attracted to him. Ugh. I hate that I'm admitting that—even if it's just to myself. But it's not like it means anything. It's all chemicals. It's just science.

Or maybe it's a bit of culture shock coupled with some loneliness. Nothing to write home about on my postcard. My plan is just buried under Italy's mayhem and madness right now. I'll dig through the shitheap and dust off the plan when it's time to go home. Get right down to it. Back in the game.

James lets out a low chuckle at something he's read. I cross my legs tighter and force myself to work.

VENTI

Ava

I wake up with a note taped to my face.

Kindly, the taper of the note avoided my eyebrow and I lose only a few ungainly chin hairs in the process of ripping it off. The handwriting is a work of art, a study in calligraphy—it's the same perfectly crafted cursive from the MacBook note. And when I see his signature swirling beneath the dips and loops of the word "Fondly," I find my fingers tracing the word like a child learning to write for the first time. Who makes F's like that?

Fondly. I snort. Since when?

I type it into the address line on his MacBook, ignoring the annoying picture of Ethan and his temptress (unfair I know, she could be a perfectly lovely woman) that I've tortured myself with since Tuesday. Fondly. Adverb. 1. With affection or liking. Hmmm. Really? James hasn't really been tossing the affection and liking around the court. He did help me grade last night, though, but that was more out of guilt or fear of Nina.

Second definition. With foolishly optimistic hope or belief. Oooh. I like that one. What is that fool hoping for optimistically?

My lower back sends a piercing pain up into my shoulder blade and I realize what the note had distracted me from at first. I've fallen asleep at my desk. While grading. Papers with James. My eyes go to the empty space where those papers once were, and I turn, half believing that he might still be there on my floor, hair still damp, eyes intent on students' work. Or me.

But he's gone. Hence the note that dangles between my fingers. I hold it back under the desk lamp.

Ava,

Please don't forget that tomorrow is a "field day" for the students. I've arranged a tour of the Palazzo Ducale for them, but I'd like it if you did NOT attend. I'll be out of town at a shoot until Saturday, but I'd like to take you to the palace myself . . .

I let out a breath that I'd been holding. Do I always hold my breath when reading? Weird. A shoot? What kind of shoot? Is James a Calvin Klein model? Also, has a man ever asked me to go to a palace alone with him? Aladdin did once in a dream I had, but I suppose that doesn't count.

Before you let that overactive brain off the leash and start telling me you have a boyfriend again, I'd like to show you the art and architecture myself so that you can transcribe and synopsize my lectures next week so that the students can have them for the final exam. I am not trying to impress you with a palace I do not own. This is not a date . . .

Asshole. Like I'd say yes if it was a date. Aladdin is hotter than you anyway. I realize I'm speaking out loud when the words drift out the still open door of the guest house and mingle with the crickets' chirps before fading into the darkness. What time is it anyway? The MacBook tells me it's one something AM.

I stand from the desk and stretch, the note still held between my fingers, then plop into my new favorite place without bothering to change. All clothes worn after midnight become pajamas.

There's an illustration beneath the last paragraph. A makeshift map of the Piazza della Repubblica with two stars hovering over buildings that live on opposite sides of the rectangle, labeled Café Aldo and Macelleria Uvaldi.

The stars are two buildings that I know house your mother's work. Aldo, owner of the café and old friend of Leo, knew her. You could have a coffee there, then head to Uvaldi's for a quick visit . . .

Look at this man planning my day for me. I'm definitely gonna start at Uvaldi's.

Or start at Uvaldi's. Whatever you want. I know your eyebrows are in your hair right now because you hate being told what to do. And your jaw is locked . . .

I rub my jaw so it relaxes then lower my brows.

I'll see you Saturday at sundown at the entrance to the palazzo.

Fondly,
James

With foolishly optimistic hope or belief. James. Maybe I'll just stand his ass up. Not show. Or show like five minutes late. Because I really want to see the Palace.

P.S. Your comments on the students' papers are poignant and thought provoking. Next time, you do not need to write an entire page of feedback for each student.

A warm sensation crawls up my neck upon reading his praise. I give my cheek a smack. *Pull yourself together. Of course you did a good job. You don't need a man to tell you that. Especially not a man who barely tolerates you.*

I hold the note so close that it would touch my nose if another soft night breeze blew in through the open door. I study the map with my lips pressed together. He even drew the little fountain at the center of the piazza with real water droplets coming out and a woman reading a book on its outer ledge. I squint and see that there's a title on the book. Oh, Lord Voldemort. This man did not draw a cartoon of a woman reading Harry Potter beside the fountain.

Shit. I tuck the note under the pillow beside me and force myself to focus on anything but the present. I think about my next email to Tammy, how I'm going to focus only on what I've discovered here, with the exception of one note-writing, pain-in-the-ass professor. I wouldn't even know what to write about him.

A pang of guilt followed by a heavy wave of grief hits me at the thought of the postcard tucked snugly between the pages of the novella on my desk. I'm used to these waves and how they come at the most random of times—brought on by a song, a smell, the sound of laughter. They used to crash over me and make me struggle for air, but now I've learned to body surf them with only mild injury.

"There's nothing to write, Ma. Nothing to say."

The crickets chirp back.

I turn my mind to safer pastures. I think about the impressive tower of glass I'll be working in come fall, or the first pair of Jimmy Choo Romy 85s I'm gonna buy to click across the marble floors of its lobby. I can almost hear that sound. I think about Ethan groveling on his knees while I wear those pumps, telling him not to get his Chapstick on them. I think about my dad's pride when I meet him across the table as an equal but opposing force to his successful firm. I do not think about impeccable penmanship or carefully crafted treasure hunt maps delineating my mother's secret art trove that she hid in a life she never shared. Nope. I do not.

And I certainly do not read the note four more times before drifting back to sleep.

VENTUNO

Ava

I should have started at Aldo's café.

The heat has bounced back on the city like a bungee cord released in a tug-of-war. And I have walked right out of the fug into a butcher shop. From heat to meat. There are legs hanging from hooks with actual fur and hooves. If I were in my dream heels, I'd head-bump a slab of mystery animal that hovers over my head. It's like a Christmas tree in here, decorated with meat ornaments. And the smell—I'm reminded of the time in high school I had to stick my head out the window during a dissection lab.

I really should have started at Aldo's.

"Buongiorno, Signorina."

It's impossible not to smile at the man who has just popped up from behind the glass showcase filled with sausages and other unknown bits. Even though the white apron covering his impressive paunch is covered in blood. I half expect him to start singing something from *Sweeney Todd*.

"Buongiorno," I try. "Parli inglese?" I cut right to the chase. No use stumbling through my shitty Italian while the threat of a meat avalanche hovers just around the bend. What a headline. *Young Lawyer Buried by Beef Abroad.*

"Certo. Would you like to try my meat?" he asks, the smile growing a bit wider beneath his rosy cheeks. He holds up a toothpick with a slice of what might be carpaccio dangling from it.

It's too early in the morning to try this man's meat.

"Maybe some other time," I tell him. And there goes the smile. His lips turn down and puppy dog eyes doesn't even begin to cover what's happening across from me.

I step forward, hands up. "Okay. Certo. I'll try your meat," I stammer, trying to make up for what was obviously an insult.

His bushy gray brows lift and his eyes widen again.

"Perfetto. Vieni qui," he gestures me over with a huge gloved hand. "Questo è cavallo."

I take the toothpick tentatively and angle my head for a nibble. He purses his lips and shakes his head.

"Mangia," he says with a flourish of hand movement.

So no nibbling in Italy then. I shove the whole piece of meat in my mouth.

It's a bit gamy for me, but the sweetness and tenderness of it are surprising. I swallow.

"Ti piace?" he asks.

I nod. "Squisito. Grazie. But I'm actually not here for meat."

His face falls again and I realize I'm not getting out of this shop without buying some sausages.

"I'm actually looking for a painting," I quickly add before he breaks out the meat cleaver and makes me try something else.

"The museum is just up Via Frederico." He points out the window and to the left.

"Professor Massini—James—sent me. It is a painting by Annette Barrett," I say.

His eyes narrow as he leans across the counter to study me more closely.

"You know Anna?" he asks.

Anna. I'd only heard her called that once when I was very young.

"Certo," he says suddenly. "Gli occhi. Your eyes are hers." He's hurrying around the counter, removing his apron as he goes. "You are her sister? Cousin?"

"Daughter. Ava," I hold out my hand to shake. He takes off his gloves and throws them in a little bin, then puts both hands on my shoulders, ignoring my hand.

"How is she?" he asks, kissing each of my cheeks.

Oh God. Here we go again. I shake my head and look down at my shoes.

"She died almost six years ago," I say to the tile, too scared to look up and find this man's exuberance sucked out by me.

His big rough hand moves from my shoulder and tips up my chin.

"Sincere condoglianze," he whispers. "Anna was una forza—she swept you away."

His eyes are filled. Or my eyes are filled and everything looks wet. I nod and blink hard.

"Come. I will show you," he says, patting my cheek.

He hurries away and I nearly sprint to keep up. He is leading me out of the meat maze up a tiled staircase and into what must be his office but looks more like the study of a fifteenth-century scholar. Everything is mahogany and carved, the wall-to-wall shelves filled with books. Old books bound in leather and cloth.

And there in the center of it all, against the far wall across from his insanely large desk, is my mother's painting.

I step forward, hand extended like I'm running my fingers along those brushstrokes. It would be like touching her incredibly soft hand again.

"Amazing, no?" he says behind me.

All I can do is nod. My tongue has swollen to the size of a small balloon.

The painting is unlike anything I've seen her do, not in style, but in subject. Most of my mother's work is landscape, a few that I have in storage are of me when I was young, but otherwise she stayed away from portraits and focused on scenery. But this, this is all human through and through.

The man in the painting is so obviously the man who stands behind me, the smile, the round face, the soulful joy in his eyes. But he's young, leaner, rich deep brown where there is now gray. And he's lying on the floor with his dog. Staring down at the mangy creature like he holds the stars in his paws.

"We were students together all'università," he says. His voice low, as if anything louder might wake the sleeping dog in the painting. "She was studying art restoration and I was studying veterinary science." He chuckles, acknowledging the irony of his career choice. I feel him step beside me, his eyes also on the painting, but his mind with her. Just like mine.

"We met at the market while I was helping my father—this was all his," he says pointing downward to the shop below. "She came up to me from behind the booth, asking for scraps for some stray dog on campus. And we were instant—"

He claps his hands together and I look toward him. Lovers? Did my mother love this man?

"Friends," he clarifies, meeting my gaze. I nod.

"There are people you meet in life that seem to just fit into a place inside of you. It's almost as if you, or He"—he points upward—"built that place knowing who would come to fill it. It was like that. Anna just fit. And that stray—Dante," his eyes fill again and I reach for his arm. "That dog took his place in my soul just as your mother did."

His huge hand covers mine and I forget who is comforting who.

"You will take this, no?" He gestures toward the painting. "It is yours."

I shake my head so hard my ponytail holder slides back an inch.

"Absolutely not. She gave that to you. It is yours. It belongs here. In Urbino." Not in the storage container that I can't seem to work up the courage to enter, with the rest of her paintings and pictures.

"They are still there, you know," he whispers, pointing to his chest. For a moment I think he's talking about the paintings. Then I realize he means those we've lost. "Once they take their place they never leave. Sempre con te."

Always with you.

She'd signed every note she'd ever written me with that closing, and when she passed, I can remember reading those words with anger, thinking that it was a lie—the bullshit parents feed children to help them sleep at night.

But now, standing next to this mountain of a man, staring at the picture she painted for him, his Italian words still caressing my brain with their gentle fingertips, I feel something flutter between my ribs—something yawns and stirs in the hole she left.

"Sempre con te," I repeat to the painting.

And the stranger beside me puts his arm around my shoulder. As if it belonged there all along.

VENTIDUE

James

This time of evening brings peace to the bustle of Urbino. The hours for aperitivi have passed, the piazzas have nearly emptied, and people have walked, happy and buzzed, back to their home or restaurant. They've sat down and tucked themselves around the table to enjoy a long, delicious dinner with the people they love. They are all settled in just as the sun settles down beneath the hills that sweep in every direction from Urbino's walls. The darkness falls gently, a warm blanket over a sleeping child, and the quiet in the streets brings quiet to my soul.

But then she arrives—five minutes late—in a black dress that holds her perfectly, and my soul is anything but quiet.

She gives a little curtsy and one of her golden curls falls forward over her shoulder when she dips her head. I step out from beneath the portico, some absurd instinct demanding that I tuck her hair back in place, while sanity keeps my hands firmly in my pockets.

But she ends my internal battle by twisting it behind her ear and gestures around us to the empty square.

"I feel like I'm in the opening act of a vampire film. Doesn't the museum close?" she asks, pointing to the huge closed wooden doors.

I nod, look down at my watch. "About an hour ago." I slide the keys from my pocket and dangle them. "The superintendent is an old friend. She allows after-hours access to the dean and me—"

"And the women you want to impress," she says with a smug smile as she approaches the entrance.

"And the assistant who needs to learn about the collection I'm lecturing about so she doesn't tell the students that Raffaello is a mutant turtle," I correct.

She keeps her distance as she passes by me, murmuring that Raphael *is* a mutant turtle. The sound of laughter reaches us from behind as a group of young people make their way past the square, perhaps one aperitivo too many between them. We are invisible to them, thank the darkness and their single-minded focus, and something about that makes my heart pick up its pace as I work the key into the heavy door and pull it open. I take a steadying breath and remind myself why I'm here.

We step through the door and it closes behind us with a dramatic thud and a metallic click.

Ava looks up at me with a wide smile as we step into the open-air courtyard.

"I feel like I'm doing something illegal." She rubs her hands together and bounces a little. I force myself to look away. She's fucking dangerously beautiful when her eyes twinkle with mischief like this.

"You'd think a future lawyer might take issue with that," I point out.

"At home—yes. I'm boring—"

"I doubt that."

"But Italian Ava seems to be a bit more exciting." She waggles her eyebrows at me and I shake my head.

"How was your shoot?" she asks.

I smile at the thought of her reading the note I stuck to her face.

"Wonderful. The couple rented out Villa Grenata for the ceremony—the lighting was perfect—"

"A wedding! You do weddings?" Her entire face lights up.

I nod. "I do all sorts of events—anything that involves people and emotions." I could add that the pay is great as well, but that's never been the reason why I do it. There's nothing as satisfying as capturing pure, untethered joy.

"Where's your camera now?" she asks. Her voice has dropped an octave as she gives her full focus to the courtyard for the first time.

"No photographs allowed," I tell her.

Though right now I hate that rule.

She's spinning slowly in the center of the Cortile d'Onore. Her eyes sweeping over the carved Corinthian capitals, the Latin inscription that runs along the top of the arches along every wall, the pale stone coupled with the bricks in perfect harmony. I can almost imagine the men of the court unable to take their eyes off of her as they walk along the arcade or stare down from the oversized windows of the first floor above us.

Then her voice, low and breathless, stirs the air as she begins to translate the inscription, "Federico Duke of Urbino something something of the Holy Roman Church—"

"Standard bearer," I supply.

She wrinkles her nose, the same expression my students give me when I've clarified them into confusion. She shakes it off with one finger in the air as she follows the inscription around the arcade, strolling contemplatively as if she were part of the duke's court. As if this courtyard were designed for her.

"And head of the Italian League," she continues, pausing to look over at me. "Is that like our Justice League? Was the duke a superhero like us?"

"Something like that. A Renaissance superhero," I say. "A merciful warrior, unmatched in kindness and knowledge alike. Basically the whole package."

"I guess he doesn't fit inside my American single box," she quotes me.

"I guess you don't either, since you can translate a dead language but have no ability to ask for a bathroom in Italian. Why did you study Latin?"

She shrugs as if to say *why not*. "I was obsessed with mythology. Loved Homer and Virgil—read the *Odyssey* in English before I could even understand it. So Latin seemed like a good fit. My dad gave it the okay since it helped with a lot of lawyer-ese."

She rarely speaks of her dad, but something in the sudden stiffness of her shoulders tells me to veer left. I think of her pushing my buttons on purpose the other night and put my foot on the gas and stay straight.

"Is your dad a lawyer too?" I ask.

She lets out a long breath and narrows her eyes on me.

"Yup," she says, popping the P.

"What's with the one word answers?"

"Don't even start, hypocrite," she says, lifting her chin at me. "You don't get to dig around in my shit, then get all touchy and aggressive when I stick the shovel in yours."

"Really nice imagery, Ava," I say with a smile. She's right. I have no right to dig, but watching her chest rise and fall when she gets fired up makes something wake up inside me.

She slowly returns my smile and asks with a southern drawl, "Did I offend your delicate sensibilities, James?"

I wave her off and try a new tack.

"How did your mom feel about the Latin?"

She lights up, smile doubling in perimeter, and suddenly she doesn't care that I'm digging.

"My mom loved languages and words, said they opened the world to you. She said that about literature too. And art. She supported me no matter what electives I chose," she says, her eyes unfocused as she looks up at the sky overhead. "She probably loved this courtyard. Walked just like this a hundred times."

She moves toward a column beside the well in the northeast corner, runs her finger over the curves of the carved stone. I know she's thinking that her mother touched that marble because her eyes have glazed over, filling up in that way they do when she talks about her.

"She sounds like an amazing woman," I say softly as I approach her.

Ava blinks hard and looks up at me, and I'm swallowed by the grief in her eyes.

"She was."

When a tear makes its way from the corner of her eye, my thumb wipes it away before I have a chance to think. But before I can pull away she tilts her head toward my hand so that I cup her cheek. She fits perfectly in my palm. Her lids drift shut, her lips part. What am I doing?

She's fucking beautiful. And I need to retreat.

I clear my throat and she straightens.

"We should head inside," I murmur.

She hesitates, pulls her brows together, then looks down at the intricate herringbone pattern of stones at her feet.

Shit. This was a bad idea, being here with her alone. And even worse, here she is upset about her mother and all I can think about is crushing my mouth to hers. What the fuck is wrong with me? She's driving me crazy.

"Ava—"

She puts a hand up, then gestures for me to lead the way. Her eyes have gone cool.

"I met Signore Uvaldi today." Her voice is gravelly, and I keep my eyes trained ahead of me. "At the butcher shop," she says to my back as we pass under the archways.

Uvaldi is one of the kindest men I've ever met. In the early days, when my anger ate at my insides, he'd paid me to walk his dog, insisting that the old mutt needed it four times a day, when in reality it was me who needed the peaceful strolls around the city walls and the soft, calming effects of the rolling hills. I want him to do the same for her—open her eyes to what this place has to offer.

"This is the grand staircase," I tell her, choosing the left arch and heading upward. The ramp to the west leads down, into the basement—a dark tunnel filled with shadows and nooks. Not a place to go with Ava.

"He was wonderful. He gave me some ciauscolo for Nina, and he's coming over for dinner tomorrow night," she adds.

"He's a great man. I'm glad you got to meet him," I tell her. I stop and gesture to the space around us and pull the conversation back to where we need to keep it. "No one architect can be credited for the palazzo, there are several who made significant contributions during Federico's and his son's rule. Laurana is responsible for the courtyard, but his predecessor took care of the first-floor windows overlooking it—"

"If it hadn't been for your little map you left me," she continues, almost whispering now. I know if I look back at her, her armor will still be out of place, shifted like that loose curl that keeps falling from behind her ear. She'll be softer somehow. Cookie dough fresh from the oven. I swallow again. Push on toward safety.

"—some of the additions were built on top of a standing medieval presence. In fact, all of Urbino is built in layers, like a wedding cake, the bottom layer dating back to the Roman Empire, then traces upward through the medieval era until it reached the hands of your Iron Man, Federico, in the Renaissance—"

"James," she huffs, putting her hand on my back. I stop, her fingers burning through the soft cotton of my shirt. When I turn she is staring up at me with that look of defiance—jaw tight, lashes low. I take a step backward and upward. A step away. "I'm trying to thank you—for today. For the note, and you won't shut up about architecture. Can we have a moment of civility?"

I let out a long breath and nod.

"Thank you for the note. I promise you can bore me to death now," she says, ascending the steps two at a time as she passes me.

"It was nothing," I call after her. "As I was saying, layers—"

"Yup. Got it, teach. Roman dudes in togas built the basement for beer pong, then Dark Ages ground floor for interrogation, torture, and sex dungeon, and then Federico enlightened the rest with his glorious towers and libraries and whatnot. That's what I'll write," she says, passing the pilaster at the top of the stairs. She traces her finger along an intricate design, making sure to hover above the shapes carved there, then looks back at me. "Does that about sum it up?"

I nod. "Almost perfectly. We are going to focus on Federico's enlightened 'whatnot' and not the sex dungeons." She's wandered into the library and is staring upward at the sunburst decoration in the center of the ceiling. "This is the library."

"La biblioteca," she murmurs to herself. "Do you think, James, that maybe I could just take a tour in silence first? Experience the ambience. Then we can retrace with the lecture?" she asks.

"That bad, huh? Of course. Whatever you want," I tell the side of her face. She's gnawing on her cheek as she studies the rays exploding in every direction from the sun.

"Oh please." She waves a hand at me, nearly smacking my face. "You know your lectures aren't bad. Haven't you noticed the students tipping toward you like you might touch their foreheads and grant them infinite knowledge?"

"No." I'm in the zone when I teach—completely swept away in the story of the art. She steps away and I follow.

"Well, they do. What are these gold sperm things with the horns?" she points up to the gold sperm things with the horns.

"Nope, no questions," I shake my head. "Silence, right?"

"Really mature, Professor," she murmurs. "Where are all the books and manuscripts?"

She stops. Looks up at me and waits.

I smirk and lift my shoulders, then let them fall.

She sighs and rolls her eyes, then moves onward.

"You are really annoying. I imagine they've all been sent over to the Vatican," she says to herself, rendering me absolutely useless because she's correct. Then finishes with a smug grin, "—since the papacy ultimately took over after the duchy. I bet Duke Fred had a mean collection."

He did. I bite my cheek to stop myself from blurting out the number of manuscripts housed here and the famous editions that topped the list.

"These tiles," she says, taking off her heels and sliding her feet on the floor like she's ice skating. "I want them in my bathroom at home. Could you arrange that, sir?"

"Certainly, Signorina. Would you like the golden sperm as well?"

She smiles over her shoulder, brows lifted.

"Someone thinks very highly of himself."

She disappears through the far doorway into the next room where seventy tiles are hung to replicate a famous frieze before I can finish laughing. And I follow. She studies the work, touches her face, chews on her lip, reaches out to trace the scene, stops, then moves on to the next exhibit. It takes everything in me not to point out the sequence of the bas relief—explain the years of restoration work that went into each piece. I'm torn between her and the art—the way her eyes shift and widen as she studies the portraits. The way her head tilts when she finds something interesting in the work.

She barely looks my way. But I know she's aware of me by the color that dips beneath her neckline when I stare, the way she tilts her head when I stand behind her, the shallowness of her breath when I get too close.

Through five rooms of ceramics and ancient antiques, while she reads and thinks and breathes, I watch her in silence—study her as she studies the artifacts that I could describe from memory. She touches every Montefeltro eagle—traces every pilaster on every mantel. I could write a lecture on her—on the way she responds to the art around her.

By the time she steps foot on the grand staircase and looks back at me over her shoulder, all of the heat in my chest that I've convinced myself was anger has melted into something just as consuming and even more urgent. And I know I'm fucked.

VENTITRE

Ava

Holy. Shit.

Have you ever stepped out of a shower and ventured outside wrapped in a towel? Let the air dry you—caress your skin and pull the wetness up and away—felt every shift in breeze on every inch of you, leaving trails of goose bumps—making you want to drop the towel—until your body sort of sings with sensation. It's glorious. And freeing.

I feel that way now. And James is the breeze.

His eyes—the silence. I'm drunk on it and I need out of this dimly lit space with all of the beautiful nude women staring down at me from the walls. They are telling me how good it feels to be naked. How glorious. How freeing.

It doesn't help that I've dropped my heels in some dark corner and I'm walking barefoot through the boudoir like I'm a duchessa roaming her own halls.

"James," I start, breaking the thick, prolonged silence that has tightened around us.

I touch my throat. My voice. It's heavy and breathy. It hangs in the thick air as I turn to find him leaning in an archway, his arms crossed over his chest as he watches me. He lifts his brows, but doesn't come closer. I want him closer. I want him here. Where I am. I just—want him.

And if I don't get out of here, I'm not sure I can hide it anymore.

I try again, "James, is there a way outside—an exit?"

He straightens, the soft darkness of his eyes hardens, and lines dip between his brows.

"Are you okay?" he asks, moving closer like I wanted, but suddenly not looking at me the way I wanted. Concern replaces—whatever the hell was in his eyes a moment ago.

I nod. Swallow a few more times until my tongue feels up to task.

"I just need a moment. Some air. A break," I say.

He takes me by the arm, his touch so warm around my elbow that I'm sure there'll be a mark, and he leads me through one archway, then the next—it's a labyrinth of art and vaulted ceilings and ornate mantels and tapestries and beauty. I'm Alice again. Every room of the palazzo a new world. Then he's pulling a giant wood door with iron handles toward me and ushering me through the opening out into the night air. Even the humidity is less oppressive than the silent air that was making my skin tighten. I was a kernel in a microwave. Just about to pop.

"Is that better?" he asks, watching me from the darkness beneath yet another portico.

"Much," I lie.

It's pathetic that I'm in there having hot flashes while he's wholly unaffected by my presence. His gaze is so steady. Made of the same stone and mortar that makes up these ancient walls.

I glance around at the garden he's taken me to. A small but lovely fountain sits at the middle, all paths leading diagonally inward between raised flower beds. Nothing but star-spotted sky overhead.

"I think the heat in there was too much maybe. Do they turn the AC off after closing?" I ask, making my way toward the fountain. I walk quickly, distance between us the goal, hoping that it will make my skin feel less taut—less like an overfilled water balloon. The fountain is the softest shade of green, oxidized over hundreds of years. Oh, what this water has seen. I reach my hand beneath the spout and let the cool current run through my fingers.

"No, the AC is on," he says, from behind me. "It's about ten degrees warmer out here—"

"There's a nice breeze coming off the hills," I interrupt. No need for him to be so rational while I'm all hot and bothered by a man who seems to loathe me—most of the time.

"This is beautiful," I whisper, gesturing toward the imposing wall across the way.

Three large rectangles are cut out of the far wall of the garden. The view through each looks like a painting, the middle my favorite, with the moon hanging low like a nursery rhyme, cascading light over the hills.

"That's where we stood that night that Verga stole your virtue."

I startle. His voice is closer than I thought it would be—just steps behind me as I approach the huge window in the wall. I look over my shoulder to see him pointing out at the trees through the cutout. "There on that hill," he clarifies unnecessarily.

I lean out the window and James grabs my wrist, presumably to save me again from a clumsy fall.

And suddenly my arm is on fire—pleasantly scorched. There's nothing but the sound of his breathing and the feeling of his fingers locked around my skin. I turn slowly toward him, the moonlight fans through the huge window behind my back, and I can see that his eyes have melted—milk chocolate with a caramel center.

"Ava," he whispers, his voice filled with something I can't place. Frustration? Anger?

"Hmmm?"

"This isn't a good idea," he says roughly.

"No?" It feels like a good idea. Best idea ever.

"You are leaving."

He's staring at my mouth like I stare at tiramisu.

"Not right now I'm not."

Time could go very slowly if he keeps staring at me like this.

"Do you know what you want?" he asks, his fingers moving up toward my shoulder.

Right now. Yes. I want his hands everywhere.

"I think so," I tell him. It's hard to formulate a sentence with his eyes on my lips like this.

"You think so?" he repeats. His other hand has made its way behind me and is balling up the fabric of my dress at the small of my back.

"Do you know what you want?" I ask, running my fingers along his chest.

He closes his eyes.

"Yes," he breathes.

"Are you sure? You seem not to like me." I trail my finger up his neck, down his jaw.

"I like you enough," he says.

A breathy laugh escapes me and the air is suddenly too heavy for words. He steps me back against the brick wall beside the window.

He lowers his mouth beside my ear. "I need to know," he breathes, "cosa vuoi."

"That's cheating, James. You can't use Italian against me," I say, turning my face to where his arm leans against the wall. I kiss his forearm, softly, letting my tongue barely touch his skin. He curses and I relent, returning my eyes to his.

"I want this—"

His lips are on mine, swallowing my words before I have a chance to speak them. The pressure of his mouth over mine, the taste of him, the softness and the insistence—it spills into me, fills every pore, every cubic inch of empty space. I want this. God, do I want this.

His tongue, his lips, they meet mine with precision. This kiss is a fucking work of art. It should be hung inside. Framed in gold. And somehow my legs, useless as they were before, have found their way around his hips and my free hand is tangled in his hair, never to come loose. His hands find my thighs, my dress hitching up above my hips, and he presses against me, hard and warm as I groan into his mouth.

"I want this," I repeat against his lips. "I want more."

He opens his eyes and pulls back, our breath mingling between us over the sound of tinkling water. His hands slide from behind my thighs and he slowly, gently lowers me to the ground.

"This is a bad fucking idea, Ava."

I don't give a shit. I grab his shirt and pull him back to me, kissing him hard, making him groan when I arch into him. And the sound fills me with triumph.

I can do this. I can have a fling. An affair. A romp abroad.

For the first time since I arrived, there's no stabbing pain beneath my rib where Ethan fractured my heart. And didn't he say that I had to experience all that Italy had to offer? That was his plan, not—

"Where'd you go?" James asks, narrowing his eyes on me.

"Nowhere. I was just rethinking my plan."

"While I was kissing you? You were rethinking your plan? Jesus, Ava. Just what every man wants to hear."

I open my mouth to defend myself, but he's right, so I shut it.

"I shouldn't have let this happen," he says. "Let's get back inside."

The words hit me like a backhand.

"Really, James? Of all the shitty things you've said to me, that has to be—"

"Don't flip this. You said you wanted this and then a minute later you're mapping out how I fit into your plan, like I'm a goddamn chess piece that you can slide around your board." His hand gestures are making me dizzy. He's never looked so Italian. He's pissed. I've hurt him. And that hurts me more than I'd like to admit.

"I'm sorry, I can't just jump in like you—"

"Jump in?" He laughs and steps closer, his voice low. "I've been trying to stay the hell away from you since you got into my car two weeks ago. I am not jumping in. I'm being dragged in by the hair."

"I'm sorry," I say softly, because it's the only thing left to say.

He takes a deep breath and studies my face.

"You are going to have to figure out what you want, dolcezza. Whatever this is"—he gestures between us—"it obviously needs an outlet."

But before I even have a chance to nod my understanding, he tugs me by the arm back toward the palace and says, "Now you need to listen. And stay the hell behind me out of sight."

I swallow a chuckle and then remain quiet as James starts his lecture, his smooth voice filling my head with art and beauty, while I try not to think about his lips on mine.

VENTIQUATTRO

Ava

I haven't had a moral hangover like this since the night my friends and I switched all of the holiday decorations on my street. Just like last night, it was all well and good when the adrenaline was coursing through me in the darkness as I switched the reindeer from Santa's sled on one lawn with the goats and donkeys from the manger on another front porch, but when the light of day revealed the Christmasy chaos I'd caused, my guilt had me confessing my sins to my slightly bemused mother in the kitchen before she even had a chance to take a sip of coffee.

I have no one to confess my sins to this morning. I consider writing it all out on Mom's postcard, the closest thing I have to the image of her trying not to laugh at my tears in her bathrobe that morning, but I know that will make it worse. The postcard isn't for contrition. It's for celebration.

I could confess to Tammy. Typically, she's right there beside me, my partner in crime, cheering me on in my bad decisions. But something in me wants to keep whatever happened with James last night to myself. The second it hits stateside and mingles with real life is the moment it becomes something to defend instead of something to enjoy. So Tammy's out for now.

But I need something to ease the shame spiral. Or something to distract me from the mental wagging finger in my brain and the scorching heat that comes when I close my eyes and remember how he felt. Because knowing this was all Ethan's idea doesn't seem to be easing that old spinny, out-of-control feeling in my chest that I work so hard to keep at bay.

Beside the warring guilt and desire, there's this feeling in my chest that something is stretching out and yawning, rubbing the sleep from its eyes. I can't pinpoint what it is or why, but I know being around all of that art last night made me feel like someone has pulled at a loose thread inside of me. Couple that with the intense whatever the hell it is between James and me, and I honestly have no idea how long it'll be before I unravel completely.

So, in the name of distraction, I make my way into town, the preparations for Urbino's market day in full swing by the time I drag my ass out of my heavenly bed and into the most wholesome outfit I can find. Dress the part and all that. Closed signs hang in Franco's window and on Vincenzo's door. The store-lined street leading up to the piazza has become a one-way route of pedestrians and peddlers ready to converge. James promised that there's nothing like an Italian market day. And this Italian market day holds the promise of James.

I let out a shaky breath and look up to the soft wisps of clouds scattered over the soft blue above. *Mom, can you hear me? Tell me what to do . . . Switch the decorations back? Or live with the chaos?*

A stray cat runs across the alley and nearly collides with my calves. *What the hell does that mean?* I look back down at the ground.

Maybe I should call Ethan. Admit what happened and verify that mind-numbing kisses are on the list of acceptable Italian experiences. Perhaps negotiate a few extra ones just in case. I'd checked my email last night before bed, the darkness of doubt already claiming me in her sharp claws the moment the door shut after James had left me with only a goodnight outside the guest house, but the only thing in my inbox was an e-card from Tammy with a sloth crawling across the screen that said "Time moves so slowly without you . . ." and one clipped email from my father reminding me that he was in fact still waiting for a reply. As if I didn't know.

None of the emails were enough of a distraction. I can't stop replaying last night, the way my body responded to James—as if it had been freed from years of captivity—I can't help but feel like I want to dive headfirst into the mess, hide inside of it and see what it's made of, like a kid in a leaf pile inspecting every color of foliage she sees. I'm not ready to be swept up. I don't know what I'm ready for.

I step inside of Aldo's café and stand against the back wall, avoiding the line of students and locals ordering their drinks. The man behind the counter moves like the Flash, presenting espressos and pastries on top of the bar that separates him from the throng, all while barking orders at the teenage boy who is obviously his son—same dark shiny hair and gorgeous olive skin, same soft brown eyes and imperious nose.

The smell of roasting coffee beans is enough to keep me present from the shitstorm in my brain, and the beautiful display of flaky pastries with their snowy blanket of powdered sugar spread atop them is enough to make a line of Vergaesque drool slide down my chin. I want all the things. But I'm here to ask about Mom. And this man is incredibly busy. Perhaps I picked the wrong time.

And just as I make up my mind to sneak back out the door, the Italian Flash settles his gaze on me and stops. His serious mouth presses together and he says something to his son beside him without taking his eyes off of me. He slips his apron over his head and balls it up on the counter, then ducks beneath the bar and approaches me slowly, slipping through the crowd of patrons without a glance their way.

"Sei la figlia di Anna," he says, tilting his head, studying me like an insect pinned in a shadow box.

I nod at my mother's nickname, though I've got no idea what he's just said.

"I'm Ava," I murmur.

He puts a callused hand that smells of coffee and chocolate on my cheek. Did this hand touch her cheek like this? The same warmth I felt when meeting Uvaldi and Franco and Vincenzo surges through me and settles in my chest. It's as if that warmth is her—her arms wrapping around me.

"Uvaldi told me about tua madre," he whispers.

I look down at my toes, tears ready to spill at the slightest move. And his hand pats my cheek fondly in understanding.

"Mi dispiace, cara. She was a wonderful woman," he says in my ear, pulling me into a hug. I sink into the embrace like an anchor thrown overboard. Never underestimate an Italian embrace.

"My wife will be so excited to know you are here. She will have much to tell you about your mother," he says, pushing back with his hands on my arms. "But I must give these people their espresso or they will start una rivoluzione, no?"

"Could you and your family come to dinner tonight?" I ask without thinking. Nina will whack me with a spoon. Or more likely smile and tell me to gather more peppers.

"Certo. Certo," he nods. "Dove?"

He glances over his shoulder at his son, who looks as if he's approaching total meltdown, then lifts his brows and widens his eyes at me in apology.

"I'm staying with Nina and Leo Russo—"

"Ha!" He rubs his hands together. "Perfetto. We owe them a visit." He spins with a wave and is back behind the bar with his apron back in place in one smooth move.

"Tonight, cara," he yells over the heads of the people, then lifts a plate and a tiny cup up in the air and nods at me as he places them on the far end of the bar for me to retrieve. He's back to the register with a whoosh, and I step up to the bar to drink my espresso and eat the gorgeous flaky pastry.

I'm basically Indiana Jones, tracking down relics from my mother's life. A splash of espresso lands on my floral print dress. Maybe not as smooth as Indiana. Maybe more like the Goonies. Oh Mylanta. This pastry is warm. I finish it off in three (two) dainty bites and chug the espresso like a local. Then set my sights on the door, ready to face the market.

Ready to face the man in the market. My stomach does a back handspring.

Okay. So maybe I can hang here for a bit, then head to the market.

I signal to Aldo for one more pastry and he grants me his first real smile as he flies into action.

VENTICINQUE

James

Market day in Urbino has always been my favorite day of the week. It's the time to catch up with the neighbors, make our all-important dinner plans for the week to come, and spend time with Zia while she sells her handmade casciotta. When I was a boy, I'd travel with her for market day from town to town, learning about each village's local culture, soaking in the art and architecture like a vacuum hose let loose in a dust cloud, sketching and shooting everything in sight. Markets in Italy are a work of art in their own right. The colors. The smells. The energy. All strokes of the brush that create living, breathing beauty.

But today, the patrons, our friends, some students, and a few tourists on day trips, are interrupting my view of the blonde in the short floral dress as she strolls through the tents touching the goods, smiling and talking to the locals. It's next to impossible to sit behind a table full of casciotta and engage in small talk when she's there, bare tan legs just asking to be touched. Especially now that I know how soft they are—how she looks when I touch them. Getting her home last night without kissing her against every priceless tapestry was a herculean task. All of the reasons I pushed her away seem to have set sail across the Adriatic, leaving me with the memory of how she felt pressed up against me—her fingers wrapped in my hair and her soft lips pressed against—

"Mio Dio, Gi. You just gave Gaetano the wrong change!" Nina says, jabbing me with a bony elbow between my ribs. She gestures out to where Ava is studying a table of antiques. "You are useless. Like having Verga here with his bone across the room. Just go. Vai."

I let out a sigh. She's right. Always right. She lifts my camera from the table beside her.

"Gaetano owes me from poker anyway."

She nods at my justification and I hesitate, unwilling to break our tradition. "Sei sicura?" I ask.

"Vai!" she yells, making change for another patron with one hand.

I take my camera from her and kiss her temple.

"Grazie, Zia."

She shoos me away like a mosquito. I make my way around the table, loop the camera strap over my neck, and lift the viewfinder to my eye. She's at the center of the crosshairs, as if the lens has been preprogrammed to capture her. Her head is back and she's talking to someone above her—Signora Antonelli, who is hanging out her kitchen window. It's dizzying how easily Ava has become a local even with all that armor and obstinacy in place. She'd deny it wholeheartedly—say something self-deprecating about how out of place she is here—but Urbino has accepted her with open arms.

Ava laughs, and I can imagine the breathy, joyous sound even through the murmur of conversation and movement all around me.

The smell of fresh olive oil mixes with the scent of fine leather from the tents on my left as I make my way behind them to avoid the crowd. I click away as the older woman above Ava points down Viale Bruno Buozzi, and her golden head turns with a wave goodbye.

And once again, I'm following her, though this time through a much thicker crowd—a much safer situation than the museum.

She stops beneath a white canopy, points to a basket of pepperoncini, and then opens her oversized bag while Signore Zannotti drops them inside. Who needs that many chili peppers? She probably got her Italian numbers wrong again. She fiddles with her euros, smiling and blushing at something the old man has said, and I wonder if he's flirting with her. No doubt he is. Why wouldn't he?

A light breeze finds its way down the street from the hills, and Ava's hair flies across her face. She turns her back to the breeze, her hands occupied with money and her overstuffed purse, and her eyes settle on me. She shakes her head and lifts a brow.

I snap one more for prosperity and lower the camera with a shrug and a smile.

"You'd have a police report filed by now if we were in America," she says as she heads back toward me.

"We aren't in America. And if I recall, you gave me permission," I remind her.

"I believe I was under the influence." She tilts her head, exposing the soft skin beneath her ear. I consider stepping forward to brush my lips there, but after how we left it last night, I still don't know what the hell she wants. And at least four locals are staring at me and the beautiful American woman. Small towns love to talk. Small Italian towns love to get involved. I put my arm out for her to take.

"Can I show you the best the market has to offer?"

"Are you insinuating that that's you?" she says, looping her arm in mine.

I dip my head down just close enough for her to hear without a thousand rumors popping into circulation, and whisper, "I was not, but if you have figured out what you want, dolcezza, I do know a place nearby."

She swallows and lets out a long breath, color rising from beneath the scalloped neckline of her dress up her neck. The color of her blush—softer than the bushels of tomatoes behind her, but deeper than the rosé being poured at Franco's booth—is enough to make me need to look away.

"What happened to this being a bad idea?" she murmurs beside me.

A group of students pass and we politely greet them. Ava looks up at me, nibbling on the lip that I nibbled on last night.

"Did I say that?" I know I did. And I know I need to say it again—to myself. My alarm bells have been going off since that kiss, but I can barely hear them when Ava is here in front of me. I want her. She wants me. And as complicated as that might be, it feels unavoidably simple when she's here with me.

"No. You said 'this is a bad fucking idea, Ava,'" she says, the last part in a deep voice that is supposed to be me. I can see the wall go up behind her eyes at the memory.

"We should talk," she adds, worrying at her lips.

Here we go. She's probably been up all night making PowerPoints about how to navigate this situation. This isn't going to be good.

"Do we?" I ask, pointing to a pair of gloves at Marco's leather stand. He nods and I lift them, taking Ava's hand in mine and slipping one finger at a time into the glove.

"What happened last night—oh my goodness these are soft!" She lifts her hand to her face and sniffs at the leather. Her eyes close and she smiles. "My mom had a pair like this. They were maroon and I'd put them on and pretend to be a princess or a mime."

"That's quite the range," I tell her, handing Marco the money.

"James! You can't buy me these," she says, rushing to pinch the top of her fingers and slip them off.

I put my hand on her back and guide her away from the tent before she inadvertently insults the vendor.

"I can and I did. Now put them somewhere that you won't get chili peppers all over them," I tell her, waving to a group of older women watching us from behind a table of handmade soaps.

"Seriously, you can't be giving me gifts. It feels too much like—"

"You're my mistress."

"I was going to say like you're my sugar daddy, but yeah. That works too." She is still trying to get the glove off of her hand. I stop her, shield her from view with my body against a tent flap, and lift the glove to my mouth, carefully biting the leather fingertip and slipping it off.

She grabs it from my mouth, looking up at me with round eyes.

"What's wrong with you being my mistress?" I ask, smiling at the amazing blush I've caused. I'm playing with fire. I'm almost certainly going to end up with third-degree burns.

She looks between my mouth and eyes, swallows hard.

"So many things," she says. "Number one, this wasn't part of the pl—"

"Don't you dare say it, Ava. That word is no longer allowed here."

"Number two, I have two weeks left here—"

I ignore the feeling in my gut and say, "We did this math last night. But I believe it was me with the reservations and you doing the begging."

"Begging? Please!"

"Yes, exactly like that, but the please was breathier—"

"Your memory is broken. Number three, won't you get in trouble for this?" she asks.

"Walking with you through the market?" I lift my hands.

She rolls her eyes so deep it hurts my head. "Sleeping with your assistant."

"Did we sleep together? I think I would remember that—"

She elbows me in the exact place Nina caught me minutes ago.

"I'm serious. I don't want to mess anything up for you here. At home, stuff like that can ruin reputations for life," she says, her eyes on the side of my face while I lead us toward the smell of fried meat. Uvaldi's food truck.

"Once again, we are not in America, Ava. Let it go. This is Italy. People here aren't as stuffy and uptight about sex and lo—and affairs of the heart," I finish lamely. Nothing like the L-word to send her into full retreat while she's ticking off reasons not to be near me. And all of her reasons are just good sound sense—exact replicas of the good sound sense I let fly out the window after tasting her last night. That kiss opened the floodgates, and now there's nothing to do but try not to drown until the water calms down. I lift the camera and take a few shots of a group of kids playing soccer in an alley to my right.

"You use your camera to hide," she says in a matter-of-fact tone. "Shit gets real and you find something to photograph."

I chuckle—lower it to my chest and take her in without the barrier. She's looking straight up at me, chest puffed out with that know-it-all grin.

"And you are the essence of open and forthright? It took me a week to be able to have a conversation with you that didn't raise your hackles and shut you down. Shit gets real and you start spouting off about plans."

She purses her lips.

"You're raising my hackles right now," she says.

I grin. "Come on. Let me show you the best thing you've ever tasted."

She shakes her head at the innuendo but graces me with a slow smile. I breathe out my relief that she's back with me—out of her head, where her worries seem to suck the joy right out of the air. And pull my own fears and worries right to the surface.

The moment Uvaldi sees her, he is out from the inside of the truck, lifting her in his huge arms against the apron that smells of sausage. She laughs when her sandal slips off during the greeting, but it's obvious she loves every second of the embrace.

"Gi, you sent this to me?" Uvaldi yells, arm around Ava's shoulders. She's a quarter of his size.

"I did," I tell him.

"Va bene. I owe you, no?" His smile is infectious.

I want to say I feel the same way about whoever sent her to me. But I just nod and watch while he tells her about tonight's antipasti that he's bringing to dinner, tugging her into the inside of the truck and ignoring the line that has formed outside.

"Signore, can I have my date back?" I yell toward the interior.

Her golden head pops up over the counter of meats.

"Date?"

I wave her question away and Uvaldi's laughter shakes the truck.

"I'd just like her to try la crescia, per favore," I tell him, doing my best to send him Nina's malocchio.

He winks at me over Ava's head and lifts his chin.

"Va bene, bella. Vai. Let's not upset Gi. We will see each other at dinner, no?" He pushes Ava back out the side door and she just smiles up at me.

"Date?" she asks again. "Don't you think you should have consulted me before taking me on a date?"

Uvaldi hands me the melted cheese and prosciutto on the flaky flatbread and I immediately hold it to her mouth to shut her up.

She takes a bite and her eyes roll into the back of her head with a moan.

She's forgotten all about my verbal slip.

She takes the crescia from my hand, licks her lips. Takes another bite. Another soft moan.

And I've forgotten my own name.

VENTISEI

Ava

The dinner table has doubled in size since last weekend. Nina and Leo have set up a white tent along the side of the villa to accommodate us, just near enough to the pool so that we can hear the murmur of the water falling over its edge beneath the chatter of the guests and the hum of the music from Verdi's *La Traviata* spilling from the open windows. The trays of antipasti that Uvaldi has talked me through—in far more detail than I might have liked as I now know each animal body location from whence the meat came—lay in ruins between us, waiting for the primo piatto to take its place alongside the candles James and I lit when we set the table.

James's hand rests on the white linen tablecloth between our wine glasses so that when I reach for the stem of my own glass, my fingertips just barely brush against his knuckles. The effects of the Sangiovese wine Franco has supplied for our first course has nothing on the warmth that spreads through my body as I lift the glass to my lips and feel his eyes on the side of my face. Who knew sitting at a table beside him would be this—challenging?

"Are you alright?" he whispers just low enough for me to hear.

I don't meet his gaze. I know I'll spontaneously combust or fall headlong into his irises.

"Mmmhmm. Just taking it all in," I tell him, swirling the wine in my glass to make a ruby cyclone that sends the unlikely duo of cherry and tomato out of its vortex and into my sinuses.

I see James's dark head nod in my periphery as I glance at Nina. She's smiling at me from the head of the table. The smile of a knowing mother. Or a devious sorceress.

"Just making sure you aren't all wrapped up in that head of yours," James says as he rises from his seat and grabs one of the empty trays.

I lower my wine glass to the table and stand to help, reaching for the other almost empty meat tray while Uvaldi dives to save the final pieces of prosciutto (pig's hind legs) by tugging them off onto his plate with a smile. He's informed me that his father taught him never to waste any part of the animal. And I do mean any.

I follow James into the house just as Pavarotti finishes a power duo with his soprano on the record player, and I step around Verga who is standing in front of the oven like it might burst open at any given moment and spray food at or into his mouth. I can't say I blame him. The savory smell of roasting beef is enough to make my stomach do a back handspring.

I go to place the empty meat tray at the Beast's feet for a lick-down and nearly bump heads with James, who is doing the exact same thing. I make a face to let him know how sickening our cuteness is.

He chuckles and leans back against the butcher block island, studying me in that way he knows makes me squirm.

"What now?" I ask, trying to match his pose, arms crossed, ankles crossed, but nearly topple sideways in the attempt. I reassess his positioning, then give up altogether and lift myself onto the counter across from him and sit on the edge.

"I'm wondering when you're going to ask about your mother," he says.

Ugh. He looks all concerned and kind. His eyebrows are doing the tight V thing they do when he cares. That look does more to my stomach than the smell of the roasting beef. I don't know what to make of concerned, kind James.

I shrug. "I will. I'm just letting everyone catch up before I selfishly hijack the conversation."

"You do realize that this is all you." He makes a whirlwind motion with his hand. "They are here for you. For your mom. They want to tell you about her."

"You have dinner together like this all the time," I point out.

"True, but tonight is different."

He didn't shave today. The fresh shadow of stubble runs up the side of his jaw toward his hair. My fingers flex, remembering what that jaw felt like. I grip the counter edge a bit harder.

I need to deflect and distract. Distract and deflect.

"You know, we never talk about your parents," I say, and immediately I want the words back.

The jaw I was just admiring hardens so quickly that I can hear the click.

"There's nothing to talk about. Dad left. Mom chose chasing a dream over motherhood. The only parents I've ever known are Nonna, Nina, Leo, and the adults around that table." He points over his shoulder toward the window.

It feels like someone is hanging on the bottom of my heart, tugging and pulling it down into my stomach. He told me about his Nonna—that she'd passed when he was young—but the parent piece had remained under the rug, until I reached my big tactless broom in there and swept it out of course. I imagine a ten-year-old James, confused and abandoned by the two people that are meant to anchor you—protect you and support you.

"I'm so sorry. I—"

"Gi! Le tagliatelle!" Nina's voice manages to boom through my apology despite the fact that I can see her still sitting at the table through the window over James's shoulder.

"I'm sorry," I repeat softly.

He nods and waves it away.

"It was a long time ago. Don't worry about it," he says.

Oh, I'll worry about it.

He pushes off the counter, takes a step toward me. The massive kitchen is suddenly far too small. *La Traviata* plays on. Violetta's high-pitched voice reaches us, sad and desperate.

"Stay with me—get out of your head," he says, running his finger along my cheek.

This is not part of the arrangement—this careful, cautious James—staring at me like I'm his camera, something he wants to handle and comfort. I want garden James. I want to be stared at like dessert again. To be teased and flirted with. That feels safer.

"The water is boiling over," I say, clearing my throat.

He curses and grabs the oven mitts just in time to remove the huge pot from the heat before the water reaches the rim. He pours the pot into an enormous colander in the sink with a satisfying hiss.

"Are you running away again?" he says over his shoulder, but I'm already out of the kitchen, moving through the living area.

"Yes!" I holler back.

I hear his sigh from the front porch and then his operatic ringtone just after. Italians are so dramatic.

Nina throws me another unsettling smile and a wink as I start to slip back into my seat beside Aldo, freezing halfway when I see James's face as he steps out onto the porch with the phone against his ear.

"Certo. Subito," he says with a nod, his jaw clenched tight as he ends the call and meets my eyes.

"What's wrong?" I ask, a thousand irrational fears take flight in my mind.

"It was Luca," he says, making his way around the table. "Steven's been arrested in Pesaro."

He grabs his jacket off the back of his chair and pulls the keys out of his pocket. Steven is a jackass. Only last week he received a warning from Urbino's carabinieri for being in the fountain and the week before he sprayed a fire extinguisher through Lindsay's open dorm window screen, but no one could prove it was him. He should have been sent home by now.

I push my chair back and James stops and meets my gaze.

"Stay," he says. "You have questions that need answers."

I ignore him and look around the table, giving an all-encompassing wave.

"I'll see you all tomorrow?" I ask. "Nina, thank you as always."

There's a murmur of agreement and well wishes, then Nina throws me a wink and shoos us off.

We don't speak until we get into the car.

"You really don't need to come," he starts. "You needed to ask about—"

"Stop, James. We've had this fight already. Besides, I want to."

"It's an hour away and we have to pick up Steven's passport first," he says.

"I don't care. The Batphone rang so we are in this together."

He smiles over at me but still doesn't start the car. I lift a brow.

"Shouldn't we be hurrying?"

James's smile widens and my heart does a somersault. The silence around us feels pleasantly heavy.

"I think Steven could benefit from a little extra time in the cell."

I laugh and his gaze falls to my mouth. I stop laughing, forgetting what the hell was funny in the first place. In fact, there's nothing in my mind but the memory of that kiss in the garden and how badly I want more. I turn my body and lean back against the door, watching the way the muscle in his neck and jaw move as he grinds his teeth. If he doesn't start the car I'm going to do something reckless, like climb over the gear shift and—

"We should go," he says thickly, eyes still on me.

"Should we?"

He breathes out, lifts the keys, and puts them in the ignition. The engine revs to life and I relax into the seat, realizing that I have an hour to study James's profile and the way his strong hands work the gearshift. I put down my window and let the night air rush over my bare arms, but the space around us still feels stifling. His fingers graze the outside of my thigh as he shifts into second and I tip my head back against the seat and shut my eyes. It's going to be a long night.

VENTISETTE

James

By the time we get to Pesaro, my skin feels freshly slapped from Ava's eyes studying me for over an hour. Despite the fact that we have a lot to unload between us, our silence in the car is like a physical force pressing down and in on us, heightening every thought of what I'd do to her if I just pulled the car over into one of the many moonlit fields we pass along the autostrada. Thank goodness for manual transmission, because if my hand wasn't occupied with the gearshift it might have found its way up her thigh and—

"James," she says, and when I swivel my gaze to her it's obvious it's not the first time she's said my name.

She pulls her lips inward to suppress a smile.

"Should we get out?"

I wonder how long we've been parked here. The entrance to the Sezione polizia stradale Pesaro is dimly lit with the municipality's red-and-blue flag dangling just above. I turn off the car and start the debriefing.

"Let me do the talking," I start.

She rolls her eyes and salutes.

"The police here aren't like the police where you're from. You can't litigate us out of this," I say, pushing open the door and standing as she does the same. A rush of briny cool air floods over me and I breathe it in.

"Smells like Ocean City," Ava says, grinning at me over the car. "And no one litigates with the police, James. You litigate in a courtroom."

I wave her off as she makes her way around the car, her hair blowing softly over her shoulders. She stops and tilts her head.

"You can hear the ocean," she says, her mouth curving into an easy smile.

"I wish we were here under better circumstances," I say. "I could show you the beach."

"Maybe next week . . ."

Her voice trails off, and I know she's thinking about how little time she has left. That same thought that was once the promise of relief for me now torments me, a constant reminder of how stupid I am to let myself want her.

"Ready?" I ask, pulling her out of herself.

She nods once and I push open the door for her. She breezes by like she owns the place, leaving me to follow in her wake. There are three officers in uniform sitting behind a long counter, each in front of an oversized computer screen. Luca sits in a chair across from them and stands abruptly when he sees us. For the first time since I've met the kid, I can safely say he's a mess.

"Ho provato a dirglielo," he says, running a hand through his hair. He turns to Ava. "He would not listen."

I put a hand on Luca's shoulder and tell him everything will be fine, and before I can greet the officers I hear Ava say in a soft sweet voice, "Buonasera, signori."

Apparently "let me handle it" didn't resonate with her. Not that I'm surprised. I gesture for Luca to sit and make my way to the counter where Ava asks, "Parlate inglese?"

The officers are all leaning in toward her, nodding their heads, murmuring some variation of "Sì. Certo, bella."

Ava smiles and they all smile back like we are playing some Italian version of Simon Says.

"Perfect," she goes on. "We believe that you have one of our students in custody."

She puts her hand out to me and I narrow my eyes at her, then fish Steven's passport from my pocket and slap it against her open palm with more force than necessary.

"Grazie," she says. She tosses me a devilish grin and then turns to her audience. "This is my associate, James."

Associate? She sounds like she's reading from Sherlock Holmes. Which means I'm Watson. I glance over at Luca and all of his fear seems to have been swept out to sea, replaced by obvious amusement as he watches Ava work the room.

The officers all lift a hand in greeting but keep their eyes on Ava as she slides the passport over to them. One opens it and nods gravely.

"Sì, cara. Steven Sanford has been incarcerated for trespassing and theft," the middle officer says, opening his hands in a "what can one do?" gesture.

Ava shakes her head and purses her lips.

"May I ask where he trespassed and what he stole?"

"Certo. Certo. He climbed into an Etruscan dig site and took an artifact," the officer says.

Holy shit. What was this moron thinking? I turn to Luca and he's rubbing his hands over his face like he can scrub away Steven's stupidity. Ava lets out a low hmmmm.

"Unacceptable," she says and the men nod like bobbleheads. "An artifact? Really?"

The officer pulls a piece of paper out of a folder and pushes it over the counter at her. I can't see her face, but I can tell by the set of her shoulders that she's surprised. She lifts her head and slides the paper back.

"I wonder if we could ask you for a huge favor. It would mean so much to us if you'd allow us to handle his punishment," she says.

They stop nodding.

"Obviously, we know you have it under control, but as a student in our program, it would really help us out if you were to release him into our custody and allow us to handle the rest. I can only imagine the legal headache that would come along with this if we were to involve his lawyers and the American embassy and—"

The officers glance at one another.

"The paperwork would be endless," Ava says.

And that does it. The dreaded P word.

"Va bene, Signorina. You may have him." The middle officer stands and makes his way to the door behind him, unlocking it and pulling it open. Steven is curled up in the fetal position on a bench, with red-rimmed swollen eyes, looking almost pathetic enough to make me feel bad.

"Let's go, Steven," I say, and I've never seen anyone move so fast. He scurries out of the cell and makes it to the door when I put my hand on his shoulder.

"Apologize," I say, as one officer pushes a pile of Steven's belongings across the counter.

Steven nods and sniffles, grabs his things, then looks up and says he's sorry to the officers, who tip up their chins in a fuck-off signal.

"Grazie, signori. Tanti grazie," Ava says, tipping her blonde head forward, and the officers start their choral murmuring again. *Niente, bella. Certo. Prego.*

I shake my head and wave goodbye to them, then open the door for everyone to hustle the hell out of here before they change their mind. When we are out in the street I turn to Luca and say, "Are you okay to drive your car?"

"Sì. Sì. I did not drink. Only," he inclines his head toward Steven.

I nod. "Okay. Get him back to the dorm so he can pack." I turn to Steven, take out my phone, and check the details of what Leo arranged while we drove. "You have a flight home at seven tomorrow morning. A car will gather you at two from the university and take you to Bologna. Your parents have been notified, but I think you owe them a call."

Steven just stares at me with glassy eyes.

"If you are late or you don't show up, I will personally drive you back to these officers and hand you over."

This time he nods his understanding.

"What happens at home will be up to your college," I tell him. "Now thank Miss Graham for saving your ass."

Steven turns to her and looks like he's about to start crying again. "Thank you. Thank you so much."

She waves it off.

"Drive safe, Luca," I say and take Ava's hand and pull her toward my car.

We slip inside and I wait until her door closes to turn to her and say, "Proud of yourself?"

"Very," she says.

I try not to smile, but the smug satisfaction on her face defeats me.

"You are impossible," I tell her, reaching out to trace the three freckles on her chin. "Impressive but impossible."

She shuts her eyes and leans into my touch.

"You can't ask me to remain quiet when I'm more persuasive than you," she whispers, turning her face so her lips brush my palm

"You don't think I'm persuasive?" I ask, trailing my fingers below her ear and then winding them in her hair. I lean in so my mouth is a breath away from hers.

"You are persuasive. But I'm more persuasive."

"What did he steal, anyway?"

She lets out a throaty laugh and smiles wide, opening her eyes. "A fertility statue."

My laugh escapes me in a blast.

"What an idiot," she murmurs, shaking her head.

I close the distance and press my lips to her jawline, kissing her softly, breathing in her scent as she tilts her head for me, giving me her neck. There's a knock on her window and we jump, the side of her head smacking against the headrest.

"Jesus Christ," she murmurs, rubbing at her temple.

Luca's handsome face is in the window holding a slip of paper. He scrunches his nose as Ava puts down the window.

"Luca, if you aren't dying—"

"Mi dispiace, Professore, ma." He hands Ava the slip of paper. "There was a parking ticket on my car and I was wondering if Miss Graham might go work her magic with the—" He gestures toward the entrance of the station.

I keep my tone as flat as possible, channeling Liam Neeson in *Taken*.

"Luca, you have five seconds to take your ticket and get. The. Hell—"

He doesn't let me finish. His eyes widen, and he snatches the ticket back from Ava and takes off in a sprint.

The sound of Ava's laughter fills the car as I put it into drive and navigate us out of Pesaro. The duration of the ride passes like that, soft giggles and stupid grins, as we tell each other stories from our past, being careful to sidestep around anything heavy or painful as we drive, like two soldiers tiptoeing through a minefield. At some point, her fingers find the space between mine on the gearshift and they stay there, squeezing lightly any time I chuckle at something she says. If I thought fighting with her was fun, this—this comfortable, unforced levity—has me more relaxed than I've felt in a long time. By the time we arrive back in Urbino, my mouth hurts from smiling, but the air tastes thinner—easier to breathe. And I wonder if she can taste it too.

VENTISETTE

James

Raffaello Sanzio is perhaps the most interesting man I know. It's clear from the way the students' faces are lit up around me that he is now the most interesting man they know. And this is what I love about teaching—the transfer of passion for a topic. How a hundred students can walk into a room completely unaware that when they walk out, their minds might be set on fire with questions about something that did not exist to them an hour before.

"The most iconic work, the real masterpieces, they can be found in Rome—no, Julia, we cannot take a field trip to Rome," I say, meeting her wide eyes.

Julia puts down her hand and smiles while I continue on.

"That's a bit outside our budget. But hopefully you all have mastered Italian transportation by now. Head down over the weekend and sit for a few hours staring at Raphael's frescoes in the papal palace. The Vatican is a spiritual experience no matter what you believe. Try that instead of going out to Rimini for clubbing all weekend. And let's try to stay out of trouble."

There are a few chuckles, and many students avert their eyes toward their laps. Word travels fast in Urbino, and Steven has already become a cautionary tale that these students will tell their children before they study abroad.

"This afternoon you will be visiting the house where Raffaello was born. Your assignment is to document what you see, through both picture and prose, and to put together the young artist's story for yourself. Engage in the debate about what happened in those walls. Which art was his and which was his father's. Use what you saw at the palazzo to make your case. Santi or Raphael? You decide."

I pause while they scribble down the assignment. My eyes find Ava's as she looks down from the third to last row. Her head is tilted and she's studying me like I'm on a microscope slide. I lift a brow and she shakes herself out of the trance and smiles. A hand pops up nearby.

"If you are about to ask me for a word count, please refrain. You should know by now when something feels complete."

The hand goes down.

"Anything to add, Miss Graham?"

All necks crane her way.

"I'm excited to see what you all come up with. I wish I had assignments like this at law school," she tells them. It's the first time I've heard her come close to complaining about her career path.

"You can do my assignment," a voice calls out from the left.

Ava chuckles. "Alright, off you go. Do the learning. Be the art."

And my class is dismissed. Our class is dismissed.

The sounds of shuffling papers and rushing footsteps fill the amphitheater as Ava makes her way down the steps in my direction. Her eyes are on the screen behind me where *La Muta* is displayed in all of her glory. The green bodice of the young noble woman's dress is the exact shade of green as the eyes beholding it.

"I didn't know he lost both his parents at such a young age," she murmurs, commenting on the information I shared about Raphael during the lecture.

"Eleven," I confirm. "His uncles took him in," I say. Her eyes find mine and I know exactly what she's thinking. That this story sounds familiar. "He turned out just fine."

"Didn't he die from too much sex?"

"That rumor was born from another painter's claims," I explain.

"But it's not not true." She tilts her head a little and turns up her palms.

"Fine. It's not not true, but very unlikely. How many people do you know who have died from too much sex?"

She pretends to count on her fingers, then counters.

"How many people do you know who are engaged to the daughter of a cardinal but hide their mistress in the villa they are being commissioned to work on?"

She's been researching. Now who's an art nerd? I narrow my eyes on her.

"Engaged to the child of a prominent political figure—" I lift my brows and incline my head toward her. Her eyes widen as she connects the dots. "But having an affair with someone else. That resonates for some reason. Deeply."

She grins. "Am I Raphael in this story? Because I don't think I can die from having too much sex when I'm having no sex at all."

And before I can offer to remedy that, she puts up her hand.

"Don't you dare say you could change that."

I pretend to be offended.

"I was just going to ask if you would like to have lunch with me to discuss your transcript from the museum. Get your mind out of the gutter."

She laughs. "A working lunch?" Her lips press together, brows lift. "All about work and only work?"

"Call it what you will, but I brought us sandwiches." I lift the basket I packed from beneath my desk.

"Uvaldi's sandwiches!?" She actually jumps up and down from one foot to the other when I nod. Food will never be the same for her in America.

America.

Where she lives. Where she'll go when she leaves. Back to Senator Shithead.

I swallow past the sudden choking sensation in my throat and hand her the basket while I gather the insanely detailed transcript she put together for me. It's one hundred times better than anything I could have written myself. Organized, clear, meticulous. These students and all future students will be lucky that Ava's international law seminar never was.

"Ready?" she asks, clicking the power button on the projector and reaching out to take the picnic basket while *La Muta* fades to darkness.

I nod and watch her make her way back up the stairs.

Am I ready, though? There's a conversation to be had—a conversation that suddenly scares the shit out of me. One that I know we've both been avoiding since the market last weekend. One that I should have started in the car last night instead of falling prey to the spell of having her so close. But there are too many what ifs in the words that we need to share. Too many realities that, if spoken, will crush everything that either of us might want from the other.

She stops at the top of the steps and looks down at me, the picnic basket dangling in front of her like a lantern in the dark.

"Sandwiches wait for no man," she says seriously. "Because I'll eat them."

I smile up at her, working hard to quiet the voice telling me that following her is akin to walking into a hornets' nest. I gather up her notes and put one foot in front of the other until the scent of her drowns out the buzzing of the hornets.

VENTOTTO

Ava

James has laid out a blanket on a square of grass in Piazzale Roma just below a statue of Raphael that sits at the public garden's center. The open sky is a backdrop that the bronzed artist would have approved of—a shade of blue that he would have mixed for his own masterpieces. A high-pitched squeal from the playground in the distance draws our gaze to a father chasing his daughter around a slide. James is holding his camera to his eye, adjusting his focus as he zooms in on the two laughing figures. I smile around the mouthful of prosciutto and cheese, remembering a game my own father used to play called Daddy Monster.

You should call him.

Oh, now you show up, Mom. Nice of you to stop in. You want me to call Dad? So I can argue with him about my choice of law firm since we barely speak about anything else? Maybe I can let him know that your mark is all over Urbino? Or ask him if he knows anything about your secret life here?

You should call him.

"Should I?"

"Should you what?" James asks, offering me a third sandwich. My heart expands and I accept the delicious gift as easily as I accepted all of his compliments on the notes I wrote for him.

"Nothing, I was just thinking out loud," I say, hiding behind the semicircle of yumminess.

"You do that a lot—" He points to my cheek and I wipe off a bit of cheese. "Talk to yourself."

I don't know which is crazier, talking to myself or to my dead mom, so I let it go.

"Well, you take too many photos," I say. Excellent comeback.

He laughs and lies back on the blanket, hands folded beneath his head.

"That's almost definitely true. But when I take that many, there's always that one out of a million that captures something so perfectly it takes your breath away."

"Like the little girl at Franco's?"

He murmurs an mmhmmm.

"Or the old men walking in the market? That's my favorite. The hand gestures and facial expressions! There is so much communication between them in that shot. I can hear it."

He's turned his head to the side and is studying me with a small smile.

"You love art," he says in the same way a middle schooler might accuse his friend of having a crush on someone.

I lower my sandwich shield.

"I never said I didn't."

"No. But you really, really love art. You light up when you talk about it. There's only one other time I've seen you light up like that."

I know better than to ask when that other time was.

"I was going to be an art teacher," I say so softly I doubt he's heard me.

He sits up, resting on his elbows. The way he looks at me—I'm suddenly the most interesting woman in the world.

"You what?"

I shrug.

"I was in my second year of an education/art history double major when my mom got sick," I say, staring at the bronze Raphael above me. "The month I took off to be with her turned into two years, and then when she passed—well, art kind of lost its appeal. I couldn't even look at a painting without falling apart."

"So you switched paths," he offers.

"My dad had always wanted me to study law. He said I had a natural talent for argument." I give him a warning look so he knows not to comment. But he doesn't look interested in the low-hanging fruit. He looks like he wants to wrap me up in the blanket and put me on his lap.

"Don't look at me like that," I tell him, my voice thicker than I'd like.

"Like what?"

"You know what," I say, gesturing to his face.

"Oh, you mean with actual emotion? Like you looked at me when I told you about my parents?" He sits up, wipes his hands on his pants. "How do you want me to look at you, Ava? With indifference?"

I shake my head. How do I want him to look at me? I don't have time to decide, because the warmth of his hand finds my own as he lifts it to his mouth.

"I can't help how I look at you any more than you can help how you found your way back to art," he says as he watches me over our hands. He presses his lips to my palm, then against my wrist.

"I didn't find my way back—this was all a mistake. None of this is part—"

"If you finish that sentence I'm not letting you have the pizza dolce I brought you."

Bastardo. What in the good Madonna's name is pizza dolce?

He leans in closer, my hand still against his lower lip so that I can feel his breath against my fingertips. "Life brought you back to art. And when life brings you something, dolcezza, you take it, say grazie, and don't look back."

A breeze blows softly up Via Raffaello, rustling the needles on the cypress trees that flank the garden. I lean toward him, pulled by some invisible force, and touch my lips softly to his, then muster up every Italian cell in my body to purr "Grazie" into his mouth.

The way his mouth relents to mine makes me dizzy, and I find purchase in his hair with my free hand. He kisses me so softly—with less urgency than the night in the garden, as if we have all the time in the world, and the careful delicacy of his lips steals the breath from my lungs in a way that terrifies me so much I pull back with a sharp inhale.

My hand goes to my mouth like my fingers might find an answer to why I can't let him kiss me like that—why I can't let myself kiss him like that. But when I meet his eyes, I can tell he already has the answer. He shakes his head slowly. All the warmth and emotion that I asked him not to look at me with has disappeared. And the breeze that I welcomed only moments before is suddenly cold enough to send goose bumps over my bare arms.

"I have to get over to the museum," he tells me, reaching into the basket and peering inside. "You stay. I'll see you in class tomorrow."

He puts the wrapped-up dessert in front of me and stands, then brushes off his pants and busies himself with cleaning up around me. I want to stop him, to tell him to stay with me, but the words don't come until he's walking away, back down Via Raffaello, his hands sunk in his pockets with the basket hooked at his elbow.

And at that point he's too far away to hear me when I ask him to stay.

VENTINOVE

James

La Fornarina and *La Velata* hang before me on the far wall of the bed chamber of Battista Sforza's apartment in the palazzo. It's a fitting place for the works to hang—in the room where the great duke's beloved wife slept—because the subject is rumored to be Raphael's mistress. The love of his short life. His muse.

In both works her dark eyes penetrate me, their intensity forcing me to search for some hidden message. The portrait on the left—the half-naked painting of his lover—is soft and intimate, while the formality of *La Velata* makes you feel as if you should bow before her. Both masterpieces are haunting. As if they aren't paintings at all, but the actual spirit and soul of the woman he loved trapped within a frame.

"What do you think?"

I turn to find Zio standing behind me, his jacket draped over his arm, his eyes flitting back and forth between the two paintings.

"I think Silvia is an absolute genius to have obtained these from Barbarini and the Palatine," I say, clearing off my notes from the bench beside me to make room. "She must have had something on their curators."

"She just may. I have heard that museum curators are a scandalous bunch." He hangs his jacket on the edge of the bench and sits gesturing toward the paintings. "She is lovely, though, is she not?"

I nod. It's impossible not to find the subject beautiful, with her oval face and stunning visage—but the reverence that Raphael injected into the work—the light and contrast, the color infused in her skin tone, the attention to detail on every single part of her—that is what I can't escape. His work is always hard for me to leave, but these portraits—these are infused with passion. Everything he felt for this woman is immortalized in every brushstroke.

"I have noticed you've been a bit absent this week, Gi. Tutto bene?" Leo asks, tossing me a sidelong glance.

"Everything is fine, Zio. I've just been working on spicing up my stale lectures." I hold up my notes from my lap, and he chuckles at the dig.

"Va bene. I thought maybe you were hiding. Avoiding someone—"

Here we go. I touch my temple to preemptively stop the throb to come. It's not like I need a reminder of her right now. She sneaks into every waking moment—every sleeping moment as well.

"You rarely miss a dinner, Gi. And you are staying at the apartment. I can't remember the last time you stayed there in the summer," he adds, looking my way.

"The apartment needed repairs, so it's just easier to stay there after working on whatever the issue of the day is," I tell him.

"Forse, but Nina told me you fixed everything on Wednesday and yet here we are." He points between us.

"Do you miss me that much, Zio?"

He pushes his lips together and shakes his head. His eyes look into me like the woman's in the portraits. I let out a breath and look down at my notebook. There's no use deflecting here. Leo can see right through me. Always could.

"She will be gone before you know it," he says softly, his hand heavy on my shoulder. "Time has a funny way of haunting us when it is wasted."

Her face after that kiss, the way she pulled back as if it had somehow hurt her—it was enough to tell me exactly what I needed to know. It doesn't matter how long she'll be here if she's not willing to give what I want. And now that I know what that is, I can see that it's impossible.

"It's safer this way," I say, shutting my notebook and slipping it into my bag.

"Just like it is safe not to follow your dreams to London?"

I stand and slip the strap of my messenger bag over my shoulder, sliding my camera back into the center of my chest when it gets knocked aside.

London again. How do I explain to him that this offer that Davenport's making is just a pipe dream? Yes, when he saw that photo I took in la Basilicata years ago and recruited me, I was interested then. But I was twenty-something—young and ambitious with no finger on the pulse of what really matters. Photography was a passion that consumed me—now it's a slow burn that I've learned to control. That kind of passion is dangerous.

"I appreciate how much you care, Zio. You know I do. But everything I need is right here."

He looks up at me, his eyes sad, and I have to turn away—look out the window into the courtyard—because I know he's thinking about Nonna and my parents. Silently blaming them for all the chances I will not take.

His voice is low when the opening words of his favorite proverb reach me. "Chi non va non vede, chi non vede non sa e chi non sa se lo prende sempre in culo."

If you don't go you won't see, if you don't see you won't know, if you don't know you'll always take it in the ass.

Charming, no?

"I'll see you at dinner tonight," I tell him, making eye contact one last time. Maybe this will keep him from tossing perverted proverbs at me.

He turns his mouth down and dips his chin, lifting his hand to shoo me away.

And I take the dismissal like a get-out-of-jail-free card and hurry out of Battista's chamber before he changes his mind.

TRENTA

Ava

Who knew I liked dirt this much?

My cheeks feel toasty from the sun. My knees are dusted with earth. My fingers smell like Genovese basil. It's fantastic.

Verga lies in the corner of the garden, stretched out in the sun like he's a celebrity on a chaise lounge in Cannes. He's moved so little that every now and then I walk over to check that he's still breathing. Nina stands behind me, pointing to the tomatoes over my shoulder, explaining which are ripe and which need another day on the vine. I squeeze one to test it as she taught me and it explodes between my fingers, seeds and tomato guts spraying onto the apron with Michelangelo's *David* standing triumphantly on the front.

"Did il pomodoro offend you somehow? You must have something pent up in there, cara," Nina murmurs as she turns to her eggplants. I know she's smiling even as I stare at the way the falling sun makes the streaks of gray shine white on the back of her head.

I wipe at the goo on my hand with the hem of the apron and give a small grunt. I have so many things "pent up" in here, Nina. So. Many.

Perhaps it's the newest image of Ethan and the Viking goddess in the background of Olivia's campaign event—the way their heads are bent together like they're sharing a secret. Or perhaps it's the passive-aggressive email from my father reminding me that choosing a firm is one of the most important steps in a law career, and that he has twenty-five years of experience to help guide me. Maybe it's the white side of my mother's postcard demanding that I put a pen to it—fill it with what I'm supposed to be discovering here in Urbino. But all I'm finding is confusion.

Most likely the tension Nina senses is from dancing around the professor of the art history class I help teach each morning, being careful not to make eye contact at the wrong moment or inadvertently recall what his lips felt like on mine when he happens to be close enough to see me flush.

"Forse, you should do some exercise—to release whatever it is that is built up in there?" she suggests, waving her hand up into the air. "A swim?"

I squeeze another rich red San Marzano, and it feels just soft enough for picking. My thumb leaves a small indent on the side, the skin wrinkly and printed. Thank Dio for Nina. Gardening with her each evening has been the highlight of my shitty week, followed closely by the cooking lessons she's been patiently enduring. Time with her has been the antidote to the anxious energy coursing through me.

"Maybe after dinner," I muse. "I want pasta duty tonight. I think I've got it down."

"Brava! The only thing left is milking the sheep," she says, turning and pointing the eggplant my way.

I start to shake my head and she laughs.

"Sì. It is part of the experience," she tells me. "You must milk the sheep or you cannot leave Italy."

I run my thumb over another bright red pomodoro. Leave Italy. Of course I'll be leaving Italy. But time has been racing by and I feel like I've only just arrived. "The tip of the iceberg," as James told me. Just over a week and then life can resume the way that it was always meant to. With whom it was always meant to.

The calm of the garden is suddenly eluding me.

"He's coming to dinner tonight, cara," Nina says from beside me.

I turn to find her studying my expression.

"Who?" I ask, knowing there's no use pretending.

She laughs and plucks the tomatoes from my hand and drops them into her basket.

"Maybe he could help you with whatever this pent up—"

"Nina!"

She widens her eyes, the picture of innocence. Terrifying woman.

"Cara, you should know that Gi is very cautious—particolarmente con il suo cuore," she says softly, switching her basket to the other arm.

Cuore. Sounds like cor in Latin. Heart.

He's cautious with his heart.

"Aren't we all?" I ask the oregano beside the fence, remembering the flash of hurt I saw on his face when I pulled away from that kiss. Then the cold acknowledgment of what it meant. I can't give him what he wants—what he deserves.

"Vero, the two of you share that. What it feels like to lose someone, buonanima."

She places her free hand on my shoulder and I meet her gaze. Her eyes are the exact color of James's, caramel centers with a layer of dark chocolate.

"My sister was many things, cara—but a good mother? No. She chose her dreams and left Italy, something that I admired at the time," she says. "She was young and beautiful and brave. Urbino was too small for her spirit. But when James was born, she did the same to him as she did to our family. And that was—imperdonabile—unforgivable."

She presses her lips together and looks out over the hills. I can see the pain etched into the set of her jaw, and I know it's not just for James. She was abandoned by her sister, too.

"Ad un certo punto nella vita, sarai consapevole del fatto che alcune persone possono stare nel tuo cuore ma non nella tua vita," she continues, and I'm mesmerized by the words. I do my best with the translation, but Latin isn't helping this time.

I lift a brow and shake my head and Nina translates. "At some point in life, you will know that some people can stay in your heart but not in your life."

Ah. I nod once and look out toward the hills.

"That point in my life has come and gone," I tell her, my voice thick and dry.

I hear Nina let out a breath.

"Certo. It has," she agrees. She lifts her wide-brimmed straw hat from the bench beside her and places it on top of her head. "Which means that you should understand more than most not to waste un momento with those who are still here."

She wipes her hands together and then holds them up. Italian hand gesture for *all done here*. I watch her stroll back toward the villa, still reeling from the motherly verbal smackdown. I haven't had one of those in a long while.

Just one of the many things I've been missing in my life.

I let out a slow breath and turn my face toward the sun. I'm not wasting time. I'm making sure that life doesn't get any messier than it already is. It would be insane to get involved in anything with the timer ticking away in the back of my head. And in my defense, he seems to be perfectly fine avoiding me right now. Maybe he's the one who needs the smackdown.

Soft fur rubs against my thigh and a wet nose finds my palm at my side.

"I'm not wasting time, right?" I ask the horse-dog.

Verga yawns loudly, then plops onto my bare feet like he's been plowing the fields all day rather than lounging indulgently. I lie down beside him and rest my head on his flank and stare up at the sky. My wrist flicks an imaginary paintbrush around the edges of the clouds. My mother lay beneath this sky—painted it over and over.

"Where do I go from here, Mom? What should I do?"

Silence.

I shut my eyes, but the image of that Italian sky stays imprinted on the back of my lids.

TRENTUNO

Ava

There's a cool breeze blowing off the hills tonight, shaking the strings of bulbs that dangle overhead, sending sparks of light across the dinner table and yard. My freshly burnt skin is covered in goose bumps despite Leo's merino wool grandfather sweater I've cocooned around me. Even the Barolo, the music, and the boisterous company have failed to warm me. Perhaps because there is an extra blast of ice coming from the man to my right. He's working hard to keep his eyes off of me, but I'm failing to keep mine off of him.

All throughout dinner Nina's words from the garden have been bouncing around my skull like a sugared-up child on a pogo stick. How am I supposed to "not waste a moment" when the man in question won't even look at me? And perhaps he's right to protect himself. I've been a mess from the moment I stepped foot in Italy—nothing like the put-together, collected woman I am across the pond. James doesn't need to get sucked into this tornado only to be spat out wrecked and ruined.

"Ava?"

Uvaldi's huge hand flashes back and forth in front of my eyes, interrupting my view of James's jaw.

"Yes?" I ask, turning in my chair to find the man behind me with a huge smile and his hand outstretched.

"Dance with me," he says, apparently for the second time.

I start to tell him no and see Nina give me a look from where she sways in the arms of Leo. Aldo and Lucia move around them, as if they were trained for this moment. I don't have a moment to marvel at them before I'm being tugged out onto the grass by my partner. The music picks up and the couples create an inner and outer circle.

"La monferrina," Uvaldi yells, clapping his hands, but I don't have time to ask him what the hell he's said because he has started to do the steps across from me. His smile is contagious as all two hundred fifty pounds move with surprising grace and alacrity. I study his feet carefully and mimic the movements, just starting to feel confident when he links his elbow in mine and spins me to Leo. The sound of my own laughter mixes with the music as I'm passed from Leo to Aldo, Aldo back to Uvaldi, and round and round again.

When the music finally stops, I'm so out of breath and dizzy from laughing and spinning that Uvaldi has to keep a hand on my shoulder so I don't tip over.

"You dance just like your mother," he says, beaming.

"Terribly?"

He gives a deep breathy laugh and shakes his head.

"Senza preoccupazioni," he says. "Without a care."

I nod. I know exactly what he means. We had dance parties in the living room all the time, spinning and bouncing like we were possessed. Even my dad would swoop in and twirl us around.

"She lived like she danced," I croak. The opening chords of "Con Te Partirò" softly reach me and I lift my brows and put out a hand to my partner. He puts his hand on his chest, feigning exhaustion, and bellows over my head.

"Gi, could you keep my lovely partner company while I rest? An old man needs a break between dances."

I shut my eyes and wince, waiting for James to reject the offer, but when I open one eye again, there he is standing before me, studying my face while chewing on the inside of his cheek.

He winds his fingers between mine and cups his hand just below my ribs, then pulls me close enough that I need to arch my back or face plant against his chest.

"Hi," I say lamely.

One side of his mouth rises and he lifts a brow at me.

"How was your week?" he asks, spinning us slowly. The question is so impersonal that it strikes a nerve.

"Fine," I say. "How was yours?"

Are we really doing small talk? As if his tongue wasn't in my mouth less than a week ago. As if my chest isn't brushing against his at every step, sending shock waves straight through my core.

"Good. Just a lot of work—"

Like what? I've been doing all the grading.

"And the apartment is ready," he finishes.

I try to keep my expression neutral because he's studying me like he studies his art. Like he's writing a dissertation on my face.

Apparently, I fail, because the corners of his mouth turn down.

"You don't have to move in," he says. "Nina and Leo are happy to have you here."

"And what about you? Are you going to keep missing dinners and soccer with Maso because I'm here? I've had to pick up all the slack from your absence. She's making me milk sheep, James."

He presses his lips together and lifts his gaze back out to the hills, and I'm left staring at the way the light leaves a fleck of white in his iris—the way his five o'clock shadow creeps down below his collar. He lets out a breath and his fingers seem to tighten on my back, urging me closer. Not close enough.

"What do you want me to do, Ava?"

His voice is so low that only I can hear him, but the question sounds pained. Like I've twisted and wrung him out, then hung him on the clothesline.

And maybe I have.

"I don't know," I tell his chest. "I don't want you to miss time with your family."

"I have plenty of time with my family—believe me—"

"And I don't want you to miss time with me."

It's out of my mouth before I have time to think about the consequences. There's that voice telling me how foolish I am in my brain—berating me for being selfish and reckless and seventy shades of stupid. But there's something bigger hammering inside my chest, growing louder by the second, drowning it out—something that sounds just like Nina. Something that sounds like my mother.

Silence slips between us as the song comes to a close, leaving my words to echo in the empty space. His hand lingers at my hip as he steps back, his eyes on mine the entire time, deep and dark and filled with something I can't name. There's a moment when I think he's about to lean in, to tell me something important, but then he shakes his head.

"Thank you for the dance," he says.

He lets go of my hand and turns and walks out into the dark, up the path that leads back to Urbino.

TRENTADUE

James

La Festa del Duca has descended on the streets of Urbino. Knights on horses, musicians playing harpsichords, and women dressed in full Renaissance garb meander through the crowd greeting locals and tourists alike. Street vendors selling handmade jewelry and antiques haggle across the table, while the squealing and laughing of children bounce off the cobbled stone as they gather near the archery exhibit to try their hand at the target. A fencing match breaks out to the left, while a jester juggles brightly colored fruit from a stand on the right. On any given day in this city I feel as if I've just stepped into the past, but today that feeling is compounded exponentially.

Even in my angry stage as a post-American preteen, this festival lit up my soul—the experience so heady and authentic that I became obsessed with everything about the period, most particularly the art. For the last eight years, I've been in charge of the photography for the Historical Foundation's media pages. But no matter how hard I work and how closely I pay attention to the details, I've never felt like my photographs have done the event justice.

I step into the doorway of Signore Galuscio's pelletteria as flag throwers fill the street and launch their bright banners into the air. The lens never leaves my eye as I snap away at the show, working to capture the movement of color against the bright sky as the flag spins in the air. The sound of drums crashes through people's chatter, and I snap several shots of a little boy running through the procession waving his own miniature flag—his smile equal parts joy and mischief.

The festival is a perfect distraction from the pit in my stomach about last night. I barely slept thinking about the way she looked in my arms as we danced. The way her eyes widened imploringly when she admitted she wanted more time with me and showed that rare vulnerability. The way she chewed on the corner of her lip, making me want to kiss right where she worried. But I walked away. Almost ran, really.

Coward.

I take in a deep breath, and the smell of roasting meat mingles with the scent of leather coming from the open door behind me, sending a wave of nausea from my gut to my head. I haven't eaten since early this morning. It's time to take a break.

I make my way back down the hill toward Vincenzo's trattoria, sidestepping a bard as he recites a poem to a group of women having negronis on their hotel balcony.

"Gi!"

Nina waves over the heads of a group of students huddled around a snake charmer. I smile and wave back, squeezing through the crowd headed up the hill toward the piazza. As I draw closer, I see that Nina's elbow is linked with the freshly reddened skin of the woman I can't seem to escape.

Ava turns away from her conversation with Signore Turino and fixes her narrowed eyes on me. She looks pissed.

"Hello, Zia. Ava." I nod in Ava's direction.

Nina looks between us and lets out a dramatic sigh.

"Dove vai?" Nina asks.

"Ho fame. I'm heading to Vincenzo's—"

"Perfetto. Ava was just saying how hungry she was. Weren't you, cara?"

Ava opens her mouth to speak, but Nina puts a finger to her lips.

"You are not allowed to be hungry in Italy," she tells her, and if my amygdala wasn't pumping out the signal for flight, I would enjoy the wide-eyed nodding that Ava is currently partaking in. I know that look well from years of wearing it whenever Nina uses that tone.

"Va bene, then off you go," Nina says, taking Ava's arm and linking it in mine.

The second the soft skin on the underside of her arm touches my inner elbow, my brain shuts down completely. There's nowhere to run to now, so I focus on getting us away from the crowd without thinking about how warm and right she feels beside me. Nina blows us a kiss and takes off uphill like a greyhound released from the gate.

After a moment, Ava slides her arm from mine and steps back from me.

"You don't need to eat with me. Really, it's—"

"Why don't I show you the apartment while we are here? I can whip you up something to eat in the kitchen there," I tell her.

I can't blame her for wanting to get away. Twice I've left her stranded without an explanation. She looks around, possibly considering her options for escape, then settles her gaze on me.

"Okay," she nods.

I hesitate, surprised that she's agreed. Or possibly surprised at myself for offering. Then I gesture for her to head up the alley that runs perpendicular to Borgo Mercatale. She looks up the narrow, shaded foot path and takes in a deep breath, then leads the way.

The moment we step between the buildings into the shadows, there's a sense of calm and quiet as we escape the chaos of the festival and the swelter of the late afternoon sun. Dark green shutters and oversized doors appear haphazardly at our flanks, and Ava studies the soft stone surrounding them as we walk, keeping her eyes on everything but me.

"Are you enjoying the festival?" I ask her.

The path before us splits, one way leading down and to the right, and the other leading up to Via Mazzini. I put my hand on the small of her back and she stiffens, then relaxes into my touch as I guide her left and upward.

"How could I not? It's surreal," she says.

I nod. We are passing beneath iron balconies that cling to the buildings on either side of us, so close together that if the residents were to reach out, they could touch each other across the footpath. They are filled with flowers, dripping from pots, cascading between the iron rails and through the grates. It's as if these neighbors are having some sort of competition. I lift my camera and point it directly upward. The angle gives the effect of being in the hanging purple gardens in Florence, but with more color. It reminds me of melting old crayons with Nonna's hair dryer, letting the wax slide down the white paper and—

"It is like all of the Italians in Urbino got together and decided to coordinate the exteriors of their homes to complement each other."

Ava's voice pulls me back to earth, and I lower the viewfinder and find her admiring the balconies. I get on one knee and take a few shots of her from below, her face turned up toward the waterfalls of flowers. Then my field of view goes black as Ava's palm blocks the shot.

"Italians worship beauty—always have," I tell her as I stand.

"Sounds like a recipe for narcissism," she murmurs.

"More so than the ideal of making as much money as possible and buying as many things as you can?"

She holds up her hands.

"Did I offend you? When did you become more Italian than American?" She's enjoying pissing me off. I know the tilt of her mouth and the angle of her brows when she wants to rile me up.

"I'm just pointing out the hypocrisy," I tell her, motioning for her to continue uphill. I hear her say something about pompous pricks under her breath, but I ignore her and answer the other half of her question, "And I didn't become more Italian—it was there all along—carved into something inside me. It just took some time to recognize that I was denying it."

Shockingly, this shuts her up.

"It sounds shallow, when you apply the value of beauty only to physical appearance, but if you look around—everything embodies that appreciation for beauty," I point out. "The food, the art, the language." I gesture out in front of us.

We've reached the top of the hill and we are now looking down over the north side of town, the rust-colored roofs staggering down and away like a staircase leading to the distant hills. Every shade of green stretches beyond the city walls.

"These moments—these views—they aren't arbitrary. The city was designed with this exact experience in mind." I point to the deep forest green door to our right. "This door was painted to complement the color of the boschi—woods—you see out over the wall. All of it is intentional."

"How could you possibly know why they chose this color for the door?" She is looking up at me like she does when I give a lecture, mouth slightly parted, brows tugging together.

I try not to smile.

"Because I painted it."

She looks up at the building again.

"This is the apartment?"

"Sì. My apartment," I correct.

"*Your* apartment?" she whispers. And I can see the range of emotions that pass over her face as she reddens. What is she picturing in that beautiful head of hers?

I turn my gaze away and focus on twisting the key in the door, then push it open to reveal the narrow stone staircase that leads up to the studio. I put out my hand for Ava to lead the way and she meets my eyes for a moment, breathes in deeply, then looks back at the inside and brushes past, just barely grazing my thigh with her hip. And I know the moment that whisper of a touch sends a shock up my spine that bringing her here was a very, *very* bad idea.

TRENTATRE

Ava

There's no way in hell I could have stayed in this apartment.

It's not the size. Nope, I'm used to tiny. My apartment at home is barely more than a studio, and I love that I can hit up the coffee machine in less than four strides. I knew the square footage I'd signed up for here.

And it certainly isn't the original problem with the air-conditioning because I have to wrap my arms around myself to keep the chill from spreading deep into my bones.

It's the—the James-ness of the place.

His photographs are everywhere. I've barely been able to make it past the first wall on my left without feeling like I was tossed into his mind to play a game of "Who is James Massini?" Every black-and-white moment oozes with emotion—a child holding an injured bird beneath a tree, her tears leaving a streak of shimmering light down her cheek—an older woman sitting on a bench looking out over Urbino, her face filled with memories of what she experienced on the streets below her.

It's all too much.

As I turn away to escape his work, my eyes lock on the painting that hangs on the wall above the small kitchen table, and it's like a sucker punch straight to the diaphragm. Layers of white slide over the hills surrounding Urbino, pooling and slipping up over the walls, up over the rooftops and the dual towers of the palazzo. The sky is a layer of bruises, purples and grays splitting across the canvas like the painting itself might be bleeding internally.

"When I was little, I believed that Urbino was made of ice because of this painting."

His low voice finds the back of my neck and seeps into my brain, anchoring me back to reality.

"How did you get this?" I ask, keeping my eyes fixed on my mother's work.

"Nonna," he says.

"She knew my mother?"

"She did. Before my grandmother moved to New York to help my mother with me, she worked in admissions at the university," he explains. "She met your mom there. This painting hung in our kitchen in Brooklyn. She'd stare at it while she cooked. Told me it brought her home."

I'm imagining a young James rolling rice balls with his grandmother in the kitchen beneath my mother's painting, and the thought of it has me reeling. It's as if my mother painted it with a purpose, to keep a piece of herself connected to all of the people she left behind. Like she painted it to connect *me* to the people she left behind.

I'm not sure how much time passes before James's hand finds my shoulder, sending so much warmth through my limbs that I think the AC may be broken again. He turns me slowly, studying my face as I spin. I'm a mess. I know I am—cheeks burnt, eyes swimming, hair God knows what—but he's looking at me like I'm beautiful and that look—Gesù Cristo, that look makes the tears escape.

"Too much?" he asks, putting both hands on my face, sweeping a tear away from the corner of my mouth with his thumb.

Too much is an understatement. At this point, my synapses are so overloaded they've frozen the signals to my brain in an attempt to keep my central nervous system from frying like a fork in a toaster.

I shut my eyes and tilt my face against his palm.

"Way too much," I whisper, and he chuckles softly.

I want to ask him what we are doing. Why he's not running for the hills like he did last night and the week before? But I don't want his hand to leave my face.

And before I can think of anything to say, his lips are on mine, barely touching at first, just brushing lightly, as if they are getting reacquainted or asking for permission. My body responds, pushing me onto my toes to deepen the kiss.

Permission definitely granted.

This week without kissing him must have left me starved for this, because I'm pulling him against me, one hand in his hair, the other gripping the fabric of his shirt at the bottom hem. I need him closer. And I need this kiss to go on forever.

I let my tongue slide along his bottom lip, and his grip on my hips tightens, the pressure of his fingers sending a soft moan out of me and into his mouth.

He pulls back and looks down at me, his breathing fast and raspy, his eyes three shades darker than a moment before, and I've lost my mind. Not a single wit is left between my ears. All I hear is the pounding of my pulse and the voice in my head demanding more. I arch back a little and untangle my hands from his hair and shirt, then slowly lift my tank top up and over my head.

James stops breathing altogether as he takes me in with his eyes before running one finger up from my hip to my sternum, taking his time to trace the scalloped lace that dips and rises along my breast.

"You are the most beautiful thing I've ever seen," he says, his eyes sliding up to meet mine.

And even though all of my blood is definitely pooling down below I still manage to flush at his compliment.

He reaches behind me and unclasps my bra, then slips the straps from my shoulders at a painfully slow pace. It slides to the black-and-white tile, forgotten at our feet as he lets his eyes wander over me, down and up, up and down, his gaze heating every inch of skin it touches. I know he's taking mental snapshots, and the idea of him actually photographing me like this sends a shock wave straight down below my navel.

"James, if you don't touch me, I'm going to go crazy," I tell him.

One side of his mouth tilts upward and his hands keep tracing slow lines along my torso and beneath my breast.

"I am touching you," he says in a tone that's far too reasonable for my liking.

I make a frustrated sound and lift myself onto the kitchen table behind me, pulling my cotton skirt up to my hips while I wrap my legs around him and hook my ankles at the back of his thighs. I pull him toward me, and when the hard part of him rubs against the soft part of me he lets out a sound that makes me want to spend all day getting him to make it again.

His mouth crashes down over mine and there's no space between us now. His lips know everything about my lips. His hands are everywhere, on my thighs, down the back of my skirt, circling and teasing at my nipple, and I want him inside me so badly that the thought of it already has me climbing toward an orgasm. I pull him closer, arching against him, needing more—

"Avvvvvvvvvvvvvva!"

James stills above me, his mouth a fraction of an inch from mine.

That voice was in my head right. Because no fucking way that voice could be real. That voice is back in Wayne, Pennsylvania.

But then there are footsteps and the sound of something being dragged up the stone steps on the other side of the wall, and I am scrambling off the edge of the kitchen table, trying to find my tank top and my bra, and James—well, James looks way too fucking calm and somewhat amused as he watches me try to slip into my bra and put it on upside down.

"This city is amazing but you should still lock the door, Aves. This is the worst fucking place for an apartment—how high is the elevation up here, A—Oh."

Tammy looks like she's just stepped out of Urbino's only spa and salon. Her perfectly glossed mouth is making a little O as she takes in James and me. Her brows lift when her gaze settles on the tag at the front of my tank top. Inside out and backward. Great.

"Ohhhh. Okay. I see," she says, her surprised O-shaped mouth now stretching into a grin.

James moves first. He steps forward and holds out his hand.

"I'm James."

Tammy holds his hand a little too long, shaking it a little too excitedly as she keeps that grin pinned on me.

Then she steps forward and opens up her arms.

"Surprise," she says with a laugh.

And I run so hard into her arms that I nearly knock us both back down the steps.

TRENTAQUATTRO

Ava

"What. In. The. Actual. Fu—"

"Stop. It's nothing," I tell her, reaching for the glass of white wine James poured for us before disappearing back down the spiral staircase into the apartment.

Tammy's here.

I keep telling myself this fact even though she's directly across from me. It just doesn't seem real.

We are sitting on the rooftop deck that looks down into the city streets on two sides and out over the countryside beyond Urbino's walls on the remaining two. The festivities are out of sight, but the sound of an accordion and the muffled voice of a baritone reach us from the piazza in front of the palazzo.

"Nothing my ass," Tammy whispers, her brows pulled so high they fade into her perfect hairline.

You'd think there would be some judgment in her tone, maybe even anger at the fact that I'm quasi-betraying her twin, but all I see is wide-eyed vicarious excitement.

"How the hell did you keep this from me?" she asks, reaching into the ice for the bottle of Vernaccia and topping me off even though I only took one sip.

I look up to the single cloud in the sky and try to find a solid answer to this question.

"I don't know. I didn't want to make it into a thing," I tell her.

Her brows waggle, the twinkle in her clear blue eyes reflects even brighter.

"Clearly it's a thing," she says, tapping the rim of her wine glass to mine. "And you know what—you deserve a thing, Aves. You know I love my brother, but come on. Who the hell does he think he is right now? You should hear what my mom has to say about this. She threatened to cut him out of the will. She is pissssed—"

I take a long sip of wine and watch her hands fly as she rants. She's already more Italian than I am, and she's only been here an hour.

"And she's thinking about keeping him off the campaign trail, but Ethan keeps feeding her this bullshit that it was mutual and you wanted to live this trip to its fullest." She breathes and lifts her brows. "Which apparently you are."

"You done?"

She grins and pretends to be thinking.

"Not really. How long has this been going on?" she asks.

Since the moment I arrived? I think about the way I told James off that day at the airport, about how I spilled embarrassing details of my personal life to him during a car ride from hell. About how I treated him like the hired help. About that night in the museu—

"Oh my God, Ava. Look at you," Tammy's wolfish grin changes into something else. Something I don't like. And I realize I'm smiling like an idiot.

She squints while she looks me over and lowers her wine glass, leaning back in her chair as if she's been hit by a truck. She lets out a low whistle and crosses her arms over her chest.

"Not once in all of those emails and postcards did you mention that you've fallen in l—"

"Ladies, do you need another bottle of wine up there?" James's voice cuts through Tammy's accusation, and I widen my eyes at her and mouth for her to shut up.

"It couldn't hurt," I yell back down to him even though we have barely tapped into the first bottle. Whatever will detain him down there longer so I can make sure Tammy doesn't say something that can't be unsaid.

"Tammy, please don't make this into something it's not."

She puts her hands up, but she's still studying me with a mixture of shock and awe.

"Stop looking at me like that," I hiss as James's ascending footsteps clang on the iron spiral staircase.

The tray he's holding appears first and it's an absolute work of art. The word charcuterie doesn't do it justice.

"Antipasti," he says, placing it on the table between us, and I don't hesitate to pluck a piece of prosciutto from the center, all the while ignoring the grin I'm getting from our server as I drop the meat into my mouth.

James places another bottle of white wine into the ice bin and starts to back his way toward the stairs again.

"I'm going to give you two some time to catch up," he says when he hits the top step. "Dinner at Nina's at eight thirty—unless you two want to go somewhere alone, which I can definitely set up for you—"

"We will be there!" Tammy cuts in, without looking my way.

James nods, and goes on, "Then we usually watch the fireworks from the top of the hill."

Tammy makes a soundless clap with her hands.

"I love fireworks. What perfect timing for me to show up!"

I glare at her, thinking about just how unperfect her timing was, and she tosses me a wink and a grin.

"Alright, arrivederci. Enjoy," James tells us, meeting my eyes for a long moment as the roll of his Rs shivers its way up and down my back. Should I follow him back downstairs? Discuss what just happened? Kiss him again before he decides to run away?

But before I can answer any of those questions, his dark hair ducks back down out of sight, and Tammy and I remain silent until the heavy wooden outer door pounds shut below us on the street.

She stares at me through the quiet, while I distract myself from her gaze with the spicy salami and fresh burrata. For the first time in my life, I don't know what the hell to say to her. How do I explain what is going on here when every time I think of him my thoughts scamper like rats when you turn the lights on?

Tammy finally stops staring at me like I'm pinned to the page of a scrapbook and leans forward, pulling a piece of pecorino right out from between my fingers.

"There I was, lonely as hell back in America picturing you over here holed up grading papers and obsessing over my brother when in fact you were out there"—she gestures with her hand out to the hills—"with that gorgeous piece of man in this gorgeous little town doing Lord knows what."

I open my mouth to defend myself, but she's not done.

"Screw your valedictorian speech. I have never been more impressed by you in my life."

And though I have a mouthful of meat, that doesn't stop the steady stretch of the smile that spreads across my face.

Tammy's here.

TRENTACINQUE

James

Nina's arms are wrapped around Zio's waist so that the front of her body is tucked against his side, his blazer tossed over her shoulders. Through the lens, I can just see the sides of their faces, her head resting on his shoulder, their eyes turned up toward the night sky. My finger is moving so fast that I've lost any sense of how many photos I've snapped of the people around me. Another burst of white light explodes over Urbino, branches of gold stretch in every direction, reaching and falling over each other like glowing acrobats in the sky, and Leo whispers something into Nina's ear. This picture—this moment—will be my anniversary gift to them next month when their marriage turns forty.

I turn my attention back to where Ava stands beside Uvaldi just as a dazzling display of red and blue is unleashed over the dome of the palazzo. Her arm is hooked in his, and a pang of absurd jealousy shoots through me at the fact that he gets to feel the soft skin on the underside of her arm. I'm an idiot. Letting myself get swept up in this—in her. But I know that there's no stopping this now. I tried avoidance and it failed—maybe even made things worse since the way we collided today felt twice as shattering as the first time.

I'm in a car with no brakes and the speedometer is climbing past one hundred. And I have zero willpower to let up on the gas.

I'm just hoping to survive the crash.

"Beautiful, isn't it?"

I drop the camera and find Tammy sitting beside me, grinning at me like she has a secret that I'll really want to hear. I've only spent about two hours with her, and for most of the time we were eating and drinking, but it was enough to see how good she and Ava are for each other. All of that armor Ava wore has been stripped away and replaced with this effusive, glowing warmth. I've heard Ava laugh more tonight than I have the entire time she's been here. And her laugh is my new favorite sound.

"How are you finding Urbino?" I ask her, nearly yelling so that she can hear me over the booming pops of the fireworks.

She turns her gaze out toward the city.

"What's not to love," she yells, then leans back on her elbows. "Thank you for letting me stay in your apartment," she adds.

I look back to where Ava is laughing at something Uvaldi has said, and I suppress the urge to lift the camera. Tammy is inspecting me like a rental car before it's left the lot, and I don't need to let her see the dents Ava has made.

"Technically, it was Ava's apartment for the month," I say, but Tammy waves that detail away.

"To be honest with you, I think she was ecstatic to give me the apartment so that she could stay in that bougie pool house. She's grown quite fond of being here with—" She pauses and looks over at Ava, who is giving Tammy a warning look over her shoulder, despite the fact that she can't possibly hear her. "With your family."

I bite back a chuckle when Tammy finger waves back at Ava.

"Well, my family has grown quite fond of her, believe me."

Ava is whispering something to Uvaldi, pushing up on her toes so she is even with his ear, and a series of golden light explodes over their heads.

"And you? Have you grown fond of her?" Tammy asks.

Too fond.

"She's alright," I say, and Tammy laughs.

Maso has begun to light sparklers and is waving one in circles around his head. I want to tell him his curly nest of hair is going to catch on fire, but Nina reaches out and smacks the back of his head before I get the chance. He lowers the sparkler and lights another for Ava, handing it over with a shit-eating grin. Ava takes it from him and rolls her eyes when he purposely lets his finger glide over hers.

"I've never seen her this happy," Tammy tells me.

I watch Ava spell her name with the sparkler in the air and I snap a few shots of the trail of light she creates with her wide-eyed, dazzling face behind it.

"My brother is a moron," Tammy adds and that grabs my attention away from the shot.

"Your brother?"

She tilts her head to one side.

"Yeah, my twin brother. Her boyfriend—well, ex-boyfriend," she clarifies.

Senator Douche is Tammy's twin? Che cazzo?

"I didn't realize—" I didn't realize what? That I know nothing about Ava? That there's no way she'll ever escape her ex if her best friend is his twin?

"Please don't hold it against me," Tammy says, her smile fading slightly at the corners. "Like I said. He's a moron. And I'm happy Ava is . . ."

Her voice trails off and she holds out her hand gesturing to all of me.

"Is?" I ask.

"Is happy. Is free. Is doing what *she* wants for once instead of following one of her carefully laid out plans." She lets out a breath. "Whatever the hell you two are doing—it's good for her."

I look back to the sky just as the finale starts, the rapid succession of explosions rattling inside my ears as the sky turns gold.

Whatever the hell you two are doing.

Is it good for her? Because it feels good to me. Even with the fear nagging and pulling at the edges of my thoughts, all of that goes away when I'm with her. I want everything I can get—as much of her as she'll give.

Silence stretches across the hilltop as the last flickers of light fly across the sky. I lift the camera one last time and twist the focus until the details of Ava's mouth are clear enough to me that I can taste our kiss from today. She senses me, turns her gaze back over her shoulder, and gives me the softest smile. The trails of gold slide slowly down behind her, but the angle makes it look like they are falling in her hair and on her shoulders—like she's being dusted in gold.

I lower the camera and smile back at Ava with a rush of satisfaction, knowing deep down that I just took the most beautiful photograph of my life.

TRENTASEI

Ava

Why have I not sat by this pool every day for the last three weeks?

Obviously, there are some extra bonus points today since Tammy is floating like an otter at the far end of the pool spilling details of her mother's campaign and ensuring she doesn't bring up Ethan throughout her chatter. She's slipped twice—both times I waited for some sort of chest pain or brain zap that never came. His name no longer makes my lungs collapse. And as much as that's a relief, it also scares the shit out of me.

I've spent a huge chunk of my life with him. Holidays, events, milestones—all of it has piled up between us to make the foundations of a life together. So how is it possible that the thought of leaving it in the past doesn't tear me in two?

I turn and find the answer. James is in full recline, reading a novel.

Shirtless.

So many bonus points to him. Ten for the lines that crisscross his abs. One hundred for the shadow beneath his pecs. And a million for reading Elena Ferrante—in her original language. He's broken the scoreboard.

I've been working very hard not to turn and gaze at him so that my face doesn't get quasi-sunned and look like a half-moon cookie. But I'm failing. I really should just swivel my chair toward him and settle into the view.

He looks over the top of his book at me and lifts a brow.

"Can I help you?"

Nina and Tammy are in a deep conversation about the different government parties in Italy, so I stand and drag my chaise across the stones, making an awful shriek as I go. Verga stands from the shade I'd been providing him and makes his way to the shadow beside James.

"I'm wondering why we haven't been doing this every day?" I ask him as I plop back beside him in my lounge.

He puts down the book.

"Partly because we have work and responsibilities," he says. He leans his head toward me, lowering his voice. "Mostly because it's next to impossible to see you in a bikini without wanting to put my hands all over you."

Yikes. I want that—the hands part. I swallow and search for words.

"Do you think we could find some time to be alone this week?" I ask. With Tammy in the apartment and the pool house out in the open for all to see, alone isn't as easy as it sounds.

Eight days left. Now that thought causes the collapsed lung.

"I think we can figure something out," he tells me. "Are you hungry?"

Always.

"Sì," I nod.

"Want to make pizza with me?" he asks, looking me over.

"How do you say hell yes in Italian?"

He shakes his head. "You don't."

I laugh and he smiles, then stands up and puts his shirt on before I have a chance to protest.

"Where are you two going?" Tammy asks, her tone brimming with insinuation.

"To make pizzas," I tell her as I tie my cover-up at the hip.

"To make babies," I hear her murmur, and I kick the soccer ball that is lying nearby in the grass at her. It hits the water and sends a splash over her face. Perfect shot.

"Nina, you want mushrooms on yours?" I ask, still keeping an eye on Tammy sputtering in the deep end in case she seeks revenge.

"Sì. Funghi, per favore," Nina says, squeezing my hand as I pass by her on the way to the kitchen. "Use my sauce."

"Va bene."

I turn to find James watching me with amusement.

"You know how Zia takes her pizza?"

I brush past him and tell him, "I learned a lot this week while you were hiding."

"Fair enough. I'm going to cut some basil—"

"Let me! I love the way my fingers smell after. Like fresh pesto," I say, veering out to the garden.

James watches me with a smile and I turn away before I do something stupid like fall on my face. Or fall for him.

Too late, honey.

Ah. There you are, Mom. Radio silence all week when I needed you, but you decide to chime in now. And you're wrong. I'm not in love. That would be reckless. Self-endangerment. Falling in love with James would be disastrous for all involved.

I look down in my hand and realize I've cut enough basil to stuff a mattress.

The glorious smell does nothing to distract me from my mother's voice echoing the same two words over and over as I make my way back to the villa and into the kitchen.

Too late.

Too late.

By the time I drop the leaves onto the counter where James is already working on kneading the dough, they are crumpled and sad from me gripping them so hard in my fist.

"You okay?" he asks, looking sidelong at me. "You look like you saw something terrifying in the garden."

I nod and swallow, then go to the sink to wash my hands before pushing into the dough he has set out for me on the counter. Maybe if I scrub hard enough I can wash this feeling off too.

"Alright, when you start kneading, you want the dough to be—"

I put up a wet hand and flick the droplets in his direction. "Don't even start mansplaining pizza making to me. I'm Nina's apprentice."

He lifts his brows and smirks.

"Is that so? And I suppose a week with my aunt has made you some sort of expert?"

"Yup." I slap some flour on my hands and press my fingers into the dough, ignoring his watchful gaze. "Shall we have a competition?"

"Absolutely. I love competitions. Winner gets to decide what we do for a date Friday night," he tells me, reaching out his flour-covered hand.

I look down at it, hiding my smile as the word date marinates in my mind. Dating? It doesn't feel like the right word—doesn't seem to cover the breadth of this. But I reach out and shake his hand anyway, watching the cloud of white powder poof into the air on contact.

"Deal."

He doesn't let go of my hand. His fingers slide up the inside of my wrist and he tugs me toward him, turning me so my back is pressed against the counter. His hands slide up my bare arms, leaving a trail of flour as they go.

"I like having Tammy here," he says, staring at my mouth.

Why is he talking about Tammy right now?

"You laugh more around her," he tells me. "And your laugh is . . ."

He searches my face for the word.

"Is?"

"Intoxicating," he says, his voice so low I feel it at the base of my spine.

His thumbs are running along my jawline as he lowers his mouth over my lips.

The sound of someone clearing their throat freezes his face an inch from mine. He sighs and lets me go, his hands falling to his sides as he sidesteps away from me without turning around.

"Zio, would you like eggplant on your pizza?" James asks as he returns to his dough, leaving me face to face with Leo's smirk.

"No, grazie. I ate at Vincenzo's," he says, stepping into the kitchen and hanging his gray suit jacket over one of the chairs at the island. He drops a large manila envelope on top of the counter and smiles at me. "I found more pictures for you, cara."

More intel on Mom? I bounce a little on my toes and start brushing off the flour from my hands and arms so that I don't mess up the photos. I pull up a stool at the island, slide the envelope to me, and pull out the stack of pictures.

The first few are of my mother alone—reading a book on the hill overlooking town; head bent over her sketchpad in the piazza out front of Aldo's; holding up a glass of red wine to the person taking the picture. She's so beautiful. And so obviously at one with her surroundings.

Then there's a series of images with her and the man from the picnic table picture Leo showed me weeks ago. In one they are holding hands in front of the Raphael statue in the park, my mother smiling dreamily at the camera. In another she is sitting beside him at a table in the university's library, her fingers pressed to her lips, signaling for him to be quiet while he has his head thrown back in laughter. The man is older than she is in the pictures, maybe by a decade, but he's undeniably handsome. And it's obvious from my mother's expressions that she adores him.

"Who is this?" I ask.

"Professore Genaro," Leo answers from just over my shoulder.

I glance back at him to ask if there was something between them, and I get my answer without asking because Leo presses his lips together and looks away.

So my mother fell in love here.

In all the years that we spoke of Italy, planned my study abroad as she shared her memories, not once did she mention an affair.

"He was her art restoration professor," Leo says.

"Can I meet him?" I ask without thinking.

Leo shakes his head.

"He retired from academia years ago to paint. Last I heard he had moved to Venezia," he says.

I trace my mother's figure sitting on the edge of the fountain in the piazza, her finger in the water sending ripples across the surface.

So many things that she never told me. But then again, she never expected to have so little time. No one expects that.

James's hand slides over mine, and I look up from the image. His eyes are asking me if I'm okay, and I nod slowly.

"Thank you for these, Leo," I say thickly.

"Prego, cara," he says, then presses a kiss to the top of my head. I hear his footsteps make their way through the kitchen and out the door, but I can't see much through the tears in my eyes.

The breath-stealing need to have more time with her is a feeling I know well, but right now it is swallowing me whole.

James slips his fingers between mine as he circles the island and wraps his arms around me from behind. I shut my eyes and hold onto him for dear life so that this wave of grief doesn't sweep me out too deep.

"I'm here," he says into my hair. "I'm here."

And as I inhale his scent and lean back into his chest, my mother's words echo one last time, then soak into my brain like syrup into pancakes.

Too late.

Too late.

Too late.

TRENTASETTE

James

The pizzas have been demolished, but the smell of marinara and basil still lingers around us. Tammy, Nina, and Maso have their heads bent together on one side of the table discussing the merits of each pizza, not knowing who made which. The truth of the matter is, neither of us really can take credit for how amazing it was because the sauce was Nina's, but that little tidbit doesn't seem to matter to anyone right now as they point to my empty tray on the left and comment on the crispy crust.

Ava is smiling at me, the only evidence of the sadness that just engulfed her presses against my forearm where her tears dampened the fabric of my T-shirt while I held her. My chest might have ripped in two when she broke down had I not been able to wrap her in my arms and hold her until the grief passed. I felt her pain so deeply that comforting her turned into comfort for me. And then, almost as suddenly as it began, the moment ended.

She popped right up after a few minutes and got straight to work on the dough. Her transition was so sharp it made me dizzy. It also made me a little nervous for her. It made me wonder if she ever truly allowed herself room to grieve her loss. I imagine after her mother's death, her transition was just as sudden—that she treated life just like she treated the dough, pounding and kneading it into submission—moving forward from task to task with her elaborate plans.

"We choose this one," Tammy says, pointing to Ava's pizza tray with the tiny dent on the rim.

Ava's mouth stretches in triumph, and I see Nina clapping out of the corner of my eye when she sees that smile and realizes that the American has me beat. Traitorous woman.

"What were the stakes?" Tammy asks, looking between us.

"None of your business," Ava answers just as I say, "Winner plans Friday night date."

Now all three of the judges are grinning like idiots. Maso shakes his head at me and mouths his favorite American slang, "You're her bitch."

"Alright, then, let's have it," I say and Ava shifts uncomfortably in her chair, looking at each of the people who should not be involved in our relationship but somehow are. "If you don't have a plan then I'd be more than happy to—"

She puts up a hand. "So Tammy has a flight out on Friday . . ."

She trails off and looks at Tammy, who is still grinning at her like a lunatic.

"From Venice."

She chews on her lip and looks back at me.

"Okay?"

She lets out a frustrated breath and then goes on.

"Soooo, I was thinking, instead of her hiring a driver like she did to get here, we could drive her to the airport and then you could show me around Venice."

Wow. This is way better than my dinner at the botanical gardens plan.

"You want me to take you to Venice?" I clarify.

She flushes and nods.

"Can I come?" Maso asks.

All four of the adults say no at the same time. Maso shrugs.

"I'd love to show you Venice, Ava," I tell her seriously, and her smile splits me right down the middle. I need some fresh air. Inside.

"I'll clean up," I say, grabbing the empty trays and heading for the kitchen, Verga right on my heels.

Venice. Bella Venezia. Better than that—Bella Ava in Bella Venezia.

Imagining an evening spent with her getting lost in shadowy, narrow alleys makes me want the week to fast forward to Friday. But then I remember that we have eight days left together and I want to hit pause here and now so I can watch her shaking with laughter from this kitchen window forever.

Forever.

It's a ridiculous thought—a pipe dream—the same silly delusion that had me sending my portfolio to the owner of UK's top magazine when I was younger. The same pathetic hope that had Nonna and me setting the table for my mother every night, just to put the plates and cutlery right back where we found them hours later. Forever isn't real. Especially not for Ava and me, with her life and future across the Atlantic and mine here—with her departure approaching like a freight train. No one gets forever.

We get here.

We get now.

Everything else is a gift.

TRENTOTTO

Ava

It's not that I'm not ecstatic that Tammy is here. Because I am. Ecstatic. Sitting beside her in the piazza, sipping aperitivi after class, watching the college students mingle with the locals and tourists—it's like having a missing piece of me here to soak up any moments I may have missed. Sharing this with her is everything. But the timing—well, the timing is not stellar.

I spend hours with James every day, listening to him speak, studying the way his eyes light up when he discusses some small piece of unknown art that is housed in Urbino. Unfortunately, these hours with him are shared with seventy-some college kids who also get to hang on his every word and study his impeccable bone structure. And I'm tired of sharing.

Even the evenings have proven impossible. I can't complain about being surrounded with friends and family at the dinner table every night, but stolen kisses in the hall beside the bathroom are not cutting it—even if they were mind-blowing, spectacular kisses. I'd like a kiss that isn't interrupted by the voyeur, Maso, or an unlucky passerby.

James did try to sneak out to the pool house on Monday night, but Verga went nuts, barking and growling like Cujo until he realized who it was tapping on the glass door. And by that time every light in the villa had turned on, and Nina's smiling face had popped out of the upstairs window. Ultimate cockblock.

Friday cannot come soon enough.

I have fantasized about Venice since my mother and I read *The Thief Lord* together in fourth grade. The magic of the city—the secret pathways, the endless bridges—the romance of it all pulled me in so wholly that I'm sometimes convinced I've been there before.

Imagining James beside me in that setting sends so many signals through my body that I have to shut down the thoughts or I'll melt beneath this bistro chair.

The Piazza della Repubblica is bustling with the afternoon rush. It's as if everyone in Urbino has showed up for the Italian equivalent of happy hour. Luckily, James and Aldo are tight with the bar owner, who has been kind enough to save us a table by the fountain for the past three days.

"Have you told James that you stalked your mom's old lover?" Tammy asks from behind the rim of her Aperol Spritz. She's channeling a Hepburn today—Audrey, I believe—with a silk scarf, a shift dress, and a pair of Jimmy Choos that even the Italian women are admiring.

I look up at the underside of the white umbrella hanging overhead. I have not told James about looking up Professore Genaro's actual address. He heard what Leo told me on Sunday, but I just haven't broached the subject again. I don't want him to think that this trip is only about my insane need for answers about my mother's secrets.

"It hasn't come up," I say, just as our waitress stops by to ask us if we need another drink.

We both say yes at the same time and she inclines her head and turns down her lips—a gesture I've learned means "of course."

"Well, I doubt James is just going to randomly ask if you stalked your mom's lover," Tammy says when the waitress heads back into the bar. "So I'd say ball's in your court there. Based on everything I witnessed, I'd say James would have no issue tagging along—"

The table of students beside us breaks out into raucous laughter, and I smile and nod at a girl named Lily who sits in the front row of James's—our—class and Tammy hammers on.

"—in fact, I think James would do anything you asked. He's clearly in—"

I put a hand up.

"Please don't finish that thought," I tell her before taking a long sip of prosecco.

"The two of you are going to have to come to terms with what's going on here," she says.

I avoid her eyes and count the bubbles in my glass. Coming to terms is the last thing I want to do. Coming to terms sounds terrifying.

"Why don't you push your flight back?" she asks.

I already did. I meet her stare and swallow down a huge gulp of prosecco. Tammy leans back in her chair.

"You did already, didn't you!?" She laughs and smiles, shaking her head. "Good for you, Ava. Good. For. You."

"It's just a few days," I say, sounding defensive, but knowing damn well I don't need to defend myself to Tammy. It's the voice in my head I need to defend myself from.

Her phone pings on the table for the thousandth time, and she lifts the screen and starts hammering away, her eyebrows pulled together making an angry little V as her thumbs fly.

"What does he want?" I ask, knowing that it's Ethan texting her like crazy. At least they are speaking again.

She puts the phone down with a sigh.

"Don't worry about what he wants. He's thousands of miles away. Worry about what you want," she says.

What do I want? Tammy watches me closely, awaiting a reply. She sees right through me to the other side of the piazza. Maybe she can tell me what I want.

"Did you accept the position at Grant and Stanley yet?" she asks.

"I did. What about you? Any news from the Brits?"

"Nothing yet. When does your job start?"

"September fifteenth," I say.

She nods. Presses her lips together. And I know she's holding back.

"What aren't you saying?" I ask.

She lets out a long breath and swirls the ice in her glass with the straw.

"Don't take this the wrong way, but I don't want you to come home," she says, and I laugh at the absurdity of the comment. "I'm serious, Aves. You're different here. Lighter somehow."

"Of course I am. I'm on vacation," I shoot back.

"No you aren't. You are a TA in a major university. You just enjoy what you are doing and who you are doing it with," she says.

"I enjoy what I do at home too."

"Do you?" she asks.

"Yeah. I do," I say. "I love my classes."

She nods. "But that's school. What about in practice?"

She's just trying to help. I know that. But my quills are up and out and my tone is suddenly too snappy.

"What exactly are you trying to accomplish here? I just busted my ass the last three years. And you want me to do what? Throw that away and move to Italy to be a what?"

"You could teach here," she says, sending me back to sophomore year in college. Teaching is not a thing I can do now. I left that path behind when I chose to leave school to be with my mom. Going back would be too hard for so many reasons.

"Tammy, stop."

All of my uncertainty and fear amplifies the volume of that sentence. Tammy's shoulders fall an inch and she looks toward the fountain at the center of the piazza, as if the water flowing from the simple marble chalice at the center holds all the answers. Guilt slides beneath my rib cage and sinks its claws into my heart.

"I just want you to be happy," she says softly.

And I deflate. Why am I lashing out at her? I know she's just looking out for me—like she always has.

"I know. I will be. I have a plan, remember?"

"That's what I'm scared of," she murmurs. "None of this was part of the plan and look how happy you are."

She gestures around us and I follow with my gaze, studying the columned archways where I broke down beneath the pay phones a few weeks ago, and the neon sign in front of Aldo's where my mother's friends have now become mine. I look around at the people passing by, the tourists and the locals and the students all mixed and mashed into one glorious culture, brought together by the simple pursuit of beauty and joy.

It's going to hurt like hell to leave this place.

And then I think of Nina and Leo. Of Maso and Verga. Of James.

The pain I feel at the thought of leaving them drills a hole straight into my chest. I felt this pain before. And the only way through it is forward—to grab back control from life and hold onto the reins.

I lift my prosecco to my lips and look anywhere but at Tammy's knowing stare.

TRENTANOVE

James

The final lecture series of the course has always been my favorite. Centered around *The Ideal City* of Urbino, we take each element immortalized in the painting and discuss its purpose—its symbolism and function during the Renaissance era. Once the students feel well versed in the art, they take to the streets with their phone cameras to immortalize their own ideal city using bits and pieces of what Urbino has to offer. Every year the work that I receive manages to impress me in some new way. Seeing the city I adore through the eyes of those who are newly falling in love with it is both inspiring and humbling. It reminds me that Urbino is the ultimate muse.

This year, I'm enjoying this final assignment more than I ever have, because as I roam the streets, watching our students flit here and there with wide smiles and phones held aloft, I have Ava by my side. The back of her hand brushes against my knuckles and I feel myself tense with the effort not to lace my fingers between hers.

This week has been purgatory, her leg brushing against mine while sitting beside me at dinner or watching her lean over the students to discuss the lesson, but never being able to touch her for more than a moment. Venice can't come soon enough.

"I'd photograph the pizzeria for my ideal city," Ava says, smiling at a group of girls who are trying to capture the cathedral and the duomo in the same shot. She looks back to me and catches me studying her profile. "It would stand smack dab in the center of my perfect town. What would you photograph?"

"All of it," I tell her. "There isn't a thing I would change about Urbino."

She makes a thinking noise and looks sidelong at me.

"You've never wanted to leave? See the world or go back to New York?"

I shake my head and shrug.

"There's nothing left for me in New York. Everyone I love is here," I say and a speckling of red appears across her cheekbone. Was it the L-word that has her looking beautifully uncomfortable? I take a step to close the distance between us and then stop when a group of students yells their greeting to us from the alley. Ava strolls away, hands folded behind her, perfecting the Italian art of passeggiata.

"What if Oxford calls and offers you a position? The most prestigious university in Europe and they want you? What then?" she asks, veering toward the cathedral's white stone side wall.

"I'd thank them for the opportunity and ask Nina what's for dinner," I tell her.

She laughs, her smile as bright and white as the side of the church.

"What if *National Geographic* saw your work and wanted to employ you exclusively?"

I stop following her, and she takes a moment to notice that I've lagged behind. Has she been talking to Leo? I narrow my eyes and study her, but she just lifts her brows and waits for my answer—which should come easily enough since I've been doing it for several years.

"I'd politely decline," I tell her. I don't add that I'd then ignore every subsequent offer by said publication owner.

"There must be something that would entice you to leave Urbino."

"I'm leaving Urbino tomorrow, so *something* did entice me."

She leans back against the church and watches me. I look around the piazza, finding nothing but glorious silence and empty tables. The need to kiss her shakes me so hard that I don't even bother looking around before I lower my mouth to hers. She softens immediately, the wall behind her and my hands at her hips keeping her standing. She parts her lips just enough for me to try get my fill of the way she tastes. I want her so badly it hurts, but the sound of laughter forces me to pull away. Awareness sadly seeps back over me like I'm waking up from the most wonderful dream.

"Ava," I whisper, stepping to her side and leaning against the wall so she's hidden from the piazza's view.

"Hmm?"

She turns her face toward me and I imagine mixing the color I see on her cheeks.

"Why do you want me to leave Urbino?"

She swallows—looks from my mouth to my eyes and back to my mouth.

"I pushed my flight back," she says, ignoring my question altogether.

I let out a breath and feel every muscle in my body relax. That's wonderful news. More time. More Ava.

"How long?" I ask.

Say a month. Say indefinitely.

"Three days," she says, running a finger beneath my jaw. Her touch scrambles my thoughts as I try to process three days of extra Ava.

Seventy-two hours.

"That's not enough," I say.

She shakes her head and puts her hand in the center of my chest.

"It's never enough." She lifts onto her toes and kisses me softly, and it's over before I have a chance to pull her against me.

"Show me the duomo," she commands, heading back to the front of the church.

I rub at the place where she touched me beneath my jaw and turn to follow her, watching the way her ponytail brushes against the bare skin of her back. I've been there—felt that softness and can't wait to go back. *Madonn.* I look to the sky and steel myself before following my temptation into the house of God.

QUARANTA

Ava

The three-and-a-half-hour ride to the Venice airport is a complete one-eighty from my first ride-along with James. One, I'm not spilling the secrets of my life to him as we curve through the hills topped with gorgeous villages that I wish we could stop at, stay the day, maybe even the month. And two, Tammy's annoyingly symmetrical face appears over and over again between us, hovering over the center console like a pair of fuzzy dice hung from the rearview mirror. She messes with the air-conditioning, changes stations, asks James both impersonal and personal questions, and just generally seems to want to sit on our laps. For someone who has emphatically pushed me to jump into whatever this is with James, she appears to be making a maximum effort to keep our hands from grazing on the gearshift. Which makes me question what the hell is wrong with her?

But before I have a real chance to ask her, we are standing at the curb of the departures terminal at Marco Polo airport, holding onto each other as if I'm not coming home in less than a week.

"You know I love you, right?" she asks.

I nod into her shoulder.

"And if I could, I would always choose you over everyone in the world. You aren't family, but you are the sister I'd choose."

I push back from our hug and narrow my eyes on her face. The lines above her nose are so deep that she might get a headache.

"What are you—"

"Ava, the water taxi is here," James says, gesturing to a handsome man standing beside him with a sign that reads Massini.

I look back at Tammy, my question still sitting on the back of my tongue like a timid child on a diving board, but she has already engaged herself in conversation with a porter who is struggling to wrangle her obnoxiously sized luggage.

She meets my gaze one last time and then winks at James. "Arrivederci!"

Part of me wants to run after her—grab onto the hem of her long skirt and tell her I need her here to tell me what to do. But she's already passed through the glass doors, laughing at something, moving merrily along as Tammy is wont to do. And I'm frozen at the departures curb, feeling far too panicky about getting on a boat to Venice with James and a thousand unnamed emotions.

A warm, solid hand lands softly on my shoulder, and my thoughts settle like a blanket laid over a sleeping child.

"Are you alright?" he asks.

I nod once and turn toward him. The moment I meet his eyes, I forget all about Tammy's weird behavior in the car because the answer to his question occupies all the space inside of me.

I'm alright. With you.

I don't need to say the words, because he smiles down at me, laces his fingers in mine, and then leads me where I need to go.

* * *

I've seen beauty. I've spent the last four weeks steeped in it, like an oversaturated tea bag ready to burst. But this—this is something else. This is otherworldly.

The briny spray that misted us as the boat sped across the choppy, dark blue waves has subsided and the motor drops from a roar to a purr. James has me pulled tightly into his side where we are perched on the shiny mahogany ledge at the stern of the motoscafo; one of his fingers is securely threaded through the belt loop of my jeans, the other squeezing my thigh as if I might plunge into the Adriatic at any moment. Venice rises above me—Aphrodite standing from her foam—her allure so palpable that every limestone curve and marble arch, every bronzed duomo and iron terrazzo sends a pang of some unknown sensation through me. It feels like desire infused with danger, darkness, and melancholy. It's unnamable.

As we approach, the sound of water laps softly against the stone foundations of the buildings, leaving dark stains that remind me of the things this city has seen. The great wars and great tragedies. The great joys and loves. The great Mini Cooper race with Charlize Theron and Marky Mark.

We turn from the Grand Canal down a narrow waterway, only just avoiding a gondola coming in the opposite direction. A young couple stare up at their gondolier, whose deep voice serenades them from beneath his wide-brimmed hat.

I'm in a novel.

"How are you not taking pictures of this?" I ask, just loud enough for my voice to be heard over the thrumming of the motor.

James leans in so that his mouth grazes my earlobe.

"If I were to get my camera out right now, I would only be taking pictures of you," he says, and I shut my eyes and let his words warm me.

I feel a shadow pass over us from behind my lids and open them to find the underbelly of a stone bridge. I could stand and run my finger across the smooth stone, grab onto the parapet and dangle over the water like fish bait.

"I've done plenty of shoots here over the years," James murmurs as a slosh of water broadsides the boat and sends us drifting toward a gray stone building with lilacs dripping from the window boxes. Our taxi turns down another narrow canal, this one empty and quiet, almost eerie if it weren't for James's arms around me. "Couples love to stage their engagement in Piazza San Marco," he finishes.

"With all the pigeons?" I ask.

"Yup. Pigeon shit and all," he laughs, and the sound of it sends a rush through my blood. "I'll take you there tonight if you want. It's far more enchanting in the dark—"

"When you can't see the pigeon shit," I venture.

"Exactly."

I release a small sigh and say, "My mother loved St. Mark's Square. Made me promise to sit at the white-clothed tables and order dessert while listening to dueling pianos."

James kisses the side of my head and whispers his condolences into my hair.

"If you'd like to do that—we could," he says.

Would I?

Yes, Ava. Say yes to all of it. My mother's voice drifts up from the depths of the dark water beneath us.

"I'd like that," I tell him.

Captain Marco shifts the boat into neutral and I lurch forward, but James's hands keep me from falling to the wooden planks below my feet.

"Siamo qui," Marco says, as he turns the wheel so that the boat pulls up against the brick side of a house that juts out from a corner where the water slices in two directions on either side. It's a fork in the canal.

"Grazie, Marco. A domani, sì?" James asks, and I'm immediately transfixed by the way his mouth rolls Marco's R. I try to mimic the sound with my own tongue dipping and falling, but I fail and James smiles at me over his shoulder while continuing his conversation.

"Sì. Alle sei?"

"Forse dopo. Ti telefonerò."

I stop trying to translate and look up at the building we are floating beside. Three stories of dilapidated brick tower above me, interrupted by huge arched windows with a small white stone balcony at the very top.

"Where are we?" I ask James as he tosses our bags overboard onto a stone step that leads to a huge wooden door.

"Cannaregio. This is where we are staying. A friend's second home," he says, offering his hand for me to step off the boat.

A friend's second home is a sixteenth-century palazzo? What the hell does his/her first home look like?

The stones beneath my feet are wet from the sloshing wakes of passing boats. My flat slips and James steadies me with a hand on my back. He types in a code on the keypad that looks so out of place beside this door that witnessed the bubonic plague, then heaves it open and steps to the side for me.

The space is like nothing I've ever seen before. Huge windows flank the far wall, exposing the water that snakes back toward the

Grand Canal. The walls are white, the floor is white, but the ceiling reminds me of the cathedral in Urbino. A hand-painted fresco, so bright and vivid I wonder if the paint is still wet, stretches overhead. The mix of modern and antique surrounding me is vertiginous—makes my thoughts spin as I run my hand along the soft arm of a midnight blue velvet settee.

I turn to find James watching me, our bags left by the door behind him. The way his eyes drink me in reminds me of the night at the museum when my skin sang each time he came close, and I can feel the color rising to my face as I remember how he felt pressing me against that garden wall.

He clears his throat, gestures to the space.

"What do you want to explore first?" he asks, his voice thick.

And without giving it a moment's thought, the answer flies off my tongue.

"You."

QUARANTUNO

James

I take a step toward her and force myself to freeze. She watches, shoulders pulled back, chin up, waiting for me to do what I know she wants me to do—to kiss her, to pin her against the arm of that settee, to touch her until she comes apart beneath me. But I know if we start this, there will be no end to it. We'll never get to San Marco's for dessert or to the dinner I have planned along the canal. Never browse the shelves of the bookshop around the corner or see the locals sitting on their blankets with lanterns while listening to the violinists in Piazza San Regio. I'm willing to forgo all of it for her, but I've seen it. Heard it. Tasted it.

Ava lifts a brow and tilts her head.

"If we start this, Ava, we aren't leaving here tonight," I say, my voice a bit strangled and this obviously brings her joy.

A slow smile spreads across her face and she takes the final step between us.

"I'm okay with that," she whispers, tracing a finger along the collar of my shirt.

"You're okay with spending your first night in Venice locked in a bedroom with me?"

She nods, swallowing hard as she unfastens the first button of my shirt.

"I'm okay with spending every night in Venice locked in a bedroom with you," she says, taking her time with each button while staring up at me. She looks wild. Hair windswept from the boat, skin flushed from the spray, or maybe from this pleasantly unbearable warmth pressing in on us. I let her finish what she's doing, my fingers itching to touch her as she pushes my shirt off my shoulders.

She lifts the soft cotton of my undershirt and puts both hands beneath it, splaying her fingers over my abdomen. Her breathing is shallow now, her chest rising and falling, brushing against me every time she breathes in. I shut my eyes and focus on the way her fingers burn against my skin.

"James?"

"Hmmm?"

When she doesn't answer right away, I open my eyes to find her staring up at me, her lip pulled between her teeth and two little lines between her brows.

I run my thumb below her bottom lip until she lets it go.

"What are you thinking, dolcezza?" I ask, leaning down and pressing a kiss on the top of her head.

"I'm thinking that I want you so badly it hurts."

Her words tighten every muscle in my body, and I wrap my arms around her back and pull her closer to let her know that I feel the same way. I've wanted her from the moment I saw her and every impossible moment after that.

She leans the side of her face against my chest and continues. "But I'm also thinking that once I have you it's going to hurt even more—to leave."

I squeeze her tighter against me. She's right, of course. Being with her will just make it harder to say goodbye. But there's not a single cell in my body that can resist her if she'll have me.

"Let me show you Venice," I say down into her hair.

She nods against my chest and says, "Is there going to be an art lecture?"

I squeeze her more tightly. "Undoubtedly."

She laughs, the vibration of it sending warmth through me.

"And you promise we can do that locked in a bedroom thing later?"

"Ava, when we get back here, we aren't making it to the bedroom before I do the things I want to do to you."

She leans back and looks up at me, eyes wide and cheeks flushed.

"Let's get out of here before I physically can't," I say. She swallows hard, then nods.

I grab her hand and pull her toward the door before I change my mind and do what we both really want.

QUARANTADUE

Ava

This night will forever be branded on my senses. Every time I hear *Phantom of the Opera*, I'll be transported back to this table, the pianos on either side of the square softly pulling the notes of the "Music of the Night" back and forth across the piazza. Every time I see a candle, I'll be transported to the square, hundreds of arched windows above me, a single flickering flame in each creating the most haunting glow. And every time someone touches me, I'll feel James's fingers tracing circles on the inside of my wrist. This night has ruined me.

And the day was no less ruinous.

I climbed books into a bookstore—actual stacks of novels made into a staircase to get inside the most amazing and unorthodox shop I've ever seen. Canoes and kayaks hung from the rafters, all inundated with books kept aloft to prevent acqua alta from damaging the goods. It was unreal. Much like the dozens of bridges and alleys James and I wandered down with no place to go and nowhere to be. And dinner—squisito—the word dinner doesn't do it justice. Mind-numbingly delicious cioppino aside, the setting was unlike anything I've ever seen. We ate a foot from a narrow canal, nestled in the archway of the loggia of some ancient building that apparently housed Vivaldi for some time. I couldn't have invented it if I tried. Walt Disney couldn't have invented it. The whole day was enchanting. Pure magic.

Through all of it, James smiled beside me, pointing out this or that, explaining some delectable piece of Venetian culture or history, and taking pictures of me like I might float away in the Adriatic with the vaporetti. The way he looks at me now, the candlelight catching the flecks of amber in his dark eyes, makes me want to drag him back to our palazzo and finish what we started today.

"The first time I came here the square was flooded," James says, tugging me from my trance. "It was up to my knees. There were makeshift plywood bridges and walkways everywhere. It was a mess. The couple I was photographing were so upset."

"I can imagine. She'd probably bought engagement shoot heels and an adorable dress and had to wear muckers instead," I say, grimacing at the thought of rubber overalls.

James smiles, and that familiar slow spread of heat creeps through me. I don't know what it is about his mouth that makes me melt into something resembling the leftover gelato on my plate. Which, if we're counting, is my fifth gelato today.

"The photos ended up being gorgeous. The candles' reflections in the floodwater added another dimension to the shoot. It was surreal," he says, picking up the pitcher of house red and topping off my glass.

"All of your photos are gorgeous, so no surprise there. And everything about Venice is surreal." I gesture to the crisp white awnings that run around the piazza, then to the bell tower stabbing at the blackness above. "All of this is like a dream."

James laces his fingers between mine and squeezes my hand as the couple at the table beside us stand to join the others dancing on the gray stones in the middle of the square. It's all incredibly romantic. The sort of scene you create for yourself to escape to when you're stuck behind a desk reading case law.

The thought smacks into me so hard I flinch. Is that how I feel? Stuck?

James stands, flicking my inner questioning off into space, and I think he's going to ask me to dance, but he doesn't. He tells me he'll be right back and disappears inside the restaurant leaving me to do my new favorite Italian thing. People watch and drink wine.

The melody shifts to "It's a Wonderful World," and I watch an older couple spin slowly, the woman's gray head bathed in gold as she rests it on the man's shoulder. They are perfectly at peace; I imagine years of this exact sort of intimacy is ingrained in their movements as they step in unison. Spin in unison—until a random man pushing through the dancers makes them misstep and open their eyes.

I'm vicariously annoyed for them, but they seem less so. They get right back to it while the golden-haired man in a perfectly tailored gray suit doesn't even spare them a glance. In fact, he spares no one a glance because he's staring straight at me—heading straight for me. And the warm fuzzy cloud of warmth and beauty that I'm floating on suddenly dissipates into tiny cotton ball–sized puffs that float out over the bell tower into the darkness as the handsome man shoots me a striking smile.

"Buonasera, Ava," he says when he's close enough for me to toss a bread stick at.

And the only thing I can manage to say seems to escape from somewhere deep within, my tone so tight it's barely recognizable.

"What are you doing here, Ethan?"

QUARANTATRE

James

As I step back out beneath the awning, I realize we couldn't have asked for a more beautiful night. Above the bleached white piece of fabric stretched out overhead, there isn't a cloud in the sky, making it possible to see the stars clustered over the Palazzo Ducale. On nights like this, it's hard to find the sky's end, the candles suddenly an extension of the constellations hanging above.

"Che romantico!" someone says from my left, and I turn to find a table of twenty-somethings looking out toward the dancers over Ava's head. In fact, when I glance around me as I step around another table, I see that everyone is looking out at the square where couples are stepping in time to the melody of a Bocelli song.

My eyes settle on Ava's golden hair and I swallow down the wish that this day would never end. It's useless to make wishes like that. Wishes that just make it all harder.

"Holy bling. Look at the size of that ring," one of the women murmurs, and I realize that no one is looking at the dancers. In fact, the dancers are now looking back toward us. I slide my gaze away from Ava and it lands directly on the cause of all this attention. The music stops—a rare occurrence for the dueling pianos—and the golden-haired man who is down on one knee holds the obscenely sized ring out to Ava and opens his mouth to speak for all to hear.

"I know it was a mistake to let you go without this ring, Ava. I should have told you before you left. I should have sent you here with a reminder of how much you mean to me—how much I love you."

I'm frozen. Staring at Ava's profile, her visible eye wide and glistening with—happy tears? No. She couldn't possibly be happy. This arse sent her here with a calling card. Not a ring. But her plan—

"When I heard you were coming to Venice, I couldn't think of a better place to do this. These few weeks without you just confirmed what I already knew. I want to spend the rest of my life with you. I want to be a part of every step of your plan in life. Will you marry me?"

She doesn't move her hand from where it covers her mouth. People around me are whispering, "Say yes!" in excited but hushed tones, and I want to tell them to shut up—that the admittedly good-looking guy on his knee is not what she wants. That her plans don't involve him anymore. There are flashes from a camera and I notice a woman standing beside them taking shots from every angle. A paid photographer? A reporter he's brought with him?

"Ava?" Ethan says louder, putting one hand on her thigh. I want to break every finger on that hand.

The flashing lights seem to knock Ava out of her daze, and she lowers her hand, which he immediately takes and holds in his own. I wait, my fists clenched painfully by my side. I wait for her to shake her head. To stand up and storm off. To tell this asshole what he needs to hear. But she says nothing and her silence stabs me square in the chest.

I need to get the fuck out of here. Away from the dashing douche proposing in the most romantic place on the planet. Away from the crowd soaking it all in with ignorant stars in their eyes.

Away from the woman who I've fallen in love with despite every effort to keep myself from doing so.

I turn and make my way into the shadows beneath the loggia, escaping to the darkness before I can hear her say yes to the life she's always wanted.

QUARANTAQUATTRO

Ava

When you've envisioned a moment over and over again so many times, something trippy and déjà vu-like occurs in your brain when it actually happens. Time slows down and I'm suddenly under water. St. Mark's is under water. My senses home in on the strangest minutiae. Like the small white scar on Ethan's temple where Tammy allegedly bit him when they were three. Or the sound of his Gucci loafer tapping against the gray stone beneath it. The unnatural softness of his fingers as they take my left hand off my lap and begin to push something cold onto my ring finger.

I look down to see the ring, the reflection of a thousand candles illuminating the huge rock from within. A flash momentarily blinds me, and I think the diamond has exploded, but then I realize

I'm being photographed. I'm used to that, surely, with James's lens constantly aimed on me.

James.

I pull my hand back quickly as everything starts to clear and the ring clatters to the stones beneath my chair. The water drains from St. Mark's. Time snaps back like a rubber band, and the reality of what's happening settles in. Where is James?

I look around, ignoring all the wide-eyed faces turned my way, searching for the only one I want to see. But he's nowhere to be found.

"Av—"

"Ethan, I need you to get up," I say softly, meeting his eyes.

He opens his mouth to argue but sees something on my face and lets out a long breath. I reach down and pick up Olivia's heirloom ring and place it back into the folds in the satin cushion. It should hurt, handing back the thing I wanted so desperately only a month ago, but the only thing I feel is a desperate need to find the man who isn't here in front of me.

"Alright," Ethan stands, nods, and smiles to the people around us, ever the politician. "Let's walk."

He holds out his hand and I take it, letting him tug me through the tables and the fluttering crowd that hovers and descends like the pigeons on St. Mark's Square. We stride across a bridge that runs parallel to the Grand Canal, and as the crowd dwindles I notice a woman following us with her camera.

"Ethan, we have company," I tell him and he just nods.

"Evette, could we get a bit of privacy?" he asks the woman, and she stops, rolls her eyes, digs into her pockets, and lights up a cigarette.

Ethan pulls me out of earshot and looks out over the canal.

"You hired a photographer?" I ask, watching the side of his face.

"Olivia did," he answers.

"How did you find me?" I ask, but I know the answer.

"Olivia," he confirms.

Of course. Olivia. Tammy was talking to her last night and she must have let it slip about James and me driving her to Venice. Olivia panicked and sent in the cavalry. Is any of this actually what Ethan wants?

"Before you start over-analyzing everything, this wasn't just my mother's doing. Yes, she played a part, but this was my idea." He lifts the ring box, shaking it a little. "This is what I want," he says, turning so that I can read every emotion that plays across his face.

I narrow my eyes and try to decipher what's real and what's a show, and realize I'll never know. In fact, I've never been able to tell with Ethan. The veneers were always a part of our relationship, and at the time I could handle the show. I preferred it. With all of the smoke and mirrors it was easier to hide my own wreckage—pretend it didn't exist and jump right into the role.

"It's not what I want," I tell him. "Not anymore."

He shakes his head slowly, studies me like he's never seen me before. And maybe he hasn't.

"That's ridiculous, Ava. How could a few weeks change years of history and commitment?" he asks.

It's a damn good question. A question that I'm not even sure I can fully answer. But I know without a doubt that it has changed. I have changed. Fundamentally.

"I don't know," I whisper, watching a gondola row by with a couple snuggled together in the passenger cabin. The sight of it makes my chest ache, because I know exactly where I want to be and with who. "Something in me—shifted. I'm different now. I—"

"You met someone," he says. His tone is matter-of-fact, but I can see around his eyes that there's anger. Pain. Maybe regret?

Something more than the stoic grace and easy composure he usually wears.

I nod.

But that sentence isn't enough. I've met someone, yes. I've met a whole family of someones. A whole village of someones. All of them slowly filling that space in my heart I thought would forever be vacant, like beautiful street art on a condemned building. James is so much more than that. He's not just filling space—he's adding space—knocking down walls and stretching my heart in ways I didn't think possible.

"Ava, this is crazy. You've known him for a month and you are willing to let us go?"

I nod.

"It's not just him," I say softly. But I don't go on. There's no way to make him understand and I don't owe him the attempt.

Ethan reaches for me and stops, his hand hovering midway between us like he's suddenly remembered I'm not his to touch.

"If I hadn't given you that calling card . . ."

His voice trails off. I take the hand that's still hovering between us and wind my fingers in his.

"I'm grateful that you did," I say.

If he hadn't, I might never have woken up. I would have stayed on that stage for the rest of my life, always wondering what it would be like to cut the strings and step down into the audience.

He shakes his head and looks out over the canal.

"I've got to go," I tell him and he reaches out and pulls me into his chest.

He holds me there as the sound of the water laps gently against the stone, and when he lets me go—this time it's for good.

QUARANTACINQUE

James

I've wanted impossible things before. As a boy, I wanted my mother and father to show up for the second grade art show that I'd won. That blue ribbon dangled from the bottom of my watercolor savanna on Nonna's fridge until the day she passed, but neither of my parents ever saw it.

I've wanted to chase the dream of photography as far as it could go, see my pictures on the walls of galleries or on the glossy covers of magazines, see my work elicit emotion. But unlike my second grade self, as an adult, reason has always kept me grounded enough to let that want stay locked in its cabinet where it can't hurt anyone.

But Ava and this impossible technicolor future I can't stop envisioning with her—no amount of reason is squashing that. It's too bold and bright. It's blinding.

The lights from the lanterns alongside the windows of the buildings that flank the tiny canal flicker and sway in the wake of an out-of-sight boat. I lean over the stone balustrade of the tiny bridge. Nearby, our apartment sits empty and waiting for the night I had planned that will never come to be. I can't go back there yet. The ornately decorated space was so perfect with her in it, asking me to kiss her. But now it will only feel garish and wasted.

How could I have possibly misunderstood the situation between us this badly? She was so clear about what she wanted from life—her plan. The success, the fiancé, the status. But somewhere along the line it had changed. She had softened, like frozen cookies in their fifth minute in the oven. Or maybe that was me. Maybe I projected all of it onto her.

The water beneath me is so dark it looks like an oil slick. The boats are all tucked against their buildings, ropes anchoring them in place as they knock against the stone. Clicking and clacking more rapidly now though no wake pushes—

"James!"

Ava appears from the shadows like she's been teleported. The only evidence that she hasn't is her heavy breathing and the way she puts both hands on the stone balustrade of the bridge as she catches her breath.

"Why—where did you—" She rests her forehead on her arm.

She's flushed and her skin glistens along the back of her neck. I look back out toward the water, avoiding every beautiful detail of the woman I'll never have.

"Why did you leave?" she asks, pulling herself upright.

"I think the answer to that is pretty obvious."

"Clearly it's not or I wouldn't be asking," she says, pulling my arm off the stone so that I'm forced to turn and look at her.

She's got her arms crossed beneath her chest, her shoulders puffed up. Peacock Ava.

"You are either seriously overestimating my threshold for torture or grossly underestimating how I feel—"

"James, I said no."

She steps forward, holds up her hand to show me that it's bare, and my mind refuses to believe her. I shake my head.

"Of course I said no," she repeats in a whisper, reaching out and putting her hand in mine.

"But your plans—"

"Changed," she interrupts. "They changed the moment some asshole picked me up an hour late at the airport."

"You said no." My voice sounds like I've been hypnotized.

She nods up at me with a small smile playing at the edge of her mouth.

She said no.

I pull her into me, lifting her chin so I can kiss her. This kiss is deeper—more frantic than before—filled with the fear of what could have been and the jealousy I felt watching that man nearly take her away to a life without me. She lets out a soft moan into my mouth and I pull back and stare down at her. She's as out of breath as when she arrived after sprinting through the alleys.

"Take me home, please," she says.

"Gladly," I tell her.

Then I lead the way over the bridge, through the darkness of the alley, back toward the apartment, my fingers laced so tightly through hers that nothing could force me to let go.

QUARANTASEI

Ava

I want to crawl into this kiss and start a new life. All of the anger and hurt that I saw on the bridge has given way to the demanding pressure of his lips on mine as we take and give, give and take. I'm so wrapped up in the sensation of his tongue that when I come up for air, I can't help but giggle at the fact that we've somehow made it from the foyer to the settee, James pinned beneath me while I straddle his lap, the bottom of my dress scrunched up around my hips so that nothing separates James from me but a layer of lace and his jeans.

"Something funny?" he says into my neck as he presses kisses down toward my clavicle. When his teeth graze softly against my collarbone I curse and press down against him and he lets out the most delicious sound in response.

"Dolcezza," he whispers and I pull his mouth back up to mine, graze my tongue against his lower lip. I want to taste the Italian, and he seems to sense that because he continues to say something against my mouth, all dipping vowels and rolling Rs.

"Posso toccarti?" he says softly.

I have no idea what the hell he's asking, but his hands are at my hips holding me steady so that I can't grind against him, so I answer the only way I can.

"Yes. Sì. Do whatever the hell you—"

His fingers slip beneath the lace between us and I've forgotten what I was saying. His hand—*Dio*—his hand. Who knew a hand could do this to a person—send so much pressure and pleasure through them that they might tear at the seams. But then somehow, impossibly, it gets better, and his fingers stop stroking and find a place inside of me that screams *Thank you* at the top of its lungs, and he curses on a breath as I clench around him. He works me slowly, pushing me closer and closer to the edge, one hand cupping my hip—moving me against his palm while his fingers circle deep inside, coaxing me toward release. And I'm there already—as if my body's been waiting for weeks for this.

"Let go, Ava," he whispers, then something in Italian, and his voice in my ear lights the fuse and everything explodes. The dam bursts and I'm flooded, every piece of me drenched in warmth, wave after wave of pleasure. When the last tingles float away in the tide, my limbs feel heavy and useless, and James slides his hand away from me and keeps me upright by the hips. The intensity in his gaze makes me want to give him everything I just felt and more.

He kisses me softly and whispers, "That was the most beautiful thing I've ever seen in my life."

Impossibly, the sound of his voice stokes an ember I didn't even know was still lit inside of me. I slide against him, and a new flame erupts when I feel how hard he is beneath me. He curses, and his fingers dig into my hips, and then he lifts the dress over my head slowly, taking me in like he did back in Urbino, like we've got all the time in the world. His mouth finds mine, and I barely register the fact that he's lifting me—carrying me through the darkness to—I don't care where because the taste of him, the softness of his lips and the firmness of his body—I can't think past it.

I don't unwrap my legs from around his back as he lays me on the bed. The light from the lanterns along the canal reach through the window and fall over my body, and he tries to move away to admire me, but I lock my ankles.

"You can take your mental photographs later," I say, reaching into his hair and pulling him down over me.

The vibration of his laugh makes me squirm beneath him, and I arch my hips to get closer, which immediately makes him stop laughing.

"I need you to have less clothes," I tell him.

"You need to unhook your ankles then."

I don't want to. Then there will be space between us. I hate space. I can see his brow lift in amusement as I weigh my options. And when I finally let my legs fall on either side of him, he pushes back, but I go with him, my hands at his waist making quick work of the buttons and zipper on his pants. He runs his finger along my jaw and I pull my gaze up to his.

No one has ever looked at me the way James is looking at me right now. The last time we shared this look, I wasn't ready and he ended up walking away. But now I want nothing more than for him to look at me like this—like I'm oxygen and desert, sunlight and art—everything he needs and wants in this world.

He lifts his shirt over his head and steps out of his pants and underwear.

"Jeezzz-us," I say and he laughs. When I start to trace the lines between his abs, he shuts his eyes like he did earlier today, and I let my fingers explore, lower and lower until they land where I want them and he lets out a sharp breath. I need him to make more sounds. I need to watch him get off like he watched me, but when he finds me looking up at him while I stroke, all of the sweetness from a moment before disappears and his eyes darken to the color of the canal outside the window.

His mouth crashes onto mine, and his hands are everywhere, and my body is just one giant ball of aching need as I move against him.

"Please, James. Please," I beg.

"Please what, Ava?" He's slipped the lace of my bra under my breasts and his tongue is doing wickedly amazing things; every tug on my nipple sends a shock down to my core.

When his mouth and body leave me so he can reach into the pocket of his discarded jeans, I can barely stand his absence.

"James."

The sound of a foil being ripped. He's taking too long.

"Yes, dolcezza?"

He returns to me, condom in place, and I whisper in his ear, "I need you," then take him in my hand between us as he slips the last bit of lace down over my legs. "Please."

And with that last plea he pushes into me, and everything I'd been imagining eviscerates into the ether because this—the way he feels inside of me—this is beyond anything I could have dreamed of. He's slow at first, his eyes on mine, assessing, gauging every reaction on my face as he stretches me, our bodies moving together in this exquisite rhythm that makes the dueling pianos from tonight look like amateurs. He gives me one long, lingering kiss and the touch of his tongue on mine erases my self-control. I hook my ankles around his ass, pulling him deeper, and he groans. He wants what I want. Our pace picks up—both of us climbing the same mountain—both of us wanting nothing more than to reach the top and spill over the other side.

My hands tangle in his hair, rake down his back, pull him deeper and closer as he says my name so reverently I forget it's just a name. I beg and plead and he answers—every touch a gift as everything tightens and coils, and then he's telling me again to let go and I listen. I'll do anything he says. When his lips find mine again, my release shatters me into pieces so small they might blow away with the breeze coming through the open windows from the canal. I cry out into his mouth, and the sound pulls him down with me, the pulsing of his orgasm riding the tide of warm heat that courses through me, pulling and stretching the pleasure like taffy until we are both wrung completely and deliciously dry.

Our breathing mingles in the dark—our chests still pressed together—hearts so close I can feel his beating into mine. He turns onto his side, runs his hand down my stomach.

"You have five minutes to rest," he says, and a hysterical giggle bubbles out of me as I watch his gorgeous ass head to the bathroom.

When he returns, I turn on my side and look up at him. His eyes look dark and serious—just like they did when he pushed—

"Zero minutes if you keep biting your lip like that," he says.

I push myself up onto my knees on the mattress while he stands in front of me.

"I'm ready when you are," I say, with a soft smile.

And he doesn't answer. Just lowers his mouth over mine because he's ready too.

QUARANTASETTE

James

The sun seems to be coming at me from every angle. Even with the pillow over my face, the room is unnaturally bright. Neither of us left the bed long enough to shut the heavy velvet curtains last night. And when I roll over and put my hand out to find Ava's smooth, soft skin beside me, I come up empty-handed.

I lower the pillow from my face and turn, squinting as I search the mounds of soft comforter for her perfect body—a body that I now know I will never get my fill of. There was a time where I thought maybe cutting through the tension would alleviate some of this nagging desire for her, but if anything, having her last night has only aggravated the situation. Knowing that satisfaction—the way she feels beneath me, the sounds she makes when I touch her just right—all of it has just piled up above me and buried me alive.

The sound of Ava cursing in the kitchen reaches me before I have a chance to spiral into my thoughts. I push myself up, my legs pleasantly sore beneath me as I step into the pair of sweats at the foot of the bed, then head for the noise.

She's wearing my gray T-shirt, the hem hitting her mid-thigh on her bare legs as she attempts to flip what looks like the world's most pathetic pancake. I lean against the doorjamb and watch.

The kidney-shaped, drippy pseudo-pancake slips from the spatula onto the floor at her feet.

"Motherf—"

"This is why we don't do pancakes in Italy," I laugh, taking the spatula from her hand before she smacks something with it.

She looks up at me and I pull her around the dead pancake and into my arms.

"I wanted to make you an American breakfast," she says.

"Isn't that what I had earlier when we—"

She pinches my side and pretends to be scandalized. I smile down at her and let my hands wander down her back.

"There's a bakery five doors down with brioche that melts on your tongue," I tell her.

She looks over her shoulder at the mess she's made and grimaces.

"I'll clean up while you get ready," I offer, and she squeezes me so tight my laugh comes out like a wheeze.

"Give me ten," she says, slipping out of my arms, then stopping in the doorframe and turning back toward me. "James?"

"Ava?"

She rocks back on her bare heels and up onto her toes, then fidgets with the hem of her shirt.

"Would you mind—coming with me—I found my mom's—Professor Genaro—and I know this wasn't part of the plan, but—"

"I thought we got rid of the plan," I say. "Besides, I looked up his address the night you asked me to bring you to Venice." I look down at the pancake smear, then back up at her. "I'd love to come with you."

The way she's looking at me makes my chest hurt.

"You are too amazing," she whispers, and her eyes are glassy now. I want to spend my life making her look at me like this.

"Get dressed." My voice comes out thick, and I distract myself with the fallen pancake, but I can see Ava lingering at the door in my periphery.

When the soft padding of her feet on the tile reaches me, I sit back on my haunches and let out a breath. It's getting difficult not to blurt out everything I want when she's in the room—to yell from the terrazzo how I feel about this woman—but the floor around us is covered with more than just fallen pancakes. The eggshells we are tiptoeing around are sharp as knives and I know I'll bleed out if I step on one and find out she's not there with me.

I hear the shower turn on and Ava starts singing the song she heard the gondolier belting out on our way into Cannaregio. Her Italian is still shit, but I can't help the slow smile that creeps across my face.

I stand, abandon the pancake, and head for the shower, while the sound of a thousand eggshells crunching echoes through my skull.

QUARANTOTTO

Ava

I'm more nervous than I was for my fourth grade solo when I had to dress as Pumba and sing "Can You Feel the Love Tonight" in a gym filled with parents and peers. I'm about to meet my mother's lover—a man she hid from me for my entire life, never bothering to mention that during her beloved study abroad experience she had a torrid affair with her handsome professor.

Is this why she went back to America? Did he break her heart and send her packing back to the States? Or was it worse? Oh my God! Was she pregnant with his love child? Am I an Italian love child!?

I do some quick math and debunk that theory, and James squeezes my hand tighter.

"You alright?" he asks.

I nod but keep my eyes on the giant wooden door before me.

"Are you going to ring the bell or would you like me to?"

Good question. My arms seem to be frozen by my sides.

"Can you do it, please?"

He reaches out and presses the buzzer. The longest minute of my life passes before a raspy male voice comes on and says, "Pronto."

Then James takes over in Italian, and the only thing I understand is my mother's name and the sound of us being buzzed into the building immediately after.

"Ready?" James asks, pushing the heavy medieval door inward.

"No," I say brushing past him.

I'm not too nervous to notice the way he stiffens when my hip touches his thigh as I pass. Nor to feel the flood of warmth that pools when he puts his hand on my lower back to guide me up the marble steps. Those hands—the things they can—

"Ava, if you keep looking at me like that, we're gonna need to go back to the apartment. Stat."

Ooops.

"Sorry not sorry," I tell him with a smile and then focus on getting up these steps without jumping him.

"Fourth floor," he tells me, and all I can do is breathe because there's no oxygen in the stairwell and I'm only hitting the second floor landing.

By the time we hit the final flight, I'm sucking in air like a Dyson and the shower I took (that was happily interrupted by James) is null and void. The man standing at the open door when we arrive on the landing takes away whatever breath I have left in my lungs. Salt-and-pepper waves brush against his broad shoulders, and his jaw is chiseled from the same marble this godforsaken staircase was built with. This man makes Clooney look like the boy next door.

Well played, Mom.

I accidently let out a whoosh of air that sounds like a whistle, and James clears his throat beside me.

"Mio Dio," the man says, stepping forward. "You look just like her. Ava . . ."

He trails off and wraps his arms around me, and I'm unsure how he knows my name or if this hug is for me or my mother, but it feels nice—like I'm somehow being touched by a piece of her. A secret hidden piece of her, but I'll take it.

"I'm Alessandro," he says into my hair. Then lets me go slowly and gestures toward the open door. "Come in. Come in." He holds his hand out to James to introduce himself while I step over the threshold and into a dream.

The walls are filled with art. And I mean filled. Oil paintings. Watercolors. Photographs. Canvases leaning against walls, hanging from hooks, and at least a quarter of them are the familiar strokes of the reason that I'm here.

"Are you okay?" James asks from behind me, somehow sensing that my head is spinning.

I nod absently and step toward an unfinished oil painting of St. Mark's Square at night. It radiates light, pulls me forward into the piazza. I can hear the melodies of the piano floating around me.

It's beautiful. And it's my mother's work.

"She stood in San Marco's every night for five weeks, trying to perfect that," Professor Genaro says from beside me. "The man who used to own the bar at the east corner would bring her food and drinks like she was a stray dog. He adored her. I used to joke that he might destroy the painting to keep her there in that spot."

I look away from the candles and up to find him staring down at me, his eyes filled with so much grief that the walls of my chest start to cave in.

"Mi dispiace, it's just—the resemblance is unreal," he whispers. "Why don't you sit? Would you like a drink? Something to eat?"

I must have responded because he hurries off into the kitchen. James puts both hands on my shoulders and squeezes, letting me know he's here as he guides me to the deep leather sofa at the center of the room.

"We can leave," he whispers, but I shake my head.

We can't leave. I need answers. It was obvious that my mother was on fire while she was here—the sheer volume of work she produced just in this room alone is staggering. Then why leave? What could possibly tear you away from the man you love and the place that inspires you enough to paint like this?

"I wish I had known you were in town, Ava. I would have prepared a real meal for you," Alessandro says, laying a tray of meats and cheeses that Uvaldi would approve of on the coffee table in front of us. "Per favore, mangia. I will get the drinks." He disappears and reappears, handing James and me each a glass of sparkling something before finally settling into the armchair across from us. But settling is the wrong word. There's nothing settled about him right now, and it suddenly occurs to me that Professor Genaro might be as nervous to meet me as I am to meet him.

"She painted all of this here?" I ask, gesturing to the work around me.

He nods as he takes a sip.

"She loved Venice almost as much as she loved Urbino. She said the water made it easy to paint. The colors and the reflections . . ."

He looks out the window toward the Grand Canal, giving me a chance to study his well-formed profile. James's hand reaches out and covers mine.

"Then why did she leave?"

The question comes out in a burst, and the silence that follows it fills me with something like regret. Maybe this was a mistake.

Maybe I wasn't meant to know these things. Maybe the past should stay in the past.

Alessandro turns back to me, and I can see his age in his eyes—not in the physical way, but in the haunted way of those who have experienced great loss or pain. Do my eyes look like that?

"I'm sorry," I say. "We don't have to—I know it must have been very painful for you—watching your lover leave." I choke a little on the words, suddenly thinking of James.

"My lover?" Alessandro asks. He narrows his cool blue eyes on me just as the door to the apartment flies open behind me and in storms a very handsome, very pissed-off blonde man with a basket of fresh fish.

"Sei venti minuti in ritardo, Alesso. Pensi che—"

His eyes fall on James and me, and the anger fades into a warm smile.

"David, this is Ava and James. Ava is—"

"Anna's daughter," David finishes, and his eyes immediately light up, then fill with tears as he places the fish basket on the counter and makes his way around the couch and folds me in his arms.

"I'm sorry if I smell of fish," he whispers into my hair. "It is so nice to meet you, Ava."

Fish or no fish, I melt into the hug.

"Let me put the fish away and get cleaned up," David says, releasing me and straightening, then pointing at Alessandro. "You are still on my shit list so don't think you aren't." He tosses me a smile then grabs the basket of fish and disappears into the kitchen, murmuring something about waiting for twenty minutes.

"David is my husband," Alessandro says to me, though I've already pieced that together from their rings and the photos I'd missed while distracted by my mother's art. "Your mother introduced us."

I lean into James as he puts his arm around my shoulder, somehow sensing that I need steadying.

"What you asked earlier—about why she left—" Alessandro looks down into his drink, then back up at me and lets out a breath. "Your mother left Italy because she had just found out she had cancer, Ava."

Impossible. I shake my head. My mother found out she had cancer five weeks before my twenty-first birthday. Not when she was young and carefree with her whole life ahead of her.

"That can't be," I say softly, but I can tell by the look on Alessandro's face that it can be. That it is.

"It started with a simple pain in her lower back. She blamed painting. But then she could no longer ignore it, and I took her to my physician. Fortunamente, it was early," he says. "She left for home two days after she received the news."

My eyes return to her unfinished painting of St. Mark's Square as my heart falls into my stomach.

Just like that, the buoyant pieces of wood that keep my memories afloat crack down the center, dumping the mirage of my childhood into the deep, murky water that lies beneath.

QUARANTANOVE

James

The moment we reach the alley that runs in front of Alessandro and David's apartment, she drops her armor, pacing the edge of the canal back and forth like the pendulum in Nina's grandfather clock. She was able to hold this back the entire hour we spent with Alessandro and David, but now she's unleashing that frantic energy with a vengeance.

"How could they keep that from me? She knew. *They* knew that there was a chance of it coming back and they never told me. They could have prepared me. Instead of my world falling off the edge of a cliff. A cliff they knew was there!"

She's not speaking to me. She's flinging her pain out into the sky, and I know better than to voice anything that's in my head.

They were trying to protect her—like good parents. Why would they want her to live in fear alongside them? To go to sleep every night with the thought that her mother could at any moment have something toxic and deadly inside of her. But I get it. She's hurt. Angry and hurt.

"They lied. My whole life. They lied."

To protect you.

She stops and stares at me, her eyes so narrow I can barely make out the green. Did I say that aloud?

"Protect me? From what, James? She died. How could they protect me from that?"

I put my hands up in immediate surrender.

"I'm sorry. I didn't mean to say that," I tell her.

"But you did say it. So you must believe it. And I get what you're saying. I do. But I was twenty. That's old enough to know. Old enough to be warned. I mean, she made me get my genome mapped for cancer genes! Said it ran in the family . . ."

She trails off and looks out over the water, hugging herself like she might crumble into the canal.

"If I had known, maybe I could have convinced her to take better care of herself—to see a better oncologist—anything," she whispers as the tears let loose.

I wrap my arms around her and hold her steady as she sobs.

"You did everything you could. You were there, Ava. Every day," I say into her hair. And she was. She gave up nearly two years of her life to be there—a sacrifice that no one should have to make that young. "That's what matters. You were there."

She leans back and looks up at me, her face open and raw. Four weeks ago I could barely see past the walls she put up between us. Now her pain runs through her and directly into my chest.

I run my thumb along her cheekbone.

"Can we go home?" she asks.

I nod. "Of course. I'll get us a boat back to the apartment—"

"I mean to Urbino," she says.

I bite back the smile that tugs at the corners of my mouth. Home? She called Urbino home.

"Yeah, we can," I tell her, reminding myself it's just a word.

Home.

I offer her my elbow and she slips her arm in mine as I lead her toward the vaporetto dock.

"Thank you for going with me," she says, leaning her head on my arm.

"Of course," I tell her. "Anything."

That word glides across the water around the dock and gets lost beneath the purr of the approaching boat's motor. Ava looks up at me like she wants to say something, but then her lips press together and the boat knocks into the dock, forcing her to look away, grabbing the pole to her right for balance. She holds my hand tightly as we step aboard the vaporetto and squeeze between the people bunched together on deck, the words she might have said blowing out to sea with the salty spray that kicks up around us as we push away from land.

CINQUANTA

Ava

Being back in Nina's kitchen is nearly as soothing as the sound of her and Leo's chatter streaming in through the open window. Venice was amazing—and my time with James in Venice even more so, but I needed out. After Alessandro and David, everything around me became less magical surrealism and more dismal melancholia, like the tide had shifted and dragged in all of the terrible memories of her battle along with my mom's secret.

The smell of the marinara bubbling around my spoon as I stir wafts up into my nostrils and tempts me to taste, but the risk of getting caught with my fingers in Nina's sauce keeps me upright, stirring slowly and methodically while trying not to eavesdrop on the conversation that they are doing nothing to hide from me.

"You will tell him he's here, no?" Nina says, hands flying in a way that if you stepped up behind her she might accidentally knock you out.

"I do not know," Leo says.

"What do you mean you do not know? He needs to be prepared for this—"

"Sì. Sì. Lo so. Ma forse, if he does not know . . ."

I move the blowing curtain to the side and watch Leo's bushy brows lift up into his hairline. What are these two up to?

"That is an ambush!" Nina says breathlessly. "He will not be happy if he knows you knew—"

My hand slips on the spoon and my wrist brushes against the lip of the pot.

"Shit!" I yell, pulling back from the heat.

Nina is inside within a breath, pulling me toward the sink, murmuring in Italian as she holds the burn under the cool running water.

"Are you okay, cara?" she asks me, surveying the angry red mark on the inside of my wrist.

"I'm fine. I swear." I shut off the faucet and head back to the marinara, but she guides me away.

"I will take care of the sauce. Go wake James for dinner," she tells me. "There is burn cream in the medicine cabinet in the upstairs bathroom."

I nod and head up the stone stairs, staring at the pictures of young James and baby Maso. Baptism pictures of Maso with a full head of black hair, James standing beside his aunt as she holds him out to the priest. James in a blue suit with a crown of laurel leaves around his head, a tradition for graduation from the University of Urbino. The hallway is a family shrine—every picture filled with love and happiness.

"Are you crying?"

I turn to find James leaning against the wooden doorjamb of the bathroom in nothing but a white towel wrapped around his waist.

"No. I was cutting onions in the kitchen," I lie.

"Tammy called again while I was asleep," he tells me and I wave him off.

I'm not upset with her. I know that she told Olivia about Venice, setting off the emergency protocol for Ethan's proposal. That's why she was acting like such a spaz for our final hours together in the car. And I know she supports my happiness more than any family agenda. But the real reason I'm avoiding that call is because of everything that has happened in the past two days. I'm not ready to answer questions about James—or my mom for that matter. Not ready to lay it all out and dissect it the way Tammy will want to do.

James adjusts his towel then smiles, and between the memories of the last shower we took together and the sight of him half naked, I forget what the hell I'm even doing up here in the hallway.

Oh right. Wake-up call.

"I'm here to wake you up," I tell him and he nods, but doesn't move. "And to get some burn cream—"

"Are you okay?" He's immediately hovering over me, inspecting me for damage. I hold out my wrist.

"It's nothing. My wrist hit the pot," I explain, but he's already turned away and is rummaging through the medicine cabinet like I've lost a limb.

"Your aunt and uncle are up to something," I tell him as he searches.

"When are they not up to something?" he murmurs, then turns and holds out his hand for me to give him my wrist.

"They were speaking loudly and in English about a man being here and whether or not to tell you. I assume they want me to tell you, hence the volume and the English," I say.

James is hyper-focused on rubbing the burn cream on the tiny red welt on my wrist.

"Does that hurt?" he asks.

I shake my head and he looks up from my burn and straightens, pulling me slowly to where he's leaning against the sink. My free hand finds a droplet of water that must have dripped from his hair and I trace it down over his chest toward his navel.

"Is the cream helping?" he asks.

"Mmhmmm."

I can't feel anything but his hands on my hips as he pulls me to him. I look away from the water droplet and up into his eyes, and my entire body turns to liquid. He lowers his mouth to mine, but just before his lips find mine he freezes.

"Non fermate. It was just getting good, no?"

I turn to see Maso leaning against the hallway wall, a picture of him in a white suit in church above his head.

"Maso, you little perv—"

"Better me than papà, who is on his way up now," Maso says with that painfully wide grin as he skips down the hallway toward the stairs.

I step away from half-naked James and hurry out of the bathroom. The only thing worse than voyeur Maso would be the dean of students crashing our little bathroom party.

"Ava," James says, grabbing my good wrist.

I smile, but make sure to stay outside in the hallway, as if the threshold makes it more acceptable to be ogling his goodies.

"Can we talk later? After dinner?" he asks.

And my stomach drops an inch or five.

Talk? We talk all the time. Of course we can talk.

But I know this one will be different. This is "the talk." I'm not ready.

"Yeah. Of course," I tell him, trying to give him my best reassuring smile.

He leans down and kisses my forehead just as Leo's booming voice can be heard from somewhere downstairs. James throws me one last smile and then shuts the door between us, and I hightail it back downstairs where I might get burned, but at least I'm safe.

CINQUANTUNO

James

All through dinner I can't help but notice how natural it is to have Ava at our table. She helps Nina in the kitchen without being directed, like they've been running a restaurant for years. She challenges Leo like she's his daughter. And she can silence Maso with just the lift of a single eyebrow. Not that it hasn't been this way before tonight, but now with her hand on mine as she laughs at Nina's story about the time I brought home a wild horse when I was fifteen, it has never been more obvious that Ava belongs here with me. With us.

I take another sip of wine to try to clear this terrifyingly dangerous train of thought before it derails me completely. Does she feel it too? This sense of rightness? She runs her thumb up the side of mine and then stands to clear the plates for dessert, and I follow suit.

"Do you really want to help or are you trying to have another make-out session in the kitchen?" she whispers over her shoulder as she steps over Verga. He sees the plates in her hands and immediately gets up and follows after us. He knows the drill.

"Both," I tell her.

She lays the plates down on the floor and Verga gets to work.

"Well, judging from the smell, we have about a minute and a half until Nina is in here fussing over the cakes, so—"

I absorb the rest of her words with my lips and she makes the soft little moan that I've come to love. When I pull back, she's flushed, out of breath, and the smell of warm chocolate is the only thing keeping me from dragging her out to the guest house and getting her to make that sound again.

"Le torte sono pronte, Gi!" Nina yells, and I smile down at Ava.

"Told ya," she sings just as Verga lifts his head and starts bellowing like a fire alarm. He takes off, stepping on the plates and sending them clattering against each other.

I watch him barrel out of the kitchen and through the door, barking like crazy as he goes. Even my whistle doesn't stop him as I follow him back out into the night, leaving Ava to handle the cakes.

By the time I make it off the porch, the barking has stopped and Verga is lying on his back in front of a gentleman in a three-piece suit with well-groomed silver facial hair, who is crouched over scratching the dog's belly. Both Nina and Leo are up and fussing, making apologies for the dog, though that's obviously unnecessary because the stranger is clearly enamored with him.

He looks up and sees me and straightens out of the crouch.

"You must be James," he says, and the British accent touches my brain and rings the bell. I've seen this man before—on a Google search—but still I can tell it's him from the hours of stalking I did when I was young and naïve.

"And you must be Greer Davenport," I say, taking a step forward and holding out my hand.

So this is what Leo and Nina were up to. He shakes my hand and smiles, the shadow of an apology at the corners of his mouth.

"Torta time!" Ava sings from behind me, and I turn to find her holding a tray of chocolate lava cakes aloft. She catches sight of Greer and smiles.

"Ava, this is Greer Davenport," I tell her, and she shifts the tray and puts out her hand for shaking.

"Are you staying for cake?" she asks him, and he shakes his head.

"I actually just need a quick word with James and then I have to meet someone in town," he says, glancing my way. I nod and gesture toward the side of the house.

"It was a pleasure to meet you all," he tells my family, then follows the brick path around the porch toward the back.

"So this was what they were up to," I whisper to Ava before following. She nods, and I can see she wants to ask me something, but she turns away from me and starts putting the plates of cake on the table.

"Good luck, son," Leo murmurs, clapping me on the back as he passes.

I roll my eyes and head for Greer. I'll handle him and Nina later.

When I find him, he's sitting on a chaise beside the pool scratching beneath Verga's ears.

"I'm sorry for dropping in like this, but I figured my emails and voice mails weren't up to snuff," he says watching me approach.

"I appreciate everything you've offered me—I really do—but I'm not willing to relocate," I say.

"I can see why, now." He pushes the chaise beside him out with his foot so I can get between and sit. "There's been a change in the offer. I've spoken to the dean of studies at Cambridge, and he'd like you to come on as an adjunct for a semester teaching—art history, of course—while you shoot for *The Post.*"

I let out a breath. Cambridge? Ava's voice floods my brain. *What if Oxford calls and offers you a position? The most prestigious university in Europe and they want you? What then?*

Greer keeps pushing on. "We'd start with profile pieces and branch out from there. We have some pretty big names in the lineup, James. And your talent with portraiture is exactly what we need. Obviously, you'll be well compensated for your work, and Cambridge will pay your rent."

The buzzing in my ear starts to drown out Greer's pitch as he goes on about social media following and my launch. When he starts to talk about the flat where I'll live, I put my hand up and stop him.

"Mr. Davenport, I'm very grateful for the opportunity you're offering but—"

"Don't answer. Just talk to your family and think about it. I know there's a lot riding on this decision. I'll be in town for three more days," he tells me.

I should shut this down. I don't need three days. I need to say no and move on—clip the wings on this silly hope that's floating around my head.

My family is here.

And you don't leave family.

"I'll think about it," I say, standing.

Greer puts his hand out for me to shake, gives Verga one last scratch beneath both ears, then turns and leaves me beside the pool. I plop back down in the chaise and look up to the stars.

"London is nearly two thousand kilometers and a channel away. It's too far," I whisper to Verga.

He puts his head on my lap and lets out a dramatic sigh.

I picture the stone courtyards of Cambridge—the bustling art galleries of Soho. It's a world far away from the peaceful hills of Le Marche. Far away from the laughter that makes its way around Zia and Zio's villa into the air around me. Far away from the people I love the most in this world.

But that's the thing about dreams and love. They don't give a damn about distance.

CINQUANTADUE

Ava

I'm sitting in front of my computer staring at the blinking cursor when James comes into the guest house through the open doors. I swivel in the desk chair and smile up at him, but his attempt to return it falls about a hundred yards short. He hasn't said a word since Davenport left, just ate his cake in silence, staring down into the melted chocolate center like it held the answers to the universe. Even Nina and Leo laid off him. So I followed suit.

He makes his way behind me and puts his hands on my shoulders, rubbing lightly at the tension there.

"Is that to your dad?" he asks and I look at the subject line and wince: *Why didn't you tell me?*

Tammy's rambling email is open in a separate tab. Her explanation of the conversation with Olivia before Venice is so detailed that she might have hired a freelance editor to give her notes. I'm sure she wants to kill me because my only response was 'I love you. Stop obsessing,' with zero details about the things that happened after I left her.

But Tammy will have to wait, because the lies my parents told me are gnawing away at the edges of my brain like starved rats. James had a point about the secret when I was young—they kept it to protect me—but after that. I just can't wrap my mind around keeping something like that from your daughter while she holds your hand through injections and tests. And even worse, for my dad to hide it after she was gone—well, that seems selfish and unforgivable. Cowardly, even.

I reach out and push the screen of the monitor down against the keyboard without hitting send.

"I can do this later. You ready to tell me about the handsome Brit?" I ask, swiveling around to face him. He shakes his head and sits on the edge of the bed.

"There's nothing to tell, really. Davenport owns *The Post* in London—also has more money than he knows what to do with. He wants me to move there and work exclusively for his publication," he says.

"James, that's amazing!"

But he doesn't seem to think so. Just kind of shrugs and messes with the hem of the comforter.

"Why aren't you excited? You love photography. It's your dream—"

"Was my dream," he interjects, finally making eye contact.

"Was? What does that mean?"

"It means that I'm not in a place to entertain chasing a dream I had a decade ago—"

"Because you're so old?"

He swats my leg and murmurs that I'm a smart-ass.

"I'm just experienced enough to know that I don't want to leave the people I love," he says, holding my gaze.

I stand from the rolling chair and sit beside him on the bed, intertwining my fingers with his. I know there's more to it. The people he loved—the people who were supposed to love him unconditionally—they left. And now he's hell-bent on correcting that wrong.

"And what do the people you love have to say about this?" I ask, knowing full well that Nina and Leo must be pushing him like bulldozers toward this opportunity.

He studies my face for a moment, then reaches across his body and puts a hand on my cheek, then asks softly, "I don't know. What do you have to say about it?"

The words spin around my brain, picking up all of the emotions I've been keeping tucked away like cotton candy spooling on a stick. My view of him suddenly blurs as the tears fill my eyes, and I blink hard to gain some sort of clarity, but nothing is clear.

How will this ever work? I have a life—a future in Philadelphia. A plan that I've been working toward since my mother passed. And I'm supposed to . . . what? Forget all of it? Pass up everything that I've been making vision boards for since 2019?

My tongue is suddenly paralyzed and the silence becomes too heavy to bear.

"James—" I start, but my throat is so dry it hurts to say his name.

Tell him.

My mother's voice makes the first tear fall, but I shoot back at her.

Like you told me everything?

The silence in the guest house begins to swell like a fresh bruise.

"You don't need to say it, Ava. I just want you to know. I'm in love with you—and if I'm being honest, I have been for a while. Maybe since that night in the courtyard—maybe before."

He kisses a tear that has reached my jawline and I shut my eyes.

"I have to go back," I whisper. And when I open my eyes again I know these words—the truth—is ripping through him.

"Do you?"

I nod. "Yeah. I do. Just as much as you need to stay here with your family, I need to go back. And I can't give up my pl—the future that I worked so hard for."

He holds my gaze and I can see in his eyes that he's deep in thought, but he doesn't share.

Neither of us brings up the logical next solution. Long distance. We don't need to. Because long-distance relationships have a light at the end of the tunnel. A goal to work toward. An eventuality of landing in the same country so that you can be together.

That eventuality doesn't exist here.

James looks down at my hand in his and then back into my eyes.

"Then I guess we better make the best of these last few days together." He tries to smile, but the effort's too much.

So I save him the trouble and cover his mouth with mine as he pulls me on top of him and I do everything in my power to show him how I feel without the words that I can't bring myself to say.

CINQUANTATRE

James

I shift the camera so that the lens rests between my left thumb and forefinger. Maso flicks the ball up from his toe to his chest, down to his knee, back up to his head. I snap away, the huge grin he's wearing lighting up the frame as much as the sun hanging directly overhead.

"Lose the camera and come play," he says without pausing his juggling.

"My back's bothering me," I tell him.

He makes a face and kicks the ball my way anyway.

"Did Ava hurt your back?" he asks, the joy in the grin turning to something far more devilish.

I put the camera on the chair next to me and get a toe beneath the ball to flick it back up in the air without answering his pervy question—mostly because he's right—I am sore from Ava. We've only left the bedroom for meals and passeggiata with the family. And I still haven't had enough of her.

Honestly, I don't know if I ever will.

The sting of knowing she doesn't feel the same way reminds me that there are tough days ahead. She doesn't feel the way I feel, which should make it easier to let her go—knowing that the love is one-sided. But it doesn't.

Right now she's in the guest house with my phone and computer, finally calling Tammy back and writing that email to her father. And I'm giving her plenty of space.

Massimo clears his throat and pushes a hand through his curly hair.

"You should focus more on getting your own life than what's going on with mine," I say, floating the ball his way.

He receives the pass effortlessly.

"Not much excitement happening in Urbino, that's why I'm pumped about—"

He meets my gaze as the ball hits off his shoulder and rolls away.

"Pumped about what, Maso?" I ask.

He shakes his head and starts to jog after the ball.

"Niente," he says. "Just some party."

Maso is a lot of things, but a good liar is not one of them. The kid is more transparent than a windshield. They tried to plan a surprise party for my thirtieth and Maso gave it away before they'd even settled on a date.

"Maso—"

He dribbles the ball in the opposite direction toward the field, waving to me over his shoulder. I could run after him, but he's too damn fast. What the hell is he up to?

I head for the barn knowing Nina is in there milking the sheep. If Maso has a secret, Nina will know it. In fact, if anyone in Urbino has a secret, Nina will know it.

The warmth in the barn hits me like a wet, hay-scented towel. The sheep let out a few nervous bleats and stomp, sending up clouds of dust, alerting Nina to my presence. She spares me a glance over her shoulder, not losing any rhythm as she grips and releases Elisabetta's udders.

"Nipote, are you here to help? I just stripped Lu so she's ready," she says, nudging a stool my way. I sit beside her facing the opposite direction, then pull an empty pail beneath Luciana, who watches me suspiciously.

"I'm here because your son is up to something," I tell her, getting to work, matching her rhythm. When I first came here, the two dairy sheep Nina had were my favorite distraction from my anger and grief. We'd sit like this twice a day, once in the morning before school and once in the late afternoon before dinner prep, and at first we barely said a word. Just sat there beside each other, working to bring the sheep relief as the pail filled up with the milk used for the delicious casciotta Nina has perfected over time.

"Certo. Maso is always up to something, no?" she says.

I study the side of her face looking for clues.

"Sì, ma questa è differente. You are up to something too." Luciana lets out a low bleat and I turn my attention to what I'm doing, making sure the pressure isn't too much on the ewe.

"And don't think you're off the hook about Davenport. I know you knew he was stopping by."

She turns down her lips and shrugs a little.

"I don't make a habit of turning down guests, Gi. Specialmente, ones who recognize my nipote for the genius that he is," she says, then stops her milking and gives the ewe a pat on the side before standing with the pail of milk and heading off to the temperature-controlled room to mix it with the cow milk and let it coagulate.

"I'm not leaving home, Zia," I say to her back, and her shoulders lift into another shrug.

"We will see, Gi," she calls back to me. "Forse, you should find your uncle and speak to him."

The door shuts behind her and I'm left dreading the conversation with Zio, staring up the wrong end of a sheep. Isn't it enough that the woman I love—who does not love me—is leaving for the other side of the world? Now we need to add on some sort of treacherous scheming from my family?

I focus on the sound of the milk hitting the pail and let it partially drown out the bellowing thoughts and fears about Davenport, Ava, and my devious family.

CINQUANTAQUATTRO

Ava

Tammy's voice fills my ear after the first ring.

"Finally," she breathes, the relief so tangible it makes my own chest relax.

"I just needed a minute," I tell her. So much has happened since we dropped her at the airport, and I'm still reeling from it all. If James weren't there to ground me every time another chunk of my heart crumbled at the thought of my parents' lies, then I'd probably have gotten on a plane to confront my father and my rage by now.

But he has been there. Steady and real.

"I bet you did. How are you?" she asks.

"I'm a mess. But also I'm happy. If that makes sense."

She makes a thinking noise and I can hear her mother saying something softly in the background.

"Did you and James—"

"Yes." I whisper it as if that might stop Olivia from finding out. Letting go of Ethan has been much less difficult than handling the idea of losing his mother and sister as parts of my life. Possibly because I think I started to let go of him the moment I met James. But I do hope that he's okay. I want him to be happy.

"Ava, I'm so sorry. I was talking to Mom, and I honestly didn't even think about what I was sharing. I'm so used to you telling her everything that I forgot for a moment I even had a brother—"

"Tammy, stop." I hear her let out a whoosh of breath. "I'm not even remotely upset with you. It had to happen."

If anything, the entire Venice situation forced me to face the truth. But I would have liked to face it without humiliating Ethan.

"How's Ethan?" I ask.

"He's okay. But I want to hear about you. Tell me about what's going on over there. When do you come home?"

I look to James's open MacBook where I have my flight info up, ready to postpone again. I'm getting killed with fees, but every time I think of leaving James and Urbino my entire body aches, so I'll pay anything not to have to face the pain that will actually hit when I step through customs and back into my life.

"Right now my flight's Thursday, but I'm thinking of pushing it to Sunday," I say, plopping back onto the comforter and looking up at the exposed beam that was built by the hands I love.

"Why not just push it back until the weekend before you start, Aves? Don't you think you should give this thing between you all of the time that you can?"

I hate it when she says smart shit.

"The longer I stay here, the harder this is going to be."

The body ache starts again. An image of me clinging to James's leg like a barnacle flashes before my eyes.

She sighs. "I think it's going to be hard no matter what you do at this point. You fell in love. It's impossible to walk away from that."

I fell in love.

It sounds so simple. Like finding a penny in the street.

"Speaking of lovers, did you find your mom's?" she asks.

My turn to sigh.

"They weren't lovers. But it turns out my mom was sick—"

"No."

"Yeah. That's why she came home. She had cancer." I can barely get the last three words out. I've said them so many times. To so many people. But it's different when I'm talking about my twenty-three-year-old mother and not my forty-eight-year-old mother.

"Jesus, Ava. I'm so sorry. Did you talk to your dad?" she asks.

I shake my head like she can see me.

"I think you should," she whispers.

I let out a long breath.

"I'm not ready to have that conversation. I'd rather focus on enjoying what I have left," I tell her, ignoring the stab to the ribs that comes with the awful countdown.

There's a ping from James's MacBook, where my email inbox sits in a rectangle on the screen. Bolded in black, the subject line of the fresh email that appeared from one of the partners at my future firm reads: **URGENT ACTION REQUIRED. OFFER UPDATE.**

I register that Tammy is talking to me about my father, but my brain can only just barely process the words of the email that now fills the screen.

Dear Ava,

The firm has taken on a high-profile case that will require the entire staff to do their part. We'd like to offer you a per diem bonus to begin Thursday, August 14th.

Oh shit, that's in two days.

The compensation will be $2,000 a day until your previous start date of September 15th when your previously negotiated salary will take precedence.

That's one month of rent. In a single day.

We look forward to your response.

Respectfully,
Serena Steinfeld
Senior Partner

"Ava?" Tammy's voice joins in with the words that I'm rereading over and over while dread and excitement play thumb-war inside my skull.

"The firm wants me to start early, T," I manage.

Silence.

Two days? That's not enough time. I look out the window at the hills, golden beneath the low hanging sun.

But this is what I worked for. This is the plan.

"How early?" Tammy asks.

I press the reply button and start typing out a response.

"Two days," I say, answering Tammy and reminding myself of the reality of the offer.

"That's not enough time," she says.

And it's suddenly very clear that, even if I stayed until September 15th, it will never be enough time.

CINQUANTACINQUE

James

Leo is missing in action.

I walked to campus to see if he was working on course designs for the spring semester like Nina said, but his secretary, Julia, informed me he has not been in the office since yesterday. I could check il museo. He's been hanging around there more than usual. Or check in with Franco. He might be holed up in the cellar taste-testing the Tuesday shipment. But I'd rather find Ava.

We've been ignoring the whole unrequited love thing and focusing on the good parts as much as we can without giving too much attention to the mobile of issues spinning over us. But today, Ava needed to check in with reality—call Tammy, reach out to her dad, check in with her new boss. And hopefully, push her flight back to next week.

Verga is sitting on a chaise lounge beside the pool with his muzzle atop his crossed paws. He doesn't even bother to lift his head as I pass, sparing his ear a scratch when I catch sight of Ava coming out of the barn in the distance. Even from a hundred yards away, the smile she's wearing catches in the sunlight and blinds me.

"I milked a goat!" she yells up the hill, her arms up in the air like she's finished a marathon.

"Sheep—" I begin to correct her, but think better of it and go with, "That's amazing."

Nina appears behind her in the doorway.

"Una naturale," Nina says. "There's a job here for her if she ever needs one."

Ava gives a little fist pump and points to the villa.

"I'm gonna wash my hands, then start on the sauce for tonight," she says as she brushes past me, purposely letting her arm graze against mine. "We're having company again."

"Are we?" I can't help the smile that comes from her words. *We* are having company.

Ava nods and looks over her shoulder at Nina, who immediately puts up her hands and turns back for the barn. Now these two are up to something. Just once would I like to be in on whatever the hell everyone is plotting.

When she turns back to me, the smile is gone and her eyes are somehow heavier—like her brain is wrapped in a weighted vest.

I take a step closer to her.

"What's going on? Did you talk to your dad?" I ask, brushing a hand over her bare upper arm.

She shakes her head.

"I think it's better to have that conversation in person," she says.

"Is it Tammy? Is she angry with you about Ethan?"

She snorts. "Hell no. She's angry with Ethan about me—" She pauses, shuts her eyes, and lets out a long breath.

And I suddenly want to run. Whatever she's about to say is going to hurt like hell.

"It's work," she says.

I focus on getting oxygen to my lungs and to my brain.

"They want me to start Thursday."

"Next Thursday?" I ask.

"This Thursday," she says.

I don't even need to ask what she wants. I can tell from the way she's standing that she's already made her choice. It's been a long time since I've seen her with that armor on, but the set of her jaw and her shoulders reminds me of the battles I fought to get through the layers and layers of bullshit she wrapped herself in.

"I'm leaving tomorrow," she whispers softly, maybe hoping that I won't hear it.

And there it is. I wonder if she can see the crack that just opened in my chest—put her hands on either side and peer inside of it.

"Tomorrow," I repeat.

She steps forward, wraps her arms around my waist, and rests her head on my chest. There's a voice in my head screaming at me to tell her no. Tell her she can't leave. Tie her up and keep her here—because surely this is where she belongs.

"I smell like a goat," she says into my chest.

"A sheep. But yes, you do," I confirm, kissing the top of her head.

"I'm sorry, James." I can feel wetness through my shirt and I know she's crying.

"There's nothing to be sorry for, Ava. This—whatever it is—has been the most amazing few weeks of my life, and I don't have a single regret."

It's not a lie. This might hurt like hell—this feeling of being left—of being less than what's needed to make her stay. It's a feeling

I've known my entire life thanks to my parents. But it doesn't change what this was—*is*—to me.

Her shoulders shake, and I squeeze her tighter. I hold her until her tears give way to something else between us. Then I guide her toward the guest house and show her just how much I'll miss her in the shower that I unknowingly built for the woman leaving tomorrow with most of my heart.

CINQUANTASEI

Ava

There are too many things here that I'm going to miss: the views, the food, the slow leisurely pace of life, James. But this—*this*—sitting around a table, dining al fresco with a group of family and friends while music plays softly to the tune of wine glasses clinking and people chatting and laughing—I will ache for this every night of my life.

James has barely stopped touching me since I told him about tomorrow. Maybe he thinks his touch will anchor me to him. Stop me from leaving him like his parents chose to do or like his grandmother did without a choice. The thought of his pain sends spiderwebbing cracks through me, and I'm worried the soft breeze will blow me away over the hills.

"Stay with me," James whispers, squeezing my hand. And for a second, I think he means stay in Italy. Don't go back to the life that I built brick by brick while wading through grief and sadness. But then he adds, "I can see you retreating into that head of yours."

And I know he means stay present. Stop overthinking. Enjoy the moment. Be Italian.

I take a sip of the wine I've barely touched. I want to be sober. I want to remember every detail of this night. The way Nina's eyes crinkle while Leo tells a story. The way Uvaldi pats Franco on the back whenever he laughs. Even the way Maso winks at me across the table when I meet his eyes.

"I'm just trying to memorize everyone," I say.

He rubs his thumb over my knuckles.

"I'm doing the same," he says, studying me.

"I'm sure you have enough pictures of me to last you a lifetime."

"I can't photograph the sound of your laugh." He leans in, his breath grazing my earlobe, "Or the way you feel when you're just about to—"

"Gi, you know there's a man staying in town who can't stop talking about your art," Franco says from across the table.

I shake off the sensation of James and rejoin the world.

"He even offered to buy one of your photographs right off my cellar wall," Franco says while dipping the bread in the ragù left on his plate.

"I hope you got enough to repair the hole in the wall from hanging it," James says with a smile.

"Che merda. Non stai umile," Uvaldi chimes in. "I've heard he arranged an assignment at Cambridge per te."

"Cambridge?" I ask, nearly sputtering my wine.

James lets out a measured breath and nods at me.

"It doesn't change anything," he says quietly.

How could it not? He's offering him two careers in one package. I know he loves it here, but surely he understands that Urbino and his family will be here when he gets back. He owes it to himself to see where this opportunity could go. I want to push him, but he's giving me a look that screams leave it be.

I'll push him later.

"Insomma, it is perfect timing with Leo's news," Franco says between mouthfuls.

James turns his head toward Leo, who is carefully studying his empty plate.

"You have news, Zio?" James asks.

Franco looks at Nina. Nina looks at Leo. Leo keeps looking at his plate.

What the hell are they up to?

Leo waves his hand in the air. "È niente," he says.

And before anyone has a chance to challenge him, he stands to clear the table, Franco right on his heels.

James locks eyes with Nina, who simply shrugs and then engages Aldo's wife in a side conversation.

"What the hell are they up to?" I ask James.

He watches Leo and Franco through the window as they put the plates down for Verga in the kitchen.

"I have no idea. But I'm starting to get nervous," he tells me quietly.

I put my hand out to him and he turns to look at me as Sara Brightman starts singing in her flawless soprano.

"Will you dance with me?" I ask, hoping I can distract him from his family's plotting.

He puts his hand in mine and pulls me out onto the grass, where I kick off my sandals and melt into his arms. We move together through the sad lyrics, me doing everything to keep the tears from starting anew, him holding me so tightly that the rest of the world blurs around us. There's nothing but the sound of the haunting music, the smell of James's soap mingling with the chocolate cakes in the oven, and the feeling in my chest that nothing will ever feel as right as it does in this moment, in his arms.

CINQUANTASETTE

Ava

Sitting beside my mother, when shit got really bad, I used to watch the clock while she slept. I'd focus so hard on the ticking hands, trying to turn them backward to a time when she wasn't vacillating between pain and being doped out of her mind to rest. I'd narrow my eyes, imagine all the energy inside of me pushing out through my pupils to send us back.

And though it obviously didn't work, I'm trying the same useless trick again on James's dashboard clock as we get closer to the Bologna airport.

"How far is ten kilometers?" I ask as the blue sign with white lettering passes by on my right.

He squeezes my hand across the center console.

"A little over six miles," he says.

Oh God. Six miles.

Goodbyes aren't my thing. When you've said goodbye to a loved one, every goodbye after that just puts you right back into that pain, like a reused tea bag. I nearly couldn't let go of Nina this morning. James had to take my hand and sort of pry me off of her. Not that she was letting go either.

And last night, saying goodbye to the Urbino family I made, that was just as bad.

But this.

I look at James's profile and he lifts the corner of his mouth in a half smile—an attempt to comfort me.

This is going to rip me to shreds.

"There's something for you behind my seat," he says, sensing I need a distraction.

I reach behind him and Verga immediately puts his head in my hand for scratching. James tried to leave him, but the dog saw the luggage and wasn't having it. He hopped right into the car that he barely fits in and sat decisively in the middle of the back seat so I could see his giant head in the rearview mirror the entire drive.

I finish scratching and lower my hand to the floor behind James's seat, searching for the "something" he was talking about. My fingers find the solid spine of a book, and I pull it into my lap.

It's an album.

I flip the soft suede cover to the first page and see myself confronting James in the driveway that first day. He's staring down at me with heated amusement and I am like a puffer fish—all my spines out and ready to poke. I run my finger along the edge of the page and laugh.

"That's when you called me a villainous sponge," he says softly.

My throat is too thick to respond so I just nod and turn the page. It's a photo of my mother's painting of Urbino in a storm, the one that hangs in James's apartment over his kitchen table.

Then there's me sitting on a blanket, my knees pulled into my chest, students spread out around me on towels covering the hilltop while we look down over Urbino.

Then there's the market, me looking up toward a window while the people and colors blur around me in the stalls. I can hear the sound of the locals chattering in their beautiful language. I can smell the piadinas from Uvaldi's truck.

I wipe away the tears that are streaming now, making sure they don't fall onto any of the pages.

Me in the garden with Nina—the sunlight visible in streaks between us. A photo of my mom's painting of Uvaldi and his dog, side by side with a photo of me being clobbered by Verga, his eyes looking into my soul. Me floating in the pool like a starfish, the color of the water so bright it pops off the page and eases my aching chest.

"James—"

The one of me spinning in Piazza San Marco knocks the breath right out of my lungs. He somehow managed to capture the reverence and awe I felt while staring up at the architecture. And the photo of me tucked into Uvaldi's side with the fireworks exploding over Urbino—I can feel the warmth of his arm wrapped around me.

"Whenever you need a reminder," he says beside me, "you can just open it up and you'll be back."

I realize, as his words pull me from the photos, that we are idling at the curb. We are here.

I turn the final page and see myself lying in white sheets, my back and shoulder bared to the camera as I stare out the open windows overlooking the canal in Venice. It's a photo I didn't know he'd taken, but it makes me feel like a goddess.

I touch the page, wishing I could dive back into that moment—relive the last four weeks and feel everything all over again.

"The pictures from your mother's trip are in the envelope on the back cover," he tells me, and I softly shut the book and place it on the dashboard.

"This," I keep my fingers on the soft suede. "This is everything, James. You are so unbelievably talented. I think you need to consider what Davenport has to say."

He touches the side of my face and I put my hand over his.

"I think you should stay in Italy," he counters, and I can't help but smile at his deflection skills.

"I have something for you too," I say, reaching into my purse at my feet, grabbing the cardstock and extending it to him.

He looks down at the white paper and back up at me.

"Your mom's postcard?" he asks.

I nod. I can see in his face that he's floored. He knows what this postcard means to me.

"Don't read it until I'm gone," I say, my voice so shaky it makes me dizzy. "I need you to stay in the car."

"I'm walking you to—"

"James. I need you to stay in the car, okay?" I say again.

He lets out a breath and leans in, kissing me slowly and softly as if we have all the time in the world.

A man in uniform pounds on the passenger side window to let us know we have to move, but I stay put, my forehead pressed to his.

James starts to say something, and I know that if he tells me he loves me again I won't be able to get out of the car, so I kiss him one more time and turn to Verga, who throws his tongue at my face, and then I twist in my seat and nearly roll out the door. James stays put while I grab my suitcases from the trunk and when I hit the back of his car twice hard. His eyes meet mine in the rearview mirror. I lift my brows and hit the bumper one more time, and I see him smile and shake his head, then shift into gear.

And just like that, the man who drove me to the best weeks of my life drives right back out of my life.

CINQUANTOTTO

James

The newlyweds are staring into each other's eyes like they are alone in a honeymoon suite. The flowering vines hang around them and overhead, framing the residual evening light that illuminates the space through the glass sides of the green house. It's a beautiful, candid moment. And I'm capturing it for them. But where my heart usually feels full and overflowing in moments like this, right now it feels like someone's chiseling into my chest, splintering and chipping away at the ruins.

I shouldn't have agreed to this job. Ava was still here when I accepted the gig, and I wanted more than anything for her to see a traditional Urbino wedding—to experience that unbridled happiness with the locals and, of course, with me. However; here I stand with nothing but my camera to keep me company. And that used to be enough. Now I only feel her absence.

"Va bene. È ora. They are calling you to the dance floor," I tell them and they startle at the sound of my voice. Yeah, I'm still here.

"Grazie," the bride smiles, yanking her husband out through the door toward the tent.

I follow. First dance, then cutting of the cake, and I'm free to go. When will other people's happiness not feel like a wet towel smothering my face.

You could go after her, Nina had told me. As if the thought had never occurred to me.

And then what?

Drag her back to Italy? Set up shop in Philadelphia while she works eighty-hour weeks at her new firm?

That's if she's even happy to see me.

I reach into my suit jacket pocket and take out the postcard, running my finger around the worn edges of the once-white cardstock. I flip it, take in her soft curving letters and imagine her at the desk in the guest house, bent over the paper with narrowed, hyper-focused eyes. I don't need to read the words again. They are carved deep into the folds of my brain. But my eyes pass over them anyway and her voice floods my skull.

James,

I've had this postcard in my possession for six years, five months, and twenty-two days. When she handed it to me, she said, "You'll know when to write on it when you have someone you want to share it with," and I rolled my eyes like I always did when she made those vague, romantic comments. But, as usual, she was right.

She wanted me to have what she had in Urbino—to be inspired by the place that she claimed "transformed" her and learn who I was and what I was capable of. And when that became impossible the first time around, she made me promise to find a way there. I thought this trip was just another task to fulfill. It was an obligation. Another box on my checklist.

I didn't know that I'd be part of a family again.

I didn't know that I'd find a guide that could measure up to her.

You gave me Urbino—a place I will escape to every night—every moment I need a break from reality. You gave me back pieces of myself that I thought died with her.

And I'll spend my life feeling grateful to you.

Love always,
Ava

The music starts around me, and I study Ava's pencil sketch of me at the bottom right corner of the card. Every time I look at the drawing I feel a small swell of triumph inside me—to know that somehow Urbino brought her back to art, even if it is just in a tiny sketch, brings me more joy than I have a right to feel. I slip the postcard back in the inside pocket of my jacket and lift the camera to my eye, focusing on the couple dancing. The warm buzz I usually feel behind the lens eludes me as I imagine Ava in my arms on her last night here, the way the chatter of my family and friends floated around us as we spun slowly in the grass.

You could go after her.

She made her choice. She wanted to leave. Just like my mother chose her career.

We can't control how others feel. Or don't feel.

The groom dips his bride and her laughter rings out over the music. Friends and family look on behind them with blissful smiles. There's a layer of warmth and joy surrounding the couple, and I try to focus on capturing that, never once forgetting that I'm looking in on something beautiful from the outside.

CINQUANTANOVE

Ava

I've got about eight million pages of case law to get through tonight and Tammy is demanding drinks at Del Frisco's at seven. I've blown her off (with plenty of apologetic groveling) at least five times since I started last week, but I think bowing out tonight might be the detonation button. And no one wants to see Tammy detonate.

On the upside, having this much work has kept my mind busy enough that the ache I feel for James and Urbino only registers when I come up for air. Which I'm doing now, staring at the last text from Tammy and counting the exclamation points behind, "Don't be fucking late!!!!!"

Five.

I hover over the reply line, trying to find the courage to let her know my boss has asked me to stay and share notes at the seven thirty impromptu meeting she called. She's ordering dinner for us from Stella, as if that makes up for the total loss of life the staff is collectively experiencing again.

"Tammy again?" Jeff asks from beside me, his eyes still on the words he's been highlighting.

"She's gonna kill me. Or worse," I tell him.

There's nothing like a 120-hour work week to help you make new friends. Jeff and I hit it off immediately when he told me he'd attended the same International Law Summit in Urbino that I was meant to attend this summer. Though having that shared experience just makes that ache a little more difficult to ignore when he's around.

"She'd better get used to it," he murmurs.

I sigh and swipe away from her text, chickening out and finding the text chain Nina started with me. The text had been the first sitting in my inbox the moment I'd powered on my new phone.

"La tua cena fa fredda," it read.

I'd translated all on my own that she was telling me my dinner was cold and then cried for an hour, imagining them all sitting around that table, laughter and head-smacks being thrown around in equal measure.

We text each other every day, Nina and I. A mistake, I'm sure, based on the fact that I should be cutting the umbilical cord and moving on and letting go. But her messages are like stepping into a warm Epsom bath. They soothe the ache.

Her name on my phone is the next best thing to seeing James's appear. Even though we decided that wasn't a good idea, I can't help but feel the fluttering rush of hope in my chest every time a text comes through.

My phone buzzes again on the table beside the pages of *DeGiulio v. Stoddard* that I've reread at least fifty times today without really getting what I needed. I'm distracted. Unfocused. And if I'm being honest, I have this nagging feeling of dissatisfaction in the back of my mind.

I'm sure it's just the transition.

I touch my phone screen and the text pops up from my father.

We still on for dinner tomorrow?

I let out an actual groan like a child asked to clean her room, and Jeff looks over at me.

"You need a donut?" he asks, eyebrows raised.

"Two," I say and the angel-man actually stands, without even rolling his eyes, and heads off to the break room to bring me donuts.

He probably just needs a break from my negativity.

I text my dad back a thumbs-up emoji and lean back in the swivel chair. I haven't told him that I know about mom, yet. After writing and rewriting a confrontational email to him a dozen times, I figured it'd be best to handle it in person. Or I'd chickened out. And obviously he knows I've accepted the job here without ever consulting him. This dinner is going to require some pregaming.

I woman up and text Tammy: *Don't kill me, but can we reschedule happy hour for tomorrow? I swear I'll get my ass there by four . . .*

The triple dot appears and I'm actually wincing in apprehension.

Are you trying to get drunk before your dinner with dad?

It's terrifying how well she knows me.

Yeah.

Short and sweet. No need to waste time failing to bullshit a politician's spawn.

Fine. But your job blows.

I put my phone down beside the inch-thick packet in front of me. My job doesn't blow. It's just challenging. This is what I signed up for—the push and grind. The immersive distraction of a career that matters. The thrill of the race.

I just can't feel the thrill right now because I turned off my emotion switch to self-preserve. Selective numbing. The thrill will come.

And until then, I'll just have to settle for the donuts.

SESSANTA

James

Market day is busier than usual. Feria brings Italians from every region to Urbino, though most head out to the coast. Nina's table is nearly empty of cheese, the coolers behind us packed only with slushy melting ice, as we sit in companionable silence watching the swarm.

"Ava is doing well," she says, pretending to wipe something off the table.

She does this. Not so subtly updating me about her like I need to be reminded that she's out there existing without me.

"That's good," I say. And I mean it. Her happiness is the only thing making this separation acceptable.

"Lei ha detto che il lavoro è troppo—that she's overworked and tired already."

I glance over at my aunt, and she lifts her brows and shrugs, like she's just making small chat and not burying land mines beneath the surface of my brain.

Overworked means nothing. Ava knew exactly what she was signing up for—she wanted that push and burn. It's how she got through. At least, that's what she wanted before.

Nina meets my gaze, studying my face like she is searching for her next move on a chessboard.

"Forse, you should call her, no?" she asks, fingers and hands swirling in a why not gesture.

"I told you, Zia. Clean break was her call. Less messy." I put the last two words in air quotes.

"Ancora? She still believes that life is not meant to be messy?" She shakes her head as if she has somehow failed and then pats my face twice. "Leaving doesn't always mean not loving," she says softly.

I look back out at the market. For once, Nina has it wrong. When you love someone you stay by their side. You are there. Present, every chance you have.

"Tuo Zio wants you to stop by his office alle nove," Nina says.

Nine? I glance at my watch. It's five of nine.

I make a frustrated noise and she winks at me.

"I'll see you at dinner. Vincenzo's stanotte."

I nod and kiss her cheek, then she turns to the man approaching the booth and I'm dismissed.

The walk down the hill and out of town makes me think of the night I found Ava at Vincenzo's, more than a little tipsy, sitting with our closest friends like she'd known them for years. That was the first night her shields had lowered, maybe even the first night that I felt what I feel now. I walk the path toward campus as briskly as I can without soaking myself in sweat—the aggressive pace is mostly for my lateness, but partially because I'm trying to escape the memory of her barefoot in Franco's hat. When I arrive, Leo's office door is open and he's bent over papers, reading glasses lowered and lips pursed.

I knock lightly and he looks up over the rim of the glasses.

"Come in, Gi," he says, smiling politely.

He's been avoiding me for the entire week, avoiding whatever conversation we are about to have that is long past due.

My ass is barely in the seat when he says, "I'm announcing my resignation tomorrow."

I say the words back to myself and stare at him, waiting for the punch line. This is not a man who resigns. This is a man who bleeds academia—who smells of books and knowledge and laurel.

"What?" I say dumbly.

"Maso's been offered a spot at Queensbridge Academy," he says. "A scholarship too, per calcio." He takes off his glasses, folds them and slips them into his breast pocket. "Your aunt and I have never had a chance to live abroad, and we'd like to see the world . . ."

His voice trails off, not because he's done explaining, but because my brain can't process the words coming out of his mouth. I'm picking up bits and pieces.

Flat in Notting Hill.

Term starts in September.

Adjunct at King's College.

Uvaldi caring for the sheep.

My sabbatical secured should I choose to come.

I put my hand up and my uncle lifts his brows.

"Why are you doing this?" I ask. But I know the answer to that question.

All of these things he's saying, the opportunity for Maso, Nina's desire to travel, his own readiness to try something new—they all are only one part of the picture.

"È tempo, Gi. It's time to see where this will take you," he says.

What's left of my heart clenches tightly, like a fist squeezing a stress ball. They are doing this for me—leaving everything they know and love to force my hand and make me follow my dream.

My eyes fill up, and Leo stands, walks around his desk, and tugs me out of the chair and into his arms.

"Siamo sempre con te. Always," he says in his gruff voice as we embrace.

We are always with you.

Never have I believed those words more than this very moment.

SESSANTUNO

Ava

By the time I arrive at Del Frisco's, I want to find a corner booth and curl up and take a nap. I'm spent. There's a red streak in my left eye leashing my pupil to my tear duct, telling the world I haven't slept soundly in days. My head and neck seem to have gained twenty pounds because I can barely keep them up on my shoulders. And I feel like a fog has descended around my head, giving me zero visibility into reality.

It will get better when this case is over.

Of course it will. Then the next case will hit my desk. And the next. And the—

"Ava! Over here!" Tammy is standing on the rung of the bar stool, waving me over in a way that alerts all of center city to my arrival.

I slip through the crowd, excusing myself as I go, and then I'm wrapped in Tammy's arms and her scent.

"That was too long," she says. "If it happens again, I'm calling your boss."

I chuckle half-heartedly and sink onto the bar stool. She isn't joking.

Tammy lets out a low whistle and looks me over.

"You know, you are the most beautiful woman I've ever seen, but you look like you need a vacation already," she says, signaling to the bartender with the perfectly groomed facial hair.

"I've been living off coffee and donuts for two weeks," I murmur. "I didn't even make it to my bed last night. Passed out on the couch."

She scrunches up her nose and turns to the good-looking hipster to order a much-needed round of martinis. She gives him a bone-melting smile and then turns to me as if the smile never happened.

"You know you have options, right? My mom would love for you to work the campaign—"

"We've been here," I sing song. We've been here extensively. And while I love Olivia, politics make me itch. Not to mention the forced proximity to my ex. Extra itchy.

She rolls her eyes.

"Or you could go back to school. Or better yet, travel," she says, popping an olive into her mouth.

I stare at her. Go back to school. And throw away three years of law school and tens of thousands of dollars.

"I'm going to say something you don't want to hear, but maybe it's time to tap into the money your mom—"

I put my hand on her mouth. My mom's money and art are exactly where they should be—safely tucked away. If I spend it, that's another piece of her I'll never get back. Tammy looks down cross-eyed at my fingertips until I move it, and then she doesn't even breathe before diving in again.

"You decided on law so fast, Ava. You barely gave yourself time to breathe after she passed, let alone time to figure your shit out."

I look down at the mahogany bar so she can't see that I know she's right. But it's too late for all of that.

"It will get better," I whisper. "It's just been a hard transition. I'm having reverse culture shock."

Not to mention the whole shattered heart thing.

"Or maybe you're in the wrong culture?" she muses.

There's a long silence between us that is fortunately interrupted by the arrival of my drink.

I say thank you and take a huge sip from the filled glass, letting the gin coat my nerves and drown out Tammy's intuitive call-outs.

"Alright, enough about me. What's going on with you? Any word from the embassy?" I ask, and Tammy's face immediately lights up.

"You got the job!" I say.

"I got the job!"

"Holy shit. This is amazing!" I hold up my drink and she clinks her rim with mine, then takes a long gulp. "When do you start?"

"October twelfth," she says.

Less than two months. Tammy is leaving me in less than two months. I don't think my heart can take another separation.

"I'll be back for Christmas, and you can come stay as many times as you can escape from your torture chamber," she says softly, putting her hand on my shoulder and squeezing.

"I'm so happy for you," I tell her.

"I know you are."

My phone buzzes on the bar and we both look down to see the text from my dad.

Table's ready. Where are you?

My head and neck gain twenty more pounds at the thought of the few blocks and the dinner ahead of me.

"To getting through dinner," Tammy says, lifting up her drink with a smirk.

"To your new adventures in diplomacy," I say, attempting a smile.

I clink my glass to hers, then down the rest of my martini.

* * *

I take another bite of tiramisu and shut my eyes.

It's not perfect—the mascarpone is too sweet and the espresso isn't bitter enough—but it is still enough to bring me back to that table. I can almost feel him beside me, leaning in to whisper something—

"I spoke to Serena this afternoon," my father says, interrupting a fantasy that I most definitely shouldn't be having while sitting across from him.

More work talk. The entire meal has been work talk. And when I ordered dessert he seemed genuinely shocked that I'd want to extend our time together. I don't want rushed meals and quick goodbyes. I want to sit and eat and enjoy the moment. Even if I'm just trying to work up the courage to confront him about Mom.

"What did you two have to talk about?" I ask, trying to keep the defensive bristle from my tone. Not many people would be comfortable with their father speaking to their boss.

"We needed some documents that she was supposed to release to us weeks ago," he says, taking a sip of his coffee. "Obviously, we didn't discuss you. That would be unprofessional."

I lift a brow. As if that's ever stopped him from getting into my business before. I shove a mouthful of drowned lady fingers into my mouth and prepare for what I've been avoiding since I sat down—even though my father has asked me several times what's wrong.

He knows me well.

His eyes narrow on me as I swallow, and he leans back in his chair, the lapels of his suit jacket falling open at his flanks.

"Why didn't you tell me you had accepted the job, Ava?" he asks. "I had to find out from my partner. It was—"

"Why didn't you tell me that Mom had cancer before?" I interrupt, my voice cracking a bit on the c word.

He puts his napkin on the table and lets out a long breath.

"So many reasons," he says, looking up at the pendant light over our table. "The main one being that she asked me not to."

I can't help the sharp sting of betrayal that hits me in the gut. The idea of my mother keeping things from me stings like a jellyfish swimming inside my veins.

"She never wanted you to see her sick in the first place, Ava. She hated that you left school, even if she loved being with you. She didn't want your life to revolve around her cancer. And that's exactly what happened. You left everything behind just to care for her," he says.

"Of course I did. And thank goodness I made that choice, because she's gone now, Dad."

"I know. I know that. I'm just telling you how she felt about it. She wanted you to live without her burden—to love without the fear of what you witnessed." He pushes his lips together, his eyes glassy and unfocused as he says, "When I wanted to tell you about her history, she asked me to let her handle it. And when she never did, she asked me to let it go. Said your memories were better left unmarred."

A fat tear falls into the smear of mascarpone on my plate.

"I know you must be angry with me. But after she died, I was so scared that you'd never recover, Ava. You wouldn't leave your room for months. Barely ate. Barely spoke. You were a ghost. And one ghost in the house was enough. I didn't know what to do. She was always the one who knew how to give you what you needed emotionally."

He looks down at his lap and smiles.

"The two of you would go from tears to laughter just like that."

He snaps, and an image of me sobbing on my teal comforter after my first boyfriend broke up with me fills my blurry vision. She came into my room dressed in black and told me there were tires to be slashed.

"I could never do what she did for you. But I knew how to push you. So when you finally emerged—that's what I did," he says with a shrug. "I was terrified that you'd fall back into that hole if I stopped pushing—stopped planning. And I was terrified I'd fall right in there with you. So I worked and helped you work. That kept us afloat."

I can barely meet his gaze. The pain I see there behind his eyes is raw and real and unnerving. Some part of me needed to see that pain after she passed, to know that I wasn't alone. Was he hiding that to protect me? I reach for my water to stop the hiccups, then realize it was my heart that hiccupped.

All this time—all the controlling and the hard love and the insane hours spent at work—it was all his way of keeping me from falling back into my depression while he was avoiding his own. Just like my way was filled with plans and checklists and tunnel vision. The tears come harder now, and he reaches across the table and places his hand on mine.

"Ava, I don't care what you do for a living. I don't even care where you are while you are doing it. If you aren't happy, then you are wasting time," he says, studying me. "And you know better than most how important time is."

I nod. I know that fact so deeply that I feel it in every breath I take.

"I met her at the hospital," he whispers. He's staring at his water glass like he can see the past on the surface of the water. "I was the last thing she wanted, and she was the last thing I expected to find. I had just been brought on by St. Mary's legal team and she was in her final round of chemo there when we ran into each other in the hospital lobby. We physically collided, me in my brand new suit and her in her head scarf with her romance novels, and God did she dislike me from the onset."

He laughs and I lean forward, imagining every detail of the scene he's painting for me. They'd always told me they met in a doctor's office, but the edges of that half-truth were always blurry.

"She was too young for colon cancer. I can remember being in a state of suspended disbelief every time I found her during my lunch break during her treatment. She told me to go away the first three times, but I made her bet that if I could make her laugh during this awful experience, then I was worth keeping around. Even with that poison inside her she was stronger than anyone I'd ever met."

He swallows hard and lets out a long breath.

"She stopped telling me to go away by my fourth visit, but she told me that letting me stay was the most selfish thing she'd ever do," he says. "We were married a year later. And you came shortly after that. You were a miracle in so many ways, Ava. She wasn't supposed to be able to have children."

The tears are falling into what's left of my tiramisu, but I'm holding onto my smile with everything I've got. This is the most he's spoken of her since she passed.

"There's no right way to go through what we went through," he says, squeezing my hand. "Your mother—" His chest rises as the corner of his mouth pulls upward. "She was a force. Watching her lose that battle—"

He shakes his head.

"No words can describe what it's like to sit by while your soulmate wastes away. But I would gladly have taken that suffering and loss over and over for the years we had together. She gave me a trillion happy moments. She gave me you," he says softly.

I wipe at my face with my napkin while I squeeze his hand. I want to tell him I love him. Tell him I'm grateful for all of his support, no matter how misguided. But I can't get words out.

"When you find someone like that," he says, looking over my head into another time, "you don't let it go."

He takes a sip of his water and meets my eyes, then adds, "You fight for it. No matter what."

The waitress appears in my blurry periphery and puts the bill down on the table. My father nods at her but doesn't let go of my hand.

The tears don't stop. They just keep coming from whatever watershed of pain I'd been keeping dammed up these last few weeks. But these tears aren't for my father. They aren't even for my mother. God knows I cried for her.

These tears are for the one I didn't fight for.

SESSANTADUE

Ava

I've been in this storage container for well over three hours, and there are still dozens of paintings to unwrap. Every time I move from the swivel chair that the man at the front desk rolled out to me when he saw me sitting crisscross applesauce on the cement, a small tornado of dust swirls in the air above me in the glow of the single light bulb. The musky scent of things left too long in darkness still pervades the space despite the fact that I have the red garage door pulled all the way up on its track to let in as much natural light as I can. Every time my fingers peel back the edges of the butcher paper to reveal my mother's work, a mixture of grief, guilt, and awe sweep over me, and I force myself to remember that we all heal at different times. It might have been a crime to keep these paintings locked up, but now I'm ready to get them out into the light.

I glance at the first row leaning to my left. This pile is for my dad. Sweeping landscapes of the places they traveled together, portraits of me and him that I can remember complaining about and squirming away from while she laughed at my impatience, and beautiful still moments of our family home, painted in a way that makes me think she dipped her brush in love and caressed the canvas while she created them. There isn't a question that they belong with him.

Pile two is for Urbino and Alessandro. This pile might be the most difficult for me to part with, but there are so many paintings filled with the essence of Italy that it feels wrong for them to exist anywhere else. Each person who touched her life—and my life—will receive one, and this feels like the least I can do after they opened their arms to me without hesitation. My heart aches with every painting I stack atop this pile, but when I unwrap the piece that I know immediately belongs to James, that ache cascades out of my heart and into my chest like rapids after a dam release.

It's the perfect complement to the painting of Urbino that hangs in his kitchen. The point of view is identical, the angles exactly the same, but where the sky was an eggplant-colored bruise, now it bursts with the brightest cerulean blue. And where the ground was shrouded in snow and the stones looked gray rising from it, now an emerald green covers every inch of the earth and the stone is the softest pink, the same color I touched my first time in town when I ran my hand along that archway. *Urbino Under Sun.* I can see it hanging directly across from his Nonna's counterpart in his apartment, that space that made me feel like I was drowning in him.

I run my finger over the soft brushstrokes and imagine that James can feel my fingers wherever he is, then I place it in the Italy stack and shove all that pain back into its bottle and pick up the next painting.

My fingers slip under the brown paper, and I gently peel back the edges, exposing my mother's soft wide strokes underneath.

Immediately, I recognize the familiar rise and fall of Urbino's twin towers painted from the main entrance of town, the angle from below instead of from the hills beyond. But in the center of the towering fortress there is a woman standing beneath the arch, staring up into the city. She's just a silhouette, made of dark lines and shadow, but I know with every inch of reason I possess that she is me—that my mother painted her final wishes—her dream for me to experience what she did.

Ava and Urbino.

Her beautiful curving title confirms what I already knew, and a shiny splatter appears on the bottom corner of the painting. I lift the painting into the light, knowing that it will go in the pile to the right. My pile—the paintings that will go where I go.

When I go to stack it against the others, my eye catches on a white square taped to the back of the canvas, and I place the painting face down into my lap. The exact postcard she gave me to fill stares up at me, with the image of Urbino that is more familiar than my own reflection. I peel the tape carefully and turn the cardstock over. On the back, my mother's handwriting fills every square inch and my eyes sweep greedily over her words:

My Ava,

I've had this dream for you since I found out you were growing inside of me. Now as I paint it, I realize that this painting might be the only way I'll get to witness you visiting the place I loved so much. And I need you to know that I'm okay with that.

The lives—yes, lives plural—that I lived were a gift I could have never asked for. Finding Italy, finding my second family and friends there, then finding my art and myself—that life was never part of the plan. But somehow, I was lucky enough for all of that to find me. And the beauty that came with it—well, words were never my strength. That's why I paint.

My second life, though, Ava. The one that came with remission and meeting your father and having you, my sweet, stubborn girl—that life blew me away. It humbled me and inspired me. The joy and the satisfaction that you could give me with just the smallest giggle—a million days in Italy couldn't compare to that sound. You were the dream I never dreamed of, my love. The dream I could never have imagined for myself.

When you look at this painting, Ava, I want you to dream beyond your plans. Beyond the limits of my imagination. Say yes to it all. And always say yes to love. You just never know what life will give you when you let it.

Always with you,
Mom

I put my hand over her words and shut my eyes, then make another promise to my mother.

SESSANTATRE

James

Fall has come early to London. The biting wind leaves the cheeks of the people passing by looking freshly smacked. I've learned quickly that the weather does not keep Londoners inside. Hyde Park is still crowded by Urbino's standards—hatted heads bent toward the onslaught, gloved hands tucked into peacoat pockets. As they hurry to where they need to be, I focus the crosshairs of my camera on the subject of *The Post*'s article and let everyone else blur away around her.

Greta Stall sits with her ankles crossed on the bench in front of me, the dark water of the Serpentine a few meters behind her reflecting the thick clouds that float overhead. Her blonde curls barely budge out of place despite the gusts that whip the tree branches of a nearby weeping willow, making her appear like she's in another world. A world protected from weather and crowds. The world in which she writes.

The photographs are exactly what I need to show the readers how her first novel, *Obscurity*, came to be. She wrote it here on this bench, often beneath an umbrella, broke and determined to follow her pipe dream despite the odds being stacked against her.

"I've got what I need, Ms. Stall," I say as I lower the camera.

She turns down her mouth and shakes her head in mock frustration.

"Greta. You need to call me Greta," she says.

"I've got what I need, Greta."

She smiles and stands from the bench, tucking the notebook she had open on her lap into the purse at her feet.

"You've been wonderful, James. I cannot wait to see the finished product." She holds out her hand and I take it.

"And I cannot wait to read your next finished product."

Her next novel releases in May, and if it's anything like her debut, she'll have another massive hit on her hands. And possibly another feature in *The Post*.

"Till we meet again then," she says, pulling a glove on the hand I just shook.

I nod and smile.

"Looking forward to it. Arrivederci," I tell her, and she gives me one last grin, crouches to give Verga one last scratch, and then turns to join the rosy-cheeked strangers walking along the sand-colored path leading back toward Kensington Gardens.

I sink down onto the bench she just left and look out toward the ornate brick buildings with their white framed windows and wrought iron balconies that string together along Kensington Road. I'm still growing accustomed to the change in scenery—like a time traveler tugged straight from the Renaissance into the Victorian era. But it's no less beautiful.

My phone pings from my pocket and I slowly pull it out thanks to my stiff frozen fingers. Nina reminding me of dinner—for the fifth time this week. Some things are just like Urbino. Even the view from their rooftop deck in their two-story flat in Notting Hill, where we desperately cling to dining al fresco in sweaters and coats, is a different kind of beautiful than our views at home. None of these differences matter, though, because they are here. We are together.

As I'm typing out a response to Nina, Verga starts barking like a madman and I look up slowly from my screen.

"Hi."

I don't blink. Because if I blink I know that she'll be gone—the daydream I must be having will scatter in the wind. Her eyes are greener than I remember, which seems impossible because I look at them every day in the photographs I refuse to delete. Her cheeks are the perfect shade of red, and I'm momentarily struck mute when her mouth stretches into a smile and her eyebrows lift. Verga has both paws on her chest as if he intends to lead her in a tango.

"Mind if I join you on that bench?" she asks, and she somehow escapes the dog's clutches and scooches into the space beside me.

"Your editor told me where to find you," she tells me as she sits. There's about an inch between us, and I've never hated that unit of measurement so much in my life. I want to make it disappear and feel the warmth of her body pressed against my side. I want to put my head in her lap like Verga is.

"What are you doing here?" Good, James. Words.

She looks over her shoulder and narrows her eyes at a pair of swans that are waddling dangerously close.

"I was just in the neighborhood," she says. "I don't trust these buggers."

"Buggers?"

She looks back at me and shrugs, "Gotta learn to talk like the locals if I'm going to live here, right? That was one of the first things you taught me."

I shake my head. She's not making any sense. None of this is real.

"This isn't real," I murmur.

She slides closer and her body fits perfectly along my flank.

"I never should have left, James. I thought that I had to—that the plans I made were the only way because of the time I spent—because of how I needed them to get through after my mom." She pauses, her eyes flitting between my mouth and my gaze. "But I don't have to follow those plans. Things can change and not fall apart."

It isn't until I reach out and brush a tear from the corner of her mouth that I realize I'm not imagining this entire scene. She's actually here. On this bench. In Hyde Park. And I can touch her.

"How are you here?" I ask softly.

She lets out a little laugh.

"Try to keep up, please," she says. "I'm living with Tammy in Belgravia. She got a job at the embassy."

"For how long?" I ask.

"Indefinitely."

"And your job in the States—"

"Resigned. It wasn't for me," she says. "I mean the money was nice, but the time. It wasn't worth it. And I don't actually need all that money, thanks to my mother . . ."

Her voice trails away in the wind and she looks down at her hands. She's wearing the gloves I gave her that day in the market.

"I'm taking some time to figure out what I love. I never got a chance to do that in college. Luckily, I know someone at King's College, so I can take a few courses there while I figure my shit out."

Of course Nina and Leo would be a part of this.

Ava lifts her butt from the bench and digs into her jeans pockets, then holds out her hand to me. There's a plastic card lying flat on her palm.

"This is for you," she says, pushing it into my hand.

"A calling card?"

Just like her ex gave to her when she left for Italy. I turn it over in my hand.

"It's not just a calling card," she says quickly, reaching up and turning my face with her hand so I'm forced to see how beautiful she is as she explains. "It's an *unlimited* calling card. Infinite minutes. Bottomless. Without limits."

I'm getting it now, but I want her to say the words anyway. "And what would I use it for?"

She lets out a frustrated noise and squirms closer.

"It's symbolic, James. The whole time we were together we were counting down minutes. I'm giving you all of my minutes now—"

I don't let her finish. I press my lips to hers and kiss her so deeply that I can't tell the difference between her breathing and my own. When we finally come up for air, she smiles up at me.

"I love you," she whispers. "I should have said it a million times."

I stand up from the bench and hold up the calling card between two fingers.

"Now you have unlimited time to say it," I tell her, and she grins up at me.

I hold out my hand to her, "Would you like to have dinner at Nina and Leo's with me?"

She puts her hand in mine and I tug her up off the bench.

"Every night," she says as I wrap my arms around her and pull her close.

I hold her like that, shielding her from the wind, until where and when become meaningless, and only who remains.

ACKNOWLEDGMENTS

This might be the most difficult part of writing this novel. When you spend half your life chasing a dream, you collect an overwhelming amount of supporters along the way. Without them, you would have given up the chase after rejection number ten and missed out on rejection number two hundred fifty and acceptance numbers one and two.

Which brings us to acceptance number one, Barbara Poelle. Not only are you the funniest person I know, you are also amazing enough to find me funny in return. You are Tina Fey meets Fairy Godmother, and I'm still in shock that you represent me. Thank you a million times, Barbara!

Then there's acceptance number two, my amazing, insightful editor, Holly Ingraham. I am forever grateful for your ideas, contributions, and belief in this story. Your vision made this novel grow in ways I could never have imagined on my own. Tanti grazie, Holly.

My original readers—Kristen, Dee, and Burg—you were the reason I kept writing Urbino, year after year. With your demands for more food porn and more porn porn—you pushed me in the best way. Love you. Thank you.

Merry, there is no Urbino without you. Every memory of that time and every word in this book is infused with you. La nostra amicizia è una delle gioe più grandi della mia vita. I love you. Thank you for letting me drag you to Italy.

Liz Fenton. Summing up my gratitude for you into a paragraph is an impossible task. You have been there for every rejection letter, every moment of crushed hope, and every triumph. I'm sure you have the screenshots to prove it. You single-handedly dusted me off and kicked me (gently) in the ass through all of it while patiently guiding me through the insanity. You are endlessly kind and funny and talented. Thank you for being my mentor and friend.

To my sixth grade teacher who somehow ended up stuck with me for life, you made me believe I was capable of anything. Thank you, Mr. Powell.

Mom and Dad, thank you for teaching me to look for humor in life even when it's too dark to see. I love you both very much and I'm so grateful for all the love you've given me, even when I did everything possible not to deserve it. I love you both.

U.C., thank you for all the years of unconditional love and support that have shaped me.

And my Sis, keep on brainstorming genius meet-cute ideas like the colonoscopy. Your laugh is what I hear when I write a funny line. Knowing you are at my back has always made me stronger. Thank you for making me brave.

Stevie. Yikes. Where do I even start? You are, without a doubt, the most patient, most wonderful, and most genuinely kind human I know. You are my friends-to-lovers trope and my lifelong best friend. I'm beyond lucky to have been put in the desk in front of you in Mr. Powell's class. I love you more each year. Thank you for being beside me through it all.

And to my babies, Hadley and Roarke, you already got the dedication so I don't want to spoil you too much, but you should know you are a huge part of why I kept writing. Roarke, you waking up at the butt crack of dawn and coming down to sit in my lap when I used to write at five AM was one of my favorite moments of every day. You'd ask something so innocent, like *How's it going today?* or say something simple like *Good job writing, Mommy.* You have no idea what those few words meant to me. And Hads, my sweet little book lover—watching you devour novels every day makes me want to write stories that you'll love. One day. When you are allowed to read them.

Thank you, readers. In the end, you are why this dream came true. I hope you already booked your trip to Urbino. Who knows what adventures are waiting for you within her walls.